W9-APG-591

DIE HAPPY

Recent Titles by J.M. Gregson from Severn House

Lambert and Hook Mysteries

AN ACADEMIC DEATH
CLOSE CALL
DARKNESS VISIBLE
DEATH ON THE ELEVENTH HOLE
DIE HAPPY
GIRL GONE MISSING
A GOOD WALK SPOILED
IN VINO VERITAS
JUST DESSERTS
MORTAL TASTE
SOMETHING IS ROTTEN
TOO MUCH OF WATER
AN UNSUITABLE DEATH

Detective Inspector Peach Mysteries

DUSTY DEATH
TO KILL A WIFE
THE LANCASHIRE LEOPARD
A LITTLE LEARNING
MERELY PLAYERS
MISSING, PRESUMED DEAD
MURDER AT THE LODGE
ONLY A GAME
PASTURES NEW
REMAINS TO BE SEEN
A TURBULENT PRIEST
THE WAGES OF SIN
WHO SAW HIM DIE?
WITCH'S SABBATH
WILD JUSTICE

DIE HAPPY

A Lambert & Hook Mystery

J. M. Gregson

This first world edition published 2011
in Great Britain and in the USA by
SEVERN HOUSE PUBLISHERS LTD of
9–15 High Street, Sutton, Surrey, England, SM1 1DF.
Trade paperback edition first published
in Great Britain and the USA 2012 by
SEVERN HOUSE PUBLISHERS LTD

British Library Cataloguing in Publication Data

Gregson, J. M.
Die happy. – (A Lambert and Hook mystery)
1. Lambert, John (Fictitious character) – Fiction. 2. Hook,
Bert (Fictitious character) – Fiction. 3. Police –
England – Gloucestershire – Fiction. 4. Detective and
mystery stories.
I. Title II. Series
823.9'14-dc22

ISBN-13: 978-0-7278-8070-3 (cased)
ISBN-13: 978-1-84751-371-7 (trade paper)

Typeset by Palimpsest Book Production Ltd.,
Falkirk, Stirlingshire, Scotland.
Printed and bound in Great Britain by
MPG Books Ltd., Bodmin, Cornwall.

To Ted and Joyce Giles,
sources of encouragement and spirited
literary exchanges over many years.

ONE

Hindsight is a wonderful thing. Everyone says that, but it is true nonetheless. With the wonderful advantage of hindsight, Chief Superintendent John Lambert would never have accepted the assignment.

He could plead a particularly trying morning in his defence, but he knew that was no excuse; he would never have accepted it as an excuse from one of his subordinates. Policemen, and senior policemen in particular, were supposed to be able to deal with both ambitious young lawyers and wily old legal foxes. No one could quite say why, because little formal training in court procedures was afforded to policemen. This contrasted with the years of preparation undertaken by the sinuous minds which were recruited and rewarded handsomely to defend villains. Lawyers were well-paid and unscrupulous, in John Lambert's not entirely unbiased view. The law said everyone had a right to be defended, and lawyers interpreted that precept with energy and enthusiasm. Was not the most ancient principle of British law that a man was innocent until proven guilty? So long as a villain did not openly proclaim his guilt to his brief, he must be defended to the hilt as an innocent man, whatever the lawyer's private opinion on the case might be.

The more vicious the criminal, the more adept and versatile his counsel was likely to be. As you progressed up the unofficial hierarchy of crime, you, or those who employed you, could afford better barristers, whilst those acting for the Crown Prosecution Service were generally less experienced, less well briefed and certainly less well paid. Policemen went into court feeling they needed a cast-iron case, because the legal odds were stacked against them.

All of this was understood in every police station in the land. Indeed, it was reiterated daily in most canteens, with the addition of a few choice adjectives and adverbs for emphasis. John Lambert had been hearing the conversation and contributing to it for thirty years now. None of it was much help when you were called as a witness in the Crown Court.

Fraud was the most complicated crime of all to prove, and it was a fraud case in which Lambert was called to appear on this bright March morning. He knew his strategy: stick to the facts, say no more than you have to say and don't allow the smooth bastards with the silly wigs to ruffle you. Lambert repeated that ancient police mantra to himself as he waited to be called. He was a tall man, taking care to walk erect and eliminate his recent tendency to stoop, carrying the carapace of experience around him as he moved to the centre of this legal drama. Yet his heart beat as hard and as fast in his seasoned chest as that of the youngest and greenest constable when he was called upon to make his way to the witness stand.

The barrister was mature and experienced in his craft, and operating in his own arena. He took Lambert steadily through the first small, mutually agreed facts of his evidence. The serious charge and the exalted setting gave a strange edge to what should have been a boring but necessary recital, with every professional in the court listening to the manner rather than the content of these brief questions and responses. Each question required no more than a three or four word affirmative. Everyone was agreed about this, the tone on both sides said. It was like watching a tiger creeping stealthily along a branch, moving nearer and nearer to the spot where it might pounce most tellingly upon its prey.

Yet there was no sense of dramatic movement when that moment came. The lawyer glanced down at his notes, as if preparing himself for one more routine query. Then he said in a voice of slightly puzzled reason, 'Chief Superintendent Lambert, you obtained a search warrant and then proceeded to ransack my client's home. From where you stand now, do you now consider this action an overreaction?'

'No. The law protects members of the public against overreaction. Search warrants are not issued without due examination of the issues involved.'

A shrug of the shoulders, a slight shake of the head beneath the white curls of the wig, an amused professional smile, which counsel hoped took in the judge as well as his supporters. 'You need not remind us here of what the law dictates, Chief Superintendent.' He ruffled his papers, then looked at Lambert, like an adult disappointed by a child who has behaved badly. 'Would you not agree that your team exercised excessive force and vigour in the way they conducted this search?'

'No. Routine procedures were applied. The search was thorough and methodical, as the circumstances demanded it should be.'

'Thorough and methodical.' The defending counsel dwelt on each syllable, elongating the phrase to give it irony. Then, as though he were forced to raise an unpleasant matter against his will, 'You wouldn't attach any importance to the fact that Mr Murray's wife and daughters were terrified by the actions of your officers?'

Lambert paused in his turn, looking completely calm, but struggling to shut out the murmur of excitement in the court and to find the words for a measured refutation. 'A degree of distress is inevitable in these situations. I would dispute the word "terrified". I should also like the court to be aware that the daughters you have chosen to mention are aged nineteen and twenty-three – hardly the fearful infants your question implied.'

'I think the court will be aware that I suggested no such thing. I should be obliged if you will confine yourself to factual answers to my questions, Chief Superintendent.'

Lambert was too experienced to point out that his answer had been entirely factual. He gave the man no reaction at all, but merely stood mute and upright, awaiting further questions.

It had the desired effect. The lawyer studied him for a moment, then said, 'Would you not concede that your prolonged and aggressive attention to my client over several weeks was excessive? Did it not, in fact, amount to police harassment?'

The well-worn, even threadbare, accusation. The word 'harassment' came from prisoners when you had them defeated in the interview room; when it came from a lawyer, you knew that he was desperate, trying to abandon his attack without losing too much face. Lambert permitted himself a small, mirthless smile. 'There was no harassment involved. We conducted a methodical investigation and we observed the correct protocol. We did no more and no less than our duty to the public demanded.'

The lawyer nodded, affording Lambert the patronizing smile which acknowledged in the arcane rites of the English law that the witness had successfully defended his position. He kept any disappointment out of his voice as he said briskly, 'No further questions.'

Lambert in his turn was careful to show no sign of relief and to leave the witness stand with measured step. For him, the strange little game was over, though the case would go on for many days yet.

His mood was not improved when he returned to the police station at Oldford. His partner in anti-crime, Detective Sergeant Bert Hook, was waiting for him to lead the interrogation of a drug dealer who had been arrested over the weekend. Important, certainly, but not likely to bring any spectacular success. People like Alfie Turner were arrested every week, but they were small fish swimming in a large and murky pond. The killer sharks who controlled this evil, lucrative industry were shadowy monsters, often not even permanently resident in the UK. People like Turner, who operated the lower outlets in the trade, knew it was literally more than their lives were worth to reveal information about people higher up the chain. The anonymous bullet in a city back street, the untraceable drowning; such victims swelled the serious crime totals, with successful investigations almost impossible.

It was a situation understood on both sides of the small square table as Lambert and Hook stared into the narrow face in the interview room. Lambert did not disguise the weary indifference the situation induced in him. Low-key might be the only possibility of success: get the little scrote off his guard and then wring some unwitting admission from him. He glanced at the notes in front of him and sighed heavily. 'Well, Alfie, we meet yet again.'

He heard the old lag's whine, which was Turner's normal

interview tone. 'Don't know why I'm 'ere, Mr Lambert. Don't know why a chief super should be wasting 'is time on the likes of me. It's a miscarriage of justice, this is.'

'Not yet it isn't, Alfie. DS Hook and I haven't even decided what charges you will face yet. There is still time for you to save yourself, if you choose to offer us a little help.'

Bert Hook glanced sharply sideways and simulated surprise, even shock, at this leniency in his chief. 'That would have to be your decision, sir. I couldn't accept responsibility for that. Not with Mr Turner facing the near-certainty of a custodial sentence.'

'I ain't going down for this. It's only a minor offence, this.' But there was alarm in the high-pitched voice, as he looked from one face to the other and found no relief in this experienced duo, who had practised their tactics so often that they could play instinctively off each other.

Lambert affected to look at his notes again, though he knew there was nothing there with which to pressurize this small-time scum. He shook his head sadly. 'Dealing in class A drugs, Alfie. Offering a choice of heroin and crack and methamphetamine. Doesn't look good to me.'

'I only sold the horse. And a little crack, just for recreational use.'

'Even offered Rohypnol, our man says – at what he considered a grossly inflated price.'

The date-rape drug, the pills most in demand in the squalid twenty-first century society where men like Turner made their livings. 'It ain't bloody fair, coppers coming in filthy shirts and jeans to look for the likes of me.'

'Whereas what you do is entirely fair, I suppose, Alfie.' Lambert's tone was suddenly harsher and less laid back. 'Seen what happens to the people you sell these substances to, have you, Alfie? Seen what they do to get the money to pay the likes of you, once you have them hooked?'

Turner shrank back on his seat as if physically threatened. 'It's their own choice, Mr Lambert. No one makes 'em come to me.'

'I can take you to the morgue in Gloucester, if you like, to show you how your customers finish life.'

'It's a free country. It's their own choice.' But Turner would not look at his adversaries as he muttered the clichés.

'Sergeant Hook's right, you know. Third time in court for dealing. You'll go down this time. And probably a good thing too. One less rat in the sewer.' He didn't trouble to disguise his distaste for the man and what he represented.

'It's a minor offence. I want a brief.'

'Oh, I'd go further than that. I'd say you need a brief, Alfie. And you shall have one, as soon as we decide upon formal charges. At present you're just a member of the public helping us with our enquiries.' He allowed himself a sour smile at that thought, and Hook beside him responded with a broader one of his own.

Bert sensed that this was the moment to take over. 'You heard Chief Superintendent Lambert say that your only chance of avoiding a hefty spell in clink was to cooperate fully with us. I can't say that I agree with such leniency, but he is my senior officer. So I have to suggest to you that your only chance this morning is to offer us useful information. We might then be able to enter a plea for leniency on your behalf.'

'But I don't know nuffing.'

'Pity, that. Looks like you're going down then, Mr Turner. Still, consider it from our point of view; one less rat rooting about in the sewer, as Mr Lambert says.'

'What is it yer want?'

Lambert leaned forward. 'Names, Alfie. Names from higher up the organization. Names that would show you're helping us with our enquiries. I'm sure that your brief when he arrives would agree that a little information would be the only means by which you might help yourself.'

Except that his lawyer would probably be retained by the drug organization itself, which would certainly forbid any such revelations. Turner said hopelessly, 'I don't know nuffing. I'm small time, Mr Lambert. They don't tell me nuffing.'

It was almost certainly true. They eventually wrung two names from him, names of suppliers on the next rung of the hierarchy. Lambert was pretty sure that the specialist Drugs Squad was aware of both of them, but equally sure now that Turner had nothing more to offer. They took the name of his brief and returned him to his cell, with the assurance that charges would be proffered within the hour.

Lambert reviewed a trying morning, looked at the paperwork which had mounted inexorably on his desk during his absence, and said glumly to Bert Hook, 'Makes you look forward to retirement and cultivating your roses, a day like this does.' At that moment, he almost believed himself.

He went home for lunch, which he wasn't often able to do, and walked round the very garden he had mentioned, noting the crocus and the budding daffodils and rejoicing that another spring was at hand. He switched on the television, watched amateurs and their expert guides trying to make purchases at an antiques fair for two minutes, picked up the sports section of *The Times*, read of the latest demands of a multi-millionaire soccer player, uttered words even the most liberal editor could never have printed, and flung the newspaper petulantly aside.

His wife observed all of this surreptitiously, keeping the kitchen door ajar whilst she engaged herself in the politically highly incorrect processes of keeping her man happy. Thirty years of marriage to a policeman as he moved through the ranks to his present eminence had taught Christine Lambert many things. One of them was that men, whatever their professional successes and the accolades heaped upon them, are essentially children in the home.

This can be trying at times, even infuriating. But it is also a factor which that can be turned to a resourceful wife's advantage. It is much better to use this weakness than to fight it. Such a sentiment was a triumph of pragmatism over feminism, Christine reflected, but it made domestic control and even domestic harmony much more attainable. She only taught part-time now, after a serious illness a year or two back, but she had many years' experience of successful teaching, and she knew how to deal with children.

Cheese on toast, with slices of small, tasty cherry tomatoes blended into its amber surface. That had been John's favourite lunchtime snack throughout their marriage and he didn't change his opinions lightly. She served it to him not at the table but in his favourite armchair, a sure sign of indulgence. He ate with slow relish, his mood improving imperceptibly with each measured movement of his jaws. When she heard him switch off the television after the headlines of the one o'clock news, Christine brought her own plate in and sat down opposite him.

John Lambert glanced at her, feeling a sudden shaft of tenderness as he saw the lines in her still attractive face. As a young CID officer working round the clock and building a career, he had shut this woman out of his professional life, forcing her away from him, forcing her to retreat into her own job and the progress of her two young daughters. It had almost cost him the marriage that most of his younger colleagues now saw as rock-solid and a model for others. Those days were long gone, though on some days he still had to force himself to reveal anything to Christine of his life at work.

This was one of those days. Even with the slowly consumed cheese on toast sitting comfortably within him, he found it difficult to relay anything positive about his morning. Instead, he contented himself with gazing fondly at his empty plate and muttering with feeling, 'Bloody lawyers!'

Christine smiled. 'I'm willing to bet that some senior barrister who is enjoying a much better lunch than you is now saying, "Bloody superintendents!"'

Lambert was cheered by that thought. It had been a no-win situation, but he hadn't done badly. He'd defended his goal stoutly; now it was up to the Crown Prosecution to score a late breakaway goal and win the game. They'd had all the right service from the police, if they could only produce a striker to kill the match off. He abandoned his over-strained metaphor, took an appreciative mouthful of tea from his favourite china beaker, and said again before he was aware of the words upon his tongue, 'Bloody lawyers!'

It was good to see John's safety valve working and being used so efficiently, Christine Lambert thought. She said with a smile, 'I know all about you, John Lambert. What you need to stretch your talents is a good juicy murder!'

Lambert knew himself well enough not to disagree with the thought. He didn't endorse it directly, but he shook his head and said, 'Fraud cases are a damned nuisance. The minds lined up against you aren't just unscrupulous, they're clever as well. The investigation takes months, and just when it's getting interesting you hand it over to the Fraud Squad.'

Christine slid him a plate with a generous slice of the sponge cake with lemon curd filling she had made that morning. 'You need something else to interest you.'

He should have sensed the danger, but he was replete and relaxed, perhaps even a little drowsy. He looked out at the garden, at the industrious blackbird on his lawn, and said affably, unthinkingly, 'You could be right there.'

'We've been getting on with plans for the Oldford Literary Festival.'

He smiled. 'I can hear the capital letters as you speak. It sounds very impressive.'

'It is, for a small place. You'll be surprised at some of the speakers we've got. Authors who are nationally famous, even internationally famous, some of them. It's a tribute to the industry of Mrs Dooks.'

'And of her energetic committee,' he said loyally.

'There might even be a role for you.'

At last, too late, he was on his guard. 'Oh I don't think I could—'

'Just a small role. Nothing that would need much preparation from you.'

'Nevertheless, I think I'd reluctantly have to decline your—'

'Mrs Dooks herself suggested you. I must say I was quite pleased by that.'

'But even with the formidable Mrs Dooks behind you, I think it's only fair to say—'

'It's the kind of thing the Chief Constable would approve of. Didn't you say he was very much in favour of senior policemen being visible presences in their local communities?'

It wasn't a phrase John Lambert would have used himself, though he remembered it from some official bulletin. 'I don't think I ever said I agreed—'

'Official policy, you see. You'd be helping to improve the police image. Endorsing the policies of your Chief Constable.'

Lambert smiled benignly, marshalling his defences. 'The

days are long gone when I needed to pay lip service to the latest police manifesto.'

'You've never done that, even when you should have done. It's one of the reasons why I'm still here.'

He was affected by flattery when it popped up in unlikely places, and Christine knew it. Most children are. He smiled and said, 'I'm glad to hear there is more than one reason.'

If he hoped she would indulge him with others, he was to be disappointed. She said, 'It's only a small spot we're talking about, as I said. All we want you to do is to introduce an eminent speaker. A couple of minutes about his life and achievements, at the most. You'd be much the most appropriate person to do it.'

He tried to resist the notion of such distinction. He said with a rather patronizing air, 'What is this mysterious assignment which demands me and only me?'

With the advantage of hindsight, he saw within minutes that he should never have asked that. Hindsight, as everyone agrees, is a wonderful thing.

TWO

Marjorie Dooks was the driving force behind the Oldford Literary Festival. Everyone knew that and everyone was content that it should be so. No one would have dared to mount an assault on her pre-eminence. More importantly, no one wished to do that. Everyone recognized her ability, her vision, and, most important of all, her energy.

She was fifty-five now. She had taken early retirement from her senior position in the Administrative Department of the Civil Service with the advent of coalition government after the hung parliament of 2010. You couldn't serve two masters, she told anyone who would listen. It would compromise your principles; she would never do that. Her husband had a senior position in industry, so finance was not a problem. The country's loss was the local community's gain. Marjorie Dooks departed to apply her formidable talents to the benefit of Oldford, in the sleepiest part of Gloucestershire. The burghers of that small but ancient market town took deep breaths of anticipation, whilst the Civil Service mandarins breathed a long sigh of collective relief.

Mrs Dooks was a parish and district councillor, but she found local politics frustrating; she had been concerned with implementing national policies in her Civil Service days. 'Irredeemably parochial' was her dismissive phrase, ignoring the fact that parish council affairs in particular were meant to be exactly that. The truth was that she was used to being in charge of her own department and her own staff and to issuing orders that would be instantly obeyed. Marjorie needed to use her considerable gifts to shape and direct something of her own.

The Oldford Literary Festival was exactly that. The town had a connection with Ivor Gurney, a worthy but almost forgotten poet of World War One, who had survived that cataclysm but in a sadly diminished state. The first festival celebrated this local connection. Subsequent ones went for broader themes and brought an unexpected distinction and cultural acclaim to the small country town that few outside Gloucestershire and Herefordshire had previously heard of.

The distinguished local writer who had been the original motivating force behind the Ivor Gurney festival was dead now. Marjorie Dooks had stepped into his role and provided new force and energy when it was most needed. She had quickly identified those people among the volunteers who could be most helpful to her. Enthusiasm was not always accompanied by efficiency; Marjorie knew that and acted accordingly. She didn't mind treading on prominent local toes, if it was for the general good. And you didn't work for twenty-five years in Whitehall without developing a pretty thick skin, as she reminded people with a hearty guffaw when they bridled at her more ruthless suggestions.

She was gradually getting used to the idea that voluntary helpers must sometimes be wooed rather than brusquely ordered to do things. In the Civil Service, rank was supreme. Everyone who reached any degree of eminence understood that completely. Tact was a welcome quality, but not an essential one. Making her way in what had still been essentially a man's world when she entered it, Marjorie had found energy and efficiency much more effective weapons than tact. Often bloody-minded determination had been more effective than diplomacy. It was difficult for her to play down the qualities that had served her so well in her working lifetime, especially when they were still so effective against local government bureaucracy.

But Mrs Dooks was an intelligent woman; she saw the need for new techniques in this new situation. You couldn't simply dragoon volunteers as you could professionals. These people were giving many hours of their time to help you to implement your grand design. Sometimes you had to persuade and convince your troops before you led them into battle.

Today she was chairing a meeting of the Oldford Literary Festival committee, and here her incisive mind and brisk approach were generally welcomed. Most of the people assembled with her in the room behind the library had endured meetings that dragged on for three hours and achieved no more than could have been decided in one. Marjorie's efficient dispatch of the agenda items was collectively welcomed. Two people had already been arrested in full flow, but each time that had been a relief to the other people in the small, overheated room.

'Item four. Speakers. Mrs Lambert, please.'

Christine cleared her throat a little nervously. 'Good progress, I think. This year's theme of "Law and Order through the Centuries" has left us a wide range of possibilities, which was our intention when we chose it. Dr Grainger, the Secretary of the Trollope Society, has suggested the topic of "Trollope and Urban Crime in the Nineteenth Century". Jack Straw, the former Home Secretary, has agreed to speak about his recent book on people who have held the office since its inception. He plans to speak principally about six of the most influential holders of that office. The title of his talk is still to be finalized, but his attendance is guaranteed.'

Christine Lambert looked round the table. 'These two talks we may take as definite. I think there is progress on other fronts also, but there are people here who can give us the most up-to-date information on that.'

'Thank you, Mrs Lambert.' Mrs Dooks completed a note on the pad in front of her and looked imperiously round the table. In truth, this was the section of the meeting where she felt least at ease. This was where she had to deal directly with 'creative' people, who were notoriously temperamental and unpredictable. She tended to use the word 'arty' herself, in private at least. It had a greater ring of scepticism about it, and implied that such people weren't to be relied upon in practical matters.

No one seemed about to help her out by speaking. Marjorie looked round the ring of expectant faces and said firmly, 'Now, who would like to begin?'

A confident, almost bored voice said after a second, 'I suppose that had better be me.' Peter Preston nodded his distinguished head a couple of times as if to endorse this decision, since it seemed no one else was going to do so. He had a broad, lightly lined face and large brown eyes, which the rimless glasses he had lately adopted seemed to accentuate and make even more impressive. He was a well-known local figure, though there were conflicting reports about his achievements. His opinions were frequently quoted in the local press and occasionally on Radio Gloucester; he was invariably described there as 'a freelance BBC producer and director', though no one was able to say confidently what was the last thing he had produced or directed.

Nevertheless, he spoke with authority on drama, poetry and opera, and was invariably ready with an opinion on anything 'cultural' – in the older and proper sense of that word, as he was wont to assure anyone who would listen. Preston could be tiresome, but he had contacts, and a little judicious flattery would easily persuade him to use them. Flattery wasn't a weapon Marjorie Dooks cared to employ, but she recognized that Peter Preston might well have his uses when you were trying to set up a worthwhile literary festival with little know-how and very limited funds.

He paused, looked round the table, apparently satisfied himself that he had everyone's attention, and announced, 'Denzil Carter thinks he can fit us into his schedule. In the light of the derisory fees we are able to offer even the most eminent of our speakers, I had to call in a personal favour to get him, but I think he will come. I should be able to confirm this after further contacts in the coming week.'

'Thank you, Mr Preston. As I am sure you will remember from the minutes of our meeting on February fourth, our fees are no longer a matter for discussion. We all understand that we are working to a tight budget, but the acceptances we already have are beginning to shape into a promising programme. Ms Charles?'

Whilst Preston bristled in silence, the woman on his left nodded and looked at her notes. 'Please call me Sue. I'm not used to the formality of meetings, but I think we'll make more rapid progress if we speak frankly and informally.' She glanced round the table and found two or three heads nodding agreement and support.

Sue Charles was sixty-eight now, and unconsciously asserting the deference due to age and seniority in a gathering like this. She had written twenty crime novels, lived in the town for thirty years, and was a respected local figure. She carried her celebrity lightly and wasn't ostentatious with her money, her neighbours said approvingly. Not many of them realized how modest the returns from writing were for all but the fortunate few. Sue had helped to found the literary festival, recognizing correctly that many authors would attend for modest fees. Some of them had an evangelical streak and were eager to spread the word about their particular kind of literature; others were natural mixers and speakers who welcomed an audience as a variant to the lonely process of writing. All were anxious to publicize and talk about their latest masterworks.

Sue Charles was more conscious of the realities of the literary life than anyone else in the room. She had spoken at the first Oldford Literary Festival herself and been well received. Now she was using her acquaintance – she modestly declined the word friendship – with one of the most eminent and well-known crime writers to persuade him to speak at this year's event. 'David Knight has agreed to come in May. My only reservation is that I know he is not in good health. But I will pick him up from the station and he will stay with me. He can now be included in our programme. I should be delighted to chair that session and to introduce him myself.'

Marjorie Dooks nodded. 'That is good news indeed, Sue. Thank you for your continuing efforts on our behalf.'

From the other side of the table Peter Preston offered his most patronizing smile. 'Whilst in no way wishing to denigrate the efforts of Ms Charles – or indeed her own literary productions – I think I should query once again whether we wish to include detective fiction and its practitioners within our programme. I don't wish to appear a snob, but are we not affecting the prestige of our little cultural celebration by including the whodunit among more serious novels?'

'What would you call yourself, if not a snob, then?'

The question burst abruptly and shockingly from the youngest person in the room, twenty-two-year-old Sam Hilton. Preston allowed himself a shake of the head and a supercilious smile. 'Dear boy, I am an unashamed elitist, not a snob. I have standards. As one who has suffered the delights of modern state education, you would perhaps not understand the difference between snobbishness and elitism, but I assure you there is one.'

Marjorie Dooks spoke decisively from the chair. 'This

question has been debated in this committee several times previously, and I think each time at your insistence, Peter. With the possible exception of romantic fiction, the detective novel is more widely read than any other form of literature. At its best, it stands up beside the serious novel and certainly warrants a place in our programme.'

'I am aware that this has been discussed before and also that I seem to be a lone voice for the civilized ethic. Perhaps I shall have to consider my position.'

There was a sudden profound silence, in which tiny sounds such as breathing and the rustling of paper seemed miraculously enlarged. Then Mrs Dooks said evenly, 'Perhaps if you hold this view so strongly you should do just that, Peter. Your resignation would be regrettable, but I'm sure we should all understand.'

Preston had not expected to have his bluff called like this. He had no real wish to resign. Indeed, his continued involvement in the success of the festival was necessary to his pose as a leading cultural presence in the area. He shrugged his shoulders, sighed elaborately, and said, 'I have said my piece. I appreciate mine is not the popular stance, but minority views need voicing, unless we are to proceed along the lines of the fascist suppressions of the thirties.' Having voiced this outrageous parallel, he nodded sternly and studied his agenda.

Sam Hilton was on the point of renewing his attack, but the chair took decisive action. 'Sam, could we have the latest news on your own efforts, please?'

Young Hilton felt his protest cut off at source, almost as if he had been physically checked. He dragged his thoughts back to why he was here and contented himself with a last glare of molten hatred at Preston. 'Yes. I've been in contact with three poets. I'm happy to say that Bob Crompton has agreed to come. He will read some of his verse and try to explain how he goes about achieving his effects.'

Peter Preston had snorted when he mentioned the name. Hilton glared at him as if daring him to voice a challenge, but the older man contented himself with a renewal of his patronizing smile. Sam Hilton was not used to committees and the more formal language appropriate to them, but he strove to discipline his feelings and speak as moderately as he could.

He found himself breathing unevenly as he did so. 'Bob comes from a very different background from that of most people in Oldford. He is from a one-parent family in a great northern city. Manchester is producing a group of young poets who may well rival the influence of the Mersey poets in a previous generation. He writes about love and sex and politics with a raw edge, which many of his listeners here will find very challenging. I am sure the experience will benefit them greatly.'

He stared round the table as if inviting a challenge, but Marjorie Dooks said swiftly and smoothly, 'I am sure it will be a mutually beneficial exchange. Many of the speakers at our last literary festival said how important it was to them to have an audience and to hear the feedback on whatever form of writing they were producing. Thank you, Sam. I'm sure that without your personal contact we should not have been able to secure the attendance of so well-known and eminent a contemporary poet as Bob Crompton. She glanced automatically at Peter Preston, but that pillar of tradition was nursing his previous wounds and had more sense than to speak again. 'Ros, could we have your report, please?'

Ros Barker was only thirty herself, but she felt an almost maternal need to support and protect the man beside her. 'May I just endorse how well I think Sam's done to get Bob Crompton for us? I know Bob does a lot of poetry readings, but to get him (a) to venture south and (b) to talk about his craft are achievements indeed. My own efforts have not secured so definite a conclusion as yet. The committee will recall that I agreed to try to get Arthur Jackson to talk to us about the history of art. As you will no doubt understand, he has many demands upon his time, as most television personalities have, and it is possible that he might be abroad during the week of our festival. But he has assured me that he wants to come and that if it is humanly possible for him he will do so.'

'That is good news indeed. Once again, thank you for your efforts on behalf of the festival, Ros. I know that Mr Jackson has a high regard for you.'

Ros Barker felt that she was blushing, a sensation she had not endured for years. She spoke hastily in an attempt to divert attention from herself and back to her visitor. 'I owe him a lot.

I was about to go to art school when he saw some of my work and advised me not to go. As you may know, Arthur Jackson has a low regard for the teaching in art schools at the moment. I went and served a sort of apprenticeship with Bernard Goldberg. I think I learned a lot there. I would never have got my own exhibition so early without Mr Jackson and his advice.' She paused, looking round the table, flicking a strand of her long, straight black hair away from her eye. She was talking about herself, when she had never meant to do that. 'I should mention that the other day someone questioned whether a painter should be speaking at a literary festival. I pointed out that Mr Jackson has written several books on the history of art and would no doubt be addressing the issues he raises in them.'

Mrs Dooks nodded emphatically. 'I'm sure you were right to do so. As you say, Mr Jackson has written extensively about art. We have already agreed that a literary festival should include all forms of writing. I am sure he will prove a popular as well as a stimulating visitor.' She glanced again towards Peter Preston, but met only a disdainful smile from a man nursing his wounds. 'I should report briefly on my own efforts. Davina Cooper's new novel is due out a fortnight before our festival. Her publisher has lined up a series of radio interviews and signing sessions for her. But she is keeping the Tuesday evening of our festival week clear and is determined to honour her promise to be with us in Oldford on that day.'

Preston saw an opportunity to ingratiate himself with the chair and reassert his standing with the committee. 'I think you in turn should be congratulated on your efforts, Madam Chairman. You are the obvious person to chair that meeting and introduce your protégé.'

Marjorie smiled, well aware of what he was about but anxious to avoid an open rift in her committee. 'Hardly my protégé, Peter.' She glanced round the table and saw mystification on a couple of faces. 'Perhaps not everyone is aware that Davina Cooper was once a member of my staff in the Civil Service. In fact, she came to me some ten years ago to tender her resignation, after the modest success of her first novel. I told her to think very hard before giving up a promising career and a safe salary in the public service. Fortunately she did not heed me, or I might have aborted a promising literary career at the outset. I suspect she may take some pleasure in recalling my advice to her when she visits us.'

There was amusement around the table and a relaxing of tension, as Marjorie had intended. She closed the meeting quickly and gathered her papers whilst the members departed. 'Christine, could I have a quick word with you, please?'

Mrs Lambert liked Marjorie Dooks, but she stopped now reluctantly, because she knew what was coming. The person who had chaired the meeting waited a moment until they were alone in the room. 'Did you broach the matter of an appearance at the festival with your husband?'

'I did. He wasn't enthusiastic. Unlike some policemen, he doesn't enjoy the publicity he already receives.'

Marjorie smiled. 'Fact of life, Christine. John Lambert is a local celebrity, as we all know. Something of a local hero, indeed. A popular policeman is a rare phenomenon nowadays. We should like to exploit that.'

'But didn't Sue Charles say that she'd be happy to introduce her crime writer?'

'Indeed. And so she should. But I had an idea last night. I thought it would be good to have John on the platform with them, so that we could explore the real situation in serious crime against that depicted in fiction. It would make the question and answer session after David Knight's talk much livelier.'

'I'm not sure I could get John to do that. As I said—'

'We'd need Mr Knight's agreement, of course, but I'm sure Sue could secure that. It wouldn't need any real preparation on your husband's part.'

Mrs Dooks was in her masterful mood. It would take a braver woman than Christine Lambert to confront her with a blank refusal. She said, 'I'll talk to John about it. It's difficult for him to give definite promises about attendance, of course. He might be involved in the investigation of a murder at the very time we want him with us.'

She was merely searching for an excuse, of course. At the time, she had no idea how ironic a ring those words would have during the week of the festival.

THREE

Two days after she had chaired the literary festival committee, Marjorie Dooks attended the local council meeting. There she expressed herself forcefully on things as diverse as the appalling state of the Gloucestershire roads after the ravages of a hard winter and the need for more resources for primary schools from the local education authority.

As usual, with the end of the financial year in sight, the need to set the lowest possible level of council tax dominated all discussions, with the result that many assurances of support in principle were offered to her and no firm promises made. This was the usual state of affairs in local government; they agreed with her sentiments, but nothing was going to happen. Marjorie held her peace and refrained from voicing that thought. She recognized the dilemmas they collectively faced, but the reality was that she could see no way of securing the finance needed to implement her proposed reforms. It was immensely frustrating, but to resign and abandon ship would be an evasion. Evasions were not part of the Dooks creed.

The fact that she understood exactly why these things were as they were didn't prevent her from feeling disheartened as she drove back to the big house on the outskirts of Oldford. But she didn't allow herself to be depressed for long. It was good that she had the festival to think about and to plan. She had more control there, and the programme was shaping up promisingly. Five o'clock, the dashboard clock told her. With a bit of luck she'd have an hour, perhaps two hours, to herself before James returned. Hadn't he said that he had a meeting this afternoon which might go on for a while?

But the big BMW was in the drive when she got there. She felt a rush of resentment that she was not to have the time alone that she had anticipated. James was sitting in a chair in the conservatory with the *Telegraph* business section open upon his knee. He had not heard her come through the house;

she paused for a moment to study him and prepare her smile before she went through to the conservatory.

He was ageing well, Marjorie decided reluctantly. She had spent an unusually long time in front of the dressing table mirror before she had gone to the council meeting, noting with surprise that the crows' feet were extending around her eyes and that the lines on her neck were becoming deeper and more obvious. She had allowed herself a small moment of melancholy at the swiftness of life's passage, at the relentless advance of the body's decay. Then she had told herself with her usual brusqueness to snap out of it.

The memory of that moment four hours earlier now made her more piqued by the capacity of men to grow more handsome as the years advanced. Some men, anyway. She should probably be happy that James was one of them, but at that moment she was not. He had a good head of hair, not very much diminished in thickness or tone from the days when she had first known him thirty years ago, but silvering becomingly at the temples. His features seemed mysteriously to retain most of the tan they had acquired during their summer holiday in Tuscany; he still looked healthy and vigorous at the end of a winter that had been the longest and coldest for twenty years.

His blue eyes remained clear and sharp. He read the paper without glasses, which she could not, but she noticed now that he was holding it a long way from his face and peering at it a little. Such a small, comical vanity should have inspired affection in one who loved him. Marjorie was surprised how contemptuous she felt when she noted it.

She took a deep breath, then opened the glass-panelled door and accorded him her smile. 'You managed to get away early after all.'

'Yes. The chairman cancelled the meeting. Got back later than expected from New York. Matthew doesn't think anything can function properly without his presence. He's probably worried we might make a decision without him.'

'No. Not good at delegation, most British industrialists, are they? The papers foster the doctrine of their supremacy. The solution to the problems of an ailing firm is always a new chairman. No wonder megalomania sets in when they're continually fed the myth of their own importance by the financial press.'

He smiled, recognizing a familiar theme in her. 'Whereas in the Civil Service there was no need for autocracy. You merely advised and implemented. All the important decisions were taken by politicians.'

'That's just the myth we liked to foster. And it's a while now since I was a civil servant. You should try organizing unpaid volunteers some time, when you've no sanctions if they don't toe whatever line you've drawn for them.'

James Dooks tried to simulate the interest in local affairs he had never really felt. 'Yes. How's the literature festival coming along, by the way?'

It was two days since the meeting in the library complex. She realized now that she had been waiting for him to ask about it. When he had finally done so, dutifully and belatedly, she felt merely irritated. 'It's taking shape quite well. Dealing with the artistic temperament is a new and enlightening experience for me. I've no doubt it would be very good for you.'

He smiled. 'No thanks. Do you want to eat out, as I'm home in plenty of time?'

'No. It's only a Marks and Spencer's meal for two, but we should eat it today. It won't take very long to prepare.' Somehow she couldn't face eating out alone with him and the long silences whilst they sought for something safe to say to each other. It was much easier when they were out socializing with other people; perhaps it was easier to sustain the fiction that all was well when you had other voices to bring into the conversation.

He came into the big dining kitchen when she called him and opened the bottle of wine that had come with the meal. He glanced at the label, then said as he sat down at the table, 'How did your meeting go this afternoon?'

For a moment she was pleased that he had remembered her council concerns. Then she realized that he had looked at the calendar by the telephone where they each entered their commitments and picked up the information from there. She should have been glad even that he had taken the trouble to check on her day. Instead, she was more annoyed than if he had never asked his question. She dismissed the council meeting briskly, without commenting upon her concerns or her frustrations.

As if he sensed her mood and was anxious to dissipate it, he began clumsily loading the dishwasher when they had finished. Even that annoyed her; he was so pathetically anxious to please that he was acting outside his character. She knew she was being petty and unreasonable, but she chose to ignore that. At that moment, she just wished to be rid of him, even for a few minutes, so that she could compose herself to behave better. Thank heavens for the television! You didn't have to talk much, once the goggle box was busy.

She glanced up at the clock on the wall and said as lightly as she could, 'There's a programme about opera on BBC Four in five minutes. If you go and put it on I'll bring the coffee through on a tray.'

James smiled and said, 'That reminds me. I think we'll probably get our invitation for Glyndebourne again this year. Clive Morrison, who entertained us there last year, owes me a favour. I'll give him a ring tomorrow, if I get the chance.'

It was not until she glanced at the clock that she saw the white foolscap envelope on the unit beneath it. James followed her gaze and said, 'Oh, I forgot about that. It was behind the door when I got home. It's addressed to you, without a stamp. It must have been delivered by hand.' He went into the lounge dutifully as he had been told to do; a moment later she heard the sound of the television newsreader.

She inspected her printed name on the envelope, then slit open the end of it with the small kitchen knife beside it. It contained a single sheet of paper, neatly folded.

Her first reaction was surprise, not fear. Nothing remotely like this had happened to her before. You read about it in books, or heard other people talking about something similar. You never expected it to be part of your own experience, and when it occurred you could not quite believe it. For sixty seconds her mind raced, but she could not have said what she was thinking, what emotions were hammering in her head.

There were only twelve words on the sheet, but the print was large, black and uncompromising.

RESIGN NOW FROM THE FESTIVAL COMMITTEE IF YOU WISH TO REMAIN ALIVE

Peter Preston was nursing his wounds. That damned woman Dooks had no standards. If the citizens of Oldford had had any sense, they'd have put him in charge of the literary festival from the start and given him a free hand with budgets and speakers. But they hadn't, and it was no surprise that they hadn't. Provincial, that's what they were, so you shouldn't expect anything other than provincial attitudes.

He said as much to his wife, but she'd heard it all before. He shouldn't have got involved if he was going to get upset like this, Edwina told him. She had lost count of the number of times before when she had had occasion to tell him that. A very conventional woman, Edwina. That was both her strength and her weakness.

'I've a good mind to withdraw my support altogether,' said Peter.

'You mustn't do that.' She was assailed by visions of him around the house all day, increasingly fractious as he realized that he had lost all influence on the intelligentsia of the area. 'You'd miss the festival if you weren't involved.'

She was right, of course. Some small part of his inner self saw that quite clearly. 'This place just doesn't appreciate everything I've done for it over the years.'

'I don't know why you allow yourself to get so upset about these things. You should realize by now that you're always going to be disappointed.' Another of her hackneyed, predictable statements; he could have foretold it, word for word. Didn't she realize that stuff like that would just infuriate him? For a surprising, delicious moment, he saw himself with his hands round her throat, squeezing the life out of her, watching her eyes dilate with terror as her string of clichés was stilled for ever.

It was a glorious vision, as fleeting as it was delightful. It left him shocked but delighted. It was another sign that he wasn't as other men, when it came to the strength of his emotions. Another sign that his extra sensitivity meant that he felt things more keenly than the common run of men. Peter was wrong there, as he often was; his knowledge of human nature was nothing like as profound as he proclaimed it to be. He didn't realize that all over Britain on any single night there were thousands of married men and thousands of married women who enjoyed delicious escapist moments as they envisaged choking the life out of a perpetually irritating spouse. He would have been astonished to know that even that conventional woman Edwina occasionally thought of him with his eyes staring sightlessly at the ceiling and those too-mobile lips stilled for ever.

Fortunately for the forces of law and order, only a tiny percentage of people ever transform thought into action. Any murderous move of that sort would certainly set Peter Preston apart from other men.

Christine Lambert chose her moment and her menu with great care. They had steak and their first Jersey Royal new potatoes of the year, with purple sprouting broccoli from their own garden. She had one glass of a very agreeable Merlot and John had two. They had cheesecake for dessert; she passed him a second helping without a word after his first longing glance at what was left. She sent him into the lounge to decide upon their television viewing for the night, whilst she cleared the dishes and prepared the coffee. She poured him a brandy to drink with his, then, after a moment's consideration, set a second, token measure for herself beside it on the tray.

The feminists would have been tutting long ago, she thought. But she had her methods of achieving things, old-fashioned but generally effective. She looked at the tray and wondered if she was overdoing things, whether John might see through her obvious ploys. But men were credulous creatures, when your weapons were food and drink. That was surely a thought of which even the most modern woman could approve.

She asked him about his day and he talked to her a little about it, as he would never have done twenty years ago. When he asked her about her own day, she knew that this was the moment she had been waiting for. 'I've been tying up a few things concerned with the literary festival. I like Marjorie Dooks. She says what she thinks and doesn't say other things behind your back. She treads on a few toes, but she gets things done. And she's not afraid of work herself. She doesn't ask you to do things just because she doesn't fancy them herself. She makes you feel as if you're definitely the best person for the job.'

'That's good. I've had mixed reports about her, but nothing to contradict what you've just said.' John Lambert contemplated the big globe of his brandy glass, rolled its contents pensively around inside it, and took an appreciative sip.

She marvelled anew at his policeman's capacity for gathering information she did not think he would have. He took no obvious interest in local affairs, yet whenever anything came up, he invariably seemed to know far more than she would have expected. A CID trait, he said apologetically, whenever she remarked upon it. You kept your ears open to everything, including gossip and rumour, and filed it away for future reference. There was nothing sinister or complex about it; you just trained your memory to do these things.

Christine said as casually as she could, 'It looks as though David Knight will be coming. Sue Charles has been using her influence.'

John Lambert gazed at his brandy and said, carefully neutral, 'That's good. He's a big name in the crime-writing field. You're doing well to get him here.'

'Marjorie still wants to get you on the platform with him.'

He took an unhurried sip of the brandy, allowing himself a moment to savour its warmth in his throat and his chest. He tried not to sound sententious as he said, 'I should have thought Sue Charles was the one to introduce him, as she's done all the work to get him here. She might feel quite hurt if you brought in someone who doesn't even know the man.'

'I agree.' Nervousness had made her agreement too prompt, too eager. 'But Marjorie had a good idea. Maybe even a brilliant one. She thought if you were on the platform for the question and answer section, you'd be able to speak from the point of view of someone fighting real crime. Illustrate the differences between fact and fiction you're always so anxious to point out when you catch me watching detective series on television.'

There was a long pause, during which she began to entertain the hope that he was giving the suggestion serious consideration. He rolled what was left of the generous helping of brandy round his glass and finally allowed himself a smile. 'I wondered why we were having steak and new potatoes and cheesecake and our best Merlot. And all in midweek, too!'

'You bastard!' But there was more reluctant admiration than annoyance in the epithet. She grinned at him. 'You knew all the time, didn't you? And you just strung me along for all you could get.'

'I thought it was you who was doing the stringing along,' he protested mildly. 'But I should be grateful to you really, for reviving skills that might have atrophied in me. It's the way you lead a snout along, getting everything he has to give out of him before you fix on a price. I haven't had to do that much since I reached the exalted heights of chief superintendent.'

She wasn't sure she liked to be classed alongside police informers. 'Was it so obvious?'

'When the cheesecake followed the steak and the wine, it became so. When the brandy came in with the coffee, I thought I might as well see how far it went. I thought if I played my cards right and had a bit of luck, you might end up seducing me on the rug.'

'Remember your age and don't push your luck and your back, John Lambert. Just finish your brandy and then tell me you'll join in that session on crime writing.'

'No can do, I'm afraid. Not my scene, literary festivals.'

'Why not? You're surprisingly well read, for a copper. Probably more so than most of your audience will be.'

'Shouldn't that be "would be"? I've already said I'm not doing it.' He hugged his brandy glass to his chest, like a child who feared that his treat might be removed.

She played her last card. 'You can tell Marjorie Dooks then.'

'No go again. It's your committee. You can report back to it that you asked me to undertake the task as you said you would and I refused.'

'Marjorie doesn't accept no for an answer very easily. Everyone else on that committee seems to be achieving whatever is asked of them.'

She looked very downcast. She gazed at her feet and her head fell a little to one side. He was suddenly reminded of her as a nineteen-year-old, when some small disappointment had seemed for a moment like the end of her world. Before he knew the thought had formed itself in his head, he found himself saying, 'I'll ask Bert Hook about it. It might appeal to him, now that he's an Open University B.A.'

Sometimes the instinctive reaction worked better than all the elaborate planning, Christine Lambert decided. Showing your disappointment always had more effect on men than women. Her daughters had always been able to sway this iron man of crime when they were cast down by some teenage setback. Perhaps men, even experienced men like John Lambert, were suckers after all.

Ros Barker looked at her subject critically, her head a little on one side, her eyes narrowing a little as she gazed intently at the naked woman who half-sat and half-lay on the chaise longue she had set up in her studio for this painting. 'You need to look more relaxed. The last thing I want is someone who looks as if she's struggling to hold a pose.'

'Perhaps that's because I'm struggling so hard to hold this pose,' said Kate Merrick testily. 'And if you don't allow us to have a coffee soon the struggle might fail.'

For a few seconds, Ros appeared to ignore her completely, whilst she applied a few key brush strokes. It was the artist's supreme moment of concentration, the instant of utter selfishness when nothing and no one else matters save the need to secure some effect that might otherwise escape forever. Then, with a relaxation of tension that she felt even in herself, she glanced at the little clock on the table to her right and said, 'Is it really eleven o'clock? High time we had a coffee, I'd say.'

Kate eased herself gingerly into a sitting position, then stretched her legs gratefully. She stood up and moved with exaggerated stiffness to the kettle in the corner of the studio and extracted two beakers from the battered little cupboard on which it stood. She heard a delighted giggle at her robotic movements from behind her and was immediately pleased, despite her supposed resentment.

'It's getting warm in here now the sun's climbing,' said Ros, standing and looking at the world outside through the long window on the south wall of her studio.

'Not if you're a poor exploited model required to keep still for hours without a stitch on, it isn't! Don't you dream of putting that electric fire off, Madam Scrooge.'

Kate brought the two beakers of instant coffee across to the old sofa on the opposite side of the room from the chaise longue. Ros, after studying her painting keenly with her head tilted elaborately for a last moment, came and sat beside Kate, who had thrown her usual blanket around herself before she sat. Though they had moved only to the other side of the studio, work had been switched off for the moment, just as effectively as if they had moved from factory floor to works canteen.

'Sometimes I think we should splash out on a professional model for you,' Kate said presently. 'You could then move her around as much as you liked, and I might escape pneumonia in the present and rheumatoid arthritis in later life.'

'It's the fate of the partner throughout the centuries. And the blessing too, of course. Rembrandt's wife was immortalized because he couldn't afford a professional model.' Ros's voice softened a little. 'Or perhaps because he could convey his tenderness towards her in a way he could never have achieved with a professional model.' She ran her hand lightly and affectionately down the slim thigh beneath the shabby blanket.

'They weren't called partners then, though. Wives or mistresses. I don't know which ones were the luckier. Or the more exploited.' Kate nibbled her ginger biscuit and took an appreciative sip of the hot coffee.

'Yes. Exciting prospect for you, that. When I'm famous all over the planet, you could be one of the first partners to be immortalized in oils.'

'I can hardly wait.' A pause, during which Ros thought fondly of the curves beneath the blanket and the natural, unthinking grace with which Kate normally moved. Ros was long-limbed, and angular, with short-cut dark hair and a lean, strong-boned face. Attraction of opposites perhaps. Or simply coincidence: it didn't do to analyse these things too thoroughly, when they were working so well.

Kate finished her coffee and gazed at the bottom of her beaker reflectively. 'Do you want me to go away when Arthur Jackson comes here?'

'Certainly not. I don't go round proclaiming that we're

living together, because it's no one's business but our own. That doesn't mean that I'm ashamed of it.'

Kate Merrick grinned, showing her sense of security, stretching deliciously beneath the blanket. 'I didn't say ashamed, stupid. That went out in the last century. I just thought you might not care to proclaim us to your mentor. He seems a very conventional man.'

'He isn't. It takes a lot of guts and a lot of cussedness to take a stand against the art establishment as he has. Most of the avant-garde still hate him. He won't raise an eyebrow when he finds us together.'

'Even when he finds his favourite protégé is one of those bloody lesbians?'

That was a private joke between them, a phrase they had heard flung across a pub in their early days, before they'd decided they liked each other enough to live together and sleep together. Ros Barker smiled and said, 'I'm sure I'm not his favourite protégé. That's probably some heterosexual girl who paints apples beautifully and smiles adoringly at him. He offered me some good advice and a little judicious support at an important stage of my life, that's all. He might at some stage examine my paintings to see what effect a lasting sexual relationship has had upon them, but his interest will be purely aesthetic. That's if he finds my work good enough to justify his interest in the future.'

'His opinion is important to you, isn't it?'

'I suppose it is, yes. I wouldn't confess this to anyone else, but I suppose he's the nearest thing I have to a father figure. My own father left us when I was four and I've only the vaguest memory of him. Just a man who shouted a lot – I can't remember what about. Mum's never pretended to have any interest in art, though she's glad to see me scraping a living in it. She's never had any success with her hetero relationships, but she claims not to understand what we feel for each other.'

'She doesn't like me.'

'She doesn't dislike you. She just doesn't like to think of us sleeping together, or that's what she says. She'll accept the idea eventually, once she's had time to get used to it. She's a great one for getting used to things, is Mum.'

'What about those dragons on the literature festival committee?'

'They're not dragons, most of them. They're not what I expected at all, but I can hardly tell them that.'

'Not even Mrs Dooks? After what I'd heard about her, I expected you to come home singed with fire and smelling of brimstone.'

'I fear you probably heard most of it from me. I went to the first meeting in fear and trepidation, but after the third one I'm impressed. She's a formidable lady, but I suspect rather a sweetie underneath, though she'd hate you to say so. She knows how to run a committee. She doesn't stand any nonsense from Peter Preston.'

Kate leant forward, clasping her blanket about her knees. 'She cut Poncing Peter down to size? I must hear about this.'

Ros glanced at the little clock. 'I suppose she did, really. He turned up his nose at detective novels and she said they'd already made the decisions about that – gave him chapter and verse about when and how. Then he had a set-to with young Sam Hilton, our local poet. I spoke up for Sam, but I wasn't really needed. Marjorie Dooks sat firmly on Peter Preston again. It was all highly embarrassing and highly enjoyable at the same time.'

'You do see life, don't you, Ros? Whereas I'm just a humble and anonymous artist's model, condemned to pose forever in a freezing garret.' Kate pouted extravagantly and crossed her arms over her breasts modestly beneath the blanket.

'In a well-heated modern studio, you mean! With someone who is stretching every nerve to make you immortal.' Ros ran her hand through Kate's hair, feeling the familiar wiry strength beneath the softness that she so relished. She felt the stirrings of desire as she caressed the nape of her partner's neck, then said sternly, 'Back to work, you idle serf. Get thee to the chaise longue and distribute thyself in the approved manner.'

Kate Merrick fled in her own simulation of abject terror, then without apparent effort set her limbs into the exact pose she had left twenty minutes earlier, with her left arm over the rise of the chaise longue, her back to the artist, and her eyes looking not directly at the easel but at the ceiling above her. Once there, she sighed extravagantly and said thoughtfully, 'I should think Peter Preston could willingly murder your Mrs Dooks.'

FOUR

Sam Hilton would have been reassured to know that Ros Barker thought so kindly of him. However, the knowledge probably wouldn't have affected the action he was now taking.

He heard the phone shrilling at the other end of the line and was surprised how his pulse quickened at the sound. Then the receiver was picked up and the authoritative voice he had expected said simply, 'Marjorie Dooks.'

'Er, good morning, Mrs Dooks. It's – it's Sam Hilton here. The poet. I'm on your literary festival committee.'

An indeterminate sound. Whether it was a stifled giggle or a grunt of exasperation or something else entirely, he couldn't be certain. 'Yes, Sam. I know who you are. What can I do for you?'

'Well, nothing really. I just wanted to tell you something.' Sam decided he hated phones, but held the small mobile more tightly against his ear.

'And what would that something be, Sam?'

Marjorie was trying to be encouraging, but she came through to Sam as a woman near the edge of her patience. 'I want to resign.'

There. He had blurted it out, when he had meant to give his reasons and emphasize how entirely logical the action was. The damned woman had this effect upon him, for some reason, when he should have just despised her and everything she stood for. He wanted to explain himself, when he should have just said, 'I'm going. Peter bloody Preston and the rest of you can just piss off if you don't like it.' But they would like it, of course. They might bleat a bit about it for form's sake, but secretly they'd be damned glad to see the back of him and everything he represented.

'It would be a pity if you felt you had to leave us, Sam. Speaking personally and selfishly, it would make my job a lot more difficult.'

He tried to be aggressive. 'I should have thought it would have made it a damned sight easier. You could plan what you want to do without having any awkward fucking youngsters to get in the way.'

'But we need awkward fucking youngsters. And you're the only one we've got, Sam.'

He'd tried to shock her and she'd come straight back at him with the word, as if she used it all the time. He had meant to throw her off balance and now he was thrown himself. He said desperately, 'I'm twenty-two and I'm the only young bugger on that committee. Half the time I'm not even sure what you're fucking talking about.'

'I'm sure that's not true, Sam. And Ros Barker's only thirty, you know. That may seem old to you, but to people like Christine Lambert and me, she's much more in your age-group than ours.'

'Mrs Lambert taught me.' Why had he said that? It had been out before he knew he was going to say it. It sounded like a confession of weakness. 'It's the first time I can remember enjoying a poem.'

'That's interesting. I didn't know that. What age were you then, Sam?'

He wished she wouldn't keep using his name. Even though he wanted to sneer at her, he knew that he couldn't call her Marjorie. 'I was about ten, I suppose. It was my last year in junior school.'

'You owe her a lot, then. She helped to set you on the lonely road to becoming a poet.'

Despite himself, he liked that word 'lonely'. It made her sound almost as though she knew what it was like to spend hours on your own wrestling with words, battering your mind to come up with the phrase that you and only you could produce. Before he could stop himself, he heard himself quoting,

'"Quinquereme of Ninevah from distant Ophir, Rowing home to haven in sunny Palestine." I can't remember what quinquereme is. Some sort of Roman galley, I think. I just liked the sound of the words. They're from *Cargoes* by John Masefield. No one reads him now.'

'More's the pity if they don't,' said Marjorie staunchly. '"Dirty British coaster with a salt-caked smoke stack, Butting through the Channel in the mad March days." That poem must have made an impression on me as well, Sam.'

'You know it!' He couldn't keep the delight out of his voice, when delight was the last thing he had planned.

'I haven't thought about it for years. But we learned things by heart, in the prehistoric days when I went to school. Actually, that was out of date even then, but I went to an old-fashioned private prep school. I've been getting rid of lots of the stuff they taught me ever since, but I'm glad we learned a bit of poetry.'

'It's full of rhythm, you know, that poem. You have to have rhythm, whatever sort of verse you're writing. Even free verse has to have some sort of rhythm.' He was preaching at her, the way he preached at his poetry-reading gigs, when people asked him about verse and why what they tried to write didn't satisfy them. She'd probably choke him off now, which would be a good thing. He could get on with resigning and telling her to piss off, if the damned woman would only behave as she was supposed to.

But the damned woman said, 'That's why we need you, Sam, you see. I don't think there's anyone else in the group who understands properly what poetry is all about.'

He said sullenly, 'People round here don't want to listen to people like me.'

She went on almost as if he hadn't spoken. 'We need you to hold your corner against all this cosy middle-class satisfaction and give us access to people like Bob Crompton. I'm sure he'll be like a breath of fresh air for us. And stuffy old Oldford needs a breath of fresh air, don't you think?'

'I suppose so.' He hoped he was just agreeing to the breath of fresh air and not to staying on her damned committee. He'd meant this to be short, sweet and vulgar, but the bloody woman seemed able to take all his shots and not even realize she was under fire. He said, 'I'm no good at committees. I've never been on one before.'

'And I've been on far too many. They're a bore for a lot of the time, but they're the only way of reaching decisions when you have a group of people with different backgrounds and different opinions. We want all of them to be represented – it's one of the differences between fascism and democracy.' Marjorie wondered if 'fascism' was still the all-embracing, demonizing word it had been in her youth. Sam Hilton would have been amazed as well as consoled if he had known how hard his ogress was struggling with her own end of the conversation.

'Anyway, that's why I've decided that it's not for me.'

'I'd miss you if you did go, you know, Sam. Between you and me, I'm not sure I could hold out against the scorn of people like Peter Preston if you weren't there to express a different point of view.'

'I can't fucking stand him.' He was surprised how much relief it brought him to be able to speak with real venom.

'Peter has his uses and his contacts. And, believe it or not, he has experience none of the rest of us has. There'll be times when we need to listen to his opinions. All points of view should be represented, as I said. Including yours, Sam.'

She'd thrown that in when he had least expected it, like a boxing punch when you were coming out of a clinch. That was a simile he'd used in one of his earliest poems. Funny it should come back to him now. He made a last attempt to get rid of this for good. 'I'm not much good to you on that committee. I don't understand properly how these things work.'

'Oh, I think you underestimate yourself, Sam. I've been pleased with your contributions thus far. The important thing is that you've spoken up when you felt it was needed.'

'But you don't need me. You were the one who told Poncey Pete to get stuffed.'

'I couldn't have done that if you and Ros Barker hadn't spoken up. The chair has to be neutral. You know that much about committees, I'm sure.'

'Has to pretend to be neutral, you mean!'

'Yes! There you are, you see! You know far more about committees and the way they operate than you said you did. And who's going to speak up for poetry if you're not there?'

She had divined correctly that there was an evangelical streak in him when it came to poetry. He often surprised himself by speaking up for it and trying to explain how it worked in all kinds of unlikely places. Perhaps it was not really so surprising; when it was the most important thing you did, you needed to justify yourself. And now he'd kept himself on that bloody committee, when he'd been determined to have done with it. He said dolefully, 'All right. I'll give it a go for a bit longer. Just until you get someone else more suitable.'

'Splendid! You've been in touch with Mr Crompton?'

'Bob? Yes. He's definitely going to come. He says he'll do his usual thing, read his usual poems, and see how they take it.' Despite himself, he was absurdly pleased that the ogress had remembered Bob's name.

'That's good. I'm really looking forward to a stimulating session. Hopefully Bob Crompton will find it useful as well.'

'I'm sure he will,' said Sam grimly.

He put down the phone and stared at it balefully for a moment. He wasn't quite sure how this had happened. It was his first experience of what many servants of the nation had experienced over the years: the formidable Marjorie Dooks had secured a totally different outcome from that planned and anticipated by her colleagues.

'I see you've booked your annual leave for the last two weeks in July.'

It was best to come at this obliquely, Chief Superintendent Lambert thought. Even people cutting your hair talked about your holidays. Bert Hook surely wouldn't see any threat in such a dull and conventional conversational opening.

'Yes. We're still confined to school holidays with the boys.' Bert played it back like a straight but unthreatening first ball, wondering what more dangerous deliveries his chief had in store for him.

'Have you decided where you're going yet?'

'Yes. We've already booked the same cottage in north Cornwall which we had last year. You have to book early at that time of the year.'

They knew each other too well, these men. Like a lot of CID men, they were not good at small talk; perhaps that came from conducting too many interviews with known criminals, where you went straight for the throat and fought to close your metaphorical hands around it. When Bert Hook heard John Lambert opening with such an unthreatening enquiry, he was immediately on his guard rather than relaxed.

Consequently, when the older man said as casually as he could, 'You'll be around here at the end of May, then,' he knew that some request or order he wasn't going to like was in the offing.

'Yes. I've a feeling in my water that we'll be pretty busy around that time, though.'

'No reason why we should be, is there, Bert?'

'No obvious reason. A feeling in my water, as I said. A nudge from the instinct I've developed as a detective sergeant. The same instinct warns me that a man who is otherwise quite civilized is about to assert the brutalities of rank.'

'You're a sensitive soul, Bert.'

'And flattery won't work. Not that it isn't welcome, of course.'

'It's a very small thing I have to ask of you, Bert.'

'I like that "ask". It implies that refusal is a possibility.'

'Oh, I don't think you'll refuse this, Bert. This is something you'll quite enjoy. A change from the dull round of petty crime and criminal faces.'

Bert said stubbornly, 'It's not such a dull round. Neither young thugs nor old lags are all the same as each other. Looking for the differences can be both instructive and useful.' He was repeating the pious mantra he had voiced to a new DC earlier in the day, but he kept his face straight.

'This is something you could do better than any other officer in the CID section, Bert.'

'I doubt that.'

'What other officer among us has recently obtained an Open University degree?'

Bert sighed. 'I don't see why that should line me up for shitty jobs.'

'It makes you an intellectual, Bert. There aren't many among us who can hold their own with the Gloucestershire intelligentsia.' Lambert looked through the window of his office, weighing the thought. Then he nodded two or three times.

But Bert Hook knew his man too well. He looked at him suspiciously and said bluntly, 'This is something that was offered to you, isn't it?'

Lambert smiled ruefully. 'It was a request addressed initially to me, yes. I was happy to think of someone more suitable for a most agreeable assignation.'

'Very unselfish of you.' Bert Hook sighed again, more elaborately. He'd rumbled what the chief was up to. That didn't happen very often and he wanted to savour the moment. 'What is the shitty job you're trying to unload on to your unsuspecting junior?'

Lambert sighed in turn at this cynicism in his bagman. 'It's not at all shitty, Bert. It's a compliment to be considered. It's the Oldford Literary Festival.' He rolled off the syllables reverently. 'They've secured an eminent author of detective novels as one of their speakers. The organizer thinks it would be an excellent idea to have a real detective on the platform with him for the discussion which will follow his talk. Someone who could point out the differences between real crime and fictional crime.'

'I agree with you on one thing. It seems an excellent idea.'

'You do? Well, in that case, I'll—'

'An excellent idea that they should approach their local celebrity, Chief Superintendent Lambert, to fulfil that role. You're the man they wanted, aren't you?'

'Well, that was the original suggestion, yes. But if I can offer them someone who is much more obviously suited to the task, I'm sure they'll be happy to—'

'It's no go, John. It's you they want. I'm sure our Chief Constable will endorse that view when you tell him about it.'

Lambert gazed through the window for a moment longer, then smiled wryly at his colleague and friend. 'It was worth a try, Bert. And you'd have done it well.'

Bert shook his head decisively. 'It's you they want and you they should have, John.'

Lambert sighed. 'Maybe there'll be a serious crime to make my attendance impossible.' He spoke without much hope. But police pessimism is not always justified.

* * *

In the sharp cold of the April frost, the man struggled beneath the straggly rhododendron. He was glad of his anorak and the thick polo-necked sweater he had put on beneath it, but nothing could keep his feet warm as he waited on the damp earth. It was a good twenty minutes before the car swung into the drive; it felt much longer than that to him.

Behind the wheel was a plump woman of around forty, bottle-blonde and carefully made up. She put on the hand brake and swung herself out of the car, gasping a curse as the cold hit her bare arms and the legs exposed beneath the absurdly short skirt. At least those legs were still good, thank God. She locked the car, the orange lights flashing bright and brief as she pressed the electronic button.

She was turning away from the car when he shot her. The single bullet through the temple would have been enough, but he blasted another one through the back of her head as she lay at his feet. Professional killers left nothing to chance. The soft noise of the bullets sounded loud in the thin air, even with the silencer on. But there was no sign of a response from any of the new houses in the quiet close. He was away from the scene and back at his car within two minutes, having seen not a soul . . .

Sue Charles stared at the computer screen for a moment, then glanced at the clock and set about logging off. Sufficient for today. She liked to have something to polish when she came back to her latest book in the morning. If she added a few telling details to make the killing more convincing, it would help to ease her into the new working day. Then she could go on to develop plot and character and do more original and creative things.

When you'd been doing this for thirty years, you knew what worked for you and what didn't in the writing process. She had a variety of little tricks to prevent her writing from becoming stale. This was one of them; the process of polishing eased you into the difficult business of trying to create something new each day.

She extracted the supermarket meal for one from the fridge and slid it into the oven. It never seemed worth spending time on preparing and cooking food when you were only catering for one. And everyone said how much better these ready-prepared meals were than they had been ten years ago. Most of them were quite tasty. Especially if you had a couple of glasses of wine with them.

She grinned wryly to herself. She found herself making these excuses to be a slattern nearly every day now, when there was really no need for them. She'd only herself to answer to, hadn't she? Speaking of which – she went and looked at herself in the hall mirror. She'd found a couple of days ago that she hadn't combed her hair all day; it had been flying untidy and unchecked at seven in the evening.

It was all right today. The grey tresses were disciplined, with only a few strands daring to leave their ranks. She couldn't understand this fashion among the youngsters for irregular partings; it seemed to destroy the whole idea of dividing your hair in a certain way. But there were many things she didn't understand and almost as many of which she didn't approve about modern life. As a writer, she knew she mustn't get out of touch with the generations behind her. The radio and the television were a great help, she supposed. She tried hard to listen to all the latest news and keep an open mind about what was happening and what other people said about it.

Sue Charles didn't think she was becoming a recluse, but she was uncomfortably aware that most recluses probably thought that.

She had been a widow for almost four years now. Most people thought she had coped very well with her new status. Her work must have been a great help, everyone told her. She supposed it had, but she missed having George around when she was writing more than people knew. He had read each chapter as she wrote, correcting typing errors and making occasional tentative suggestions about character and plot. The house never felt emptier, nor writing a lonelier craft, than when she finished a chapter, breathed a sigh of relief, and realized anew that there was now no one to show it to if she printed it off.

She had been more prepared for her husband's death than many of the widows she knew. When you married a man twelve years older than you, you were vaguely aware throughout the marriage that the odds were that you would eventually bury your husband. That had been George's phrase, and she was still acutely conscious of those moments when she had stood at the graveside and looked down at the coffin with its neat gold plate in the pit below her. She recalled even the feel of the ridiculous little scoop with which she had sprinkled the damp earth at the priest's invitation, watching the earth fall on the English oak. She remembered that odd mixture of relief and irritation which her husband's religion had always brought to her; half consoling ancient rites and half mumbo-jumbo.

All the funerals she had attended since then had been cremations, as hers would be, many of them with humanist conductors. She was grateful for that, for she wanted no echoes of George's passing. She was grateful, too, to her publishers, who still wanted her work in a recession, who continued to celebrate her modest success with equally modest contracts for new detective novels. It still gave her a secret thrill after all these years to add the bright new cover of the latest Sue Charles whodunit to the shelves set aside for her work in her book-lined study.

There was a clatter of cat flap in the utility room that adjoined the kitchen. She knew every familiar sound and what it meant in this bungalow. Losing your partner was like losing some peculiar extra sense, she sometimes thought. The other ones, particularly sight and hearing, became more alert to the seasons in the garden and to the small sounds around the house than they had ever been before.

Roland, her nine-year-old neutered cat, inspected the contents of his bowl and found them unsatisfactory. He walked across the kitchen, stared at Sue accusingly for fifteen seconds, and then strode away into the sitting room with tail erect and disapproval bristling in his every movement. It was good to have an animal in the house, though a cat wasn't the companion that a dog was. But she didn't like small dogs, and she didn't think she had the time or the energy to cope with the sort of boisterous Labrador she and George had always enjoyed when they were younger.

The lasagne was almost ready now. The timer bell pinged on the cooker and she set the cutlery on the tray ready to take into the sitting room and the TV. Sloppy, but everyone did it, her friends told her, so there was no need to feel guilty. She was putting the salt and pepper pots on the tray when she heard a sound from the hall which she did not immediately recognize. Then she decided she knew what it was: the soft fall of a letter or single sheet on to the matt beside the front door. Not the heavy clunk of the postman, which usually denoted nothing more than the latest batch of junk mail. It was far too late for that, in any case, almost seven o'clock, with the sun gone behind the hill and twilight creeping in. Probably the latest leaflet from the pizza shop that had recently opened in Oldford, she decided. It was one of the little games she played with herself to offset disappointment, deciding just what the latest thing to come through her letter box might be.

She picked up the envelope as she carried her tray through to the sitting room. Addressed to her personally, so unlikely to be junk mail. Perhaps a friend who hadn't wanted to disturb her. She felt a sudden irritation that the deliverer hadn't stopped to exchange a word or two.

There was but a single sheet inside the envelope. The message was simple and stark.

RESIGN NOW FROM THE FESTIVAL COMMITTEE IF YOU WISH TO REMAIN ALIVE

FIVE

Peter Preston was in the midst of a trying day. They seemed to him to happen with increasing frequency as he grew older.

He tried the number again, with no great hope of success. But this time it was answered and a curt voice said, 'Hilary James here. How can I help you?'

'And who is Hilary James?' He tried to keep the tone light and the impatience out of his voice.

'I am Mr Carter's secretary. Whom am I addressing?'

'My name is Peter Preston. I knew Denzil in the days before he could afford to employ the services of a secretary.'

A pause whilst she scribbled the name on her telephone pad. 'I see. And what is the purpose of your call, Mr Preston?'

'I shall reveal that to Denzil. Please put me through to him.'

'I cannot do that. Mr Carter does not have a phone in his study. He prefers to have no disturbance whilst he is working.'

'Good old Denzil. I approve of that. Nevertheless, please tell him that I wish to speak to him.'

'I'm afraid that won't be possible, Mr Preston. Mr Carter makes it a rule that he will not be disturbed during working hours.'

'Again, I approve. And again, I must ask you to tell Denzil that Peter Preston wishes to speak to him. I am sure that he will make an exception for an old friend.'

'That would be most irregular. Mr Carter does not take kindly to interruptions.'

But he had caught the instant of hesitation in her voice. It was time to be firm with this wretched woman. 'He will take kindly to this one. I assume your time is valuable, as mine certainly is. Please don't waste any more of either and tell your employer that I am on the line.'

There was a pause before the secretary said, 'This is highly irregular and against my instructions. Hold the line, please, whilst I see whether Mr Carter wishes to speak to you.'

Preston tapped his fingers on the desk impatiently as the phone was put down and he heard the faint sound of departing footsteps. 'Stroppy cow!' he muttered to himself with feeling. Sometimes the modern invective he so despised could be a useful outlet. The seconds stretched into minutes. He hoped the woman was being firmly put in her place.

There was the sound of the phone being picked up and he said, 'Sorry to disturb you at your desk, Denzil, but I—'

'Mr Preston, this is Mr Carter's secretary again. I'm afraid Mr Carter is far too busy at present to interrupt his work. What is it that you wished to speak to him about?'

His instinct was to say tersely that his business was no concern of hers, but something told him belatedly to be cautious. He said stiffly, 'It is a personal matter, which I should have much preferred to discuss with Mr Carter rather than an intermediary. I am speaking from Oldford in Gloucestershire. We run a small but prestigious literary festival in the town, in which I am a prime mover. My old friend Denzil Carter has agreed to come and speak about his plays and the processes of their construction; I shall be chairing that session. I merely wish to finalize the details of this visit with Denzil himself.'

'I see. Mr Carter said that this proposed visit might be the subject of your phone call.'

'Yes. I hope you see now why I needed to speak to Denzil personally.'

'Indeed. But I have to tell you that Mr Carter's recollection of the arrangements made is rather different from yours, Mr Preston. He says that you made a tentative approach and that he gave you no firm guarantee of his attendance.'

'Ms James, I can assure you that—'

'Mr Carter is adamant that he gave you no definite undertaking to speak at your festival. Indeed, he says he warned you that the pressure of his commitments in the second half of May would probably make it impossible.'

Peter Preston knew that although he was furious he must think quickly. He was nothing like as good at that as he had once been. 'This is why I needed to speak to Denzil personally, you see. An arrangement between friends is always vague, but this one is underpinned by the regard we have built up for each other over the years. I'm sure this could be resolved in a few minutes if I could just be allowed to—'

'Mr Carter's instructions were to inform you that pressure of work and the engagements he has already committed himself to at the time of your festival mean that he is now certain that he will not be able to undertake this visit to Oldford. He asks me to remind you that he informed you at the time of your original approach that this would be the likely outcome.'

'But this is preposterous! I'm sure the misunderstanding could be resolved very quickly if you would only—'

'I am afraid that Mr Carter is quite definite about this. His further instructions were to wish you success with your festival and inform you that he regrets that pressure of work does not allow him to speak to you at this time.'

'Look, I've had quite enough of your damned impertinence! Kindly—'

'Mr Preston, I am, as you accurately pointed out to me a few moments ago, nothing more than an intermediary. As such, it is part of my duties to protect my employer from unwanted approaches. If you—'

'Unwanted approaches! I told you, we—'

'I was about to suggest that if your recollection of the arrangements made and the commitment undertaken is different from Mr Carter's, you should put your feelings in writing. I shall make sure any written communication from you is presented to Mr Carter. I cannot guarantee that his reaction will differ substantially from the one I have conveyed to you today. Good afternoon, Mr Preston.'

The line was dead, leaving Peter Preston infuriated and helpless. He had thought he would at least have had the small satisfaction of slamming his phone down to end this futile conversation. But the woman had outsmarted him even in that.

Peter went from his study into the bedroom and looked at himself in the mirror. He felt as if he had been dragged through a hawthorn hedge, but there was little sign of disturbance in the face he saw there. His colour was perhaps a little higher than normal, but his gently waving hair was as neatly parted and groomed as ever. His brown eyes were bright; he knew that was the product of frustration and indignation, but the uninformed viewer might have seen them only as pleasantly animated behind the rimless glasses. Wrinkles were inevitable at fifty-five, but anger seemed to have made them a little less prominent.

He didn't look anything like as ruffled as he had expected to look. That was some consolation, he decided. Peter Preston was unaware of his vanity, as he was unaware of many of the things that other, less talented, people might have noticed in themselves.

Ros Barker was excited. She was humming quietly but continuously to herself. Kate Merrick, the woman who shared her life, could have told anyone who was interested that this was a mark of excitement in her friend and lover. When Ros was at work on a painting, the sound was a sure sign to her sometime model that the work was coming along well, that Ros was pleased with some part of the painting, some effect she had sought for and achieved. And when Kate stretched comfortably in bed and heard Ros humming over the toaster in the kitchen, Kate knew that her partner was pleased with the night that had passed and with the life they lived together.

The source of Ros's pleasure this morning was much more worldly. She was driving to Cheltenham to discuss the exhibition of her work which was to be mounted there in May. When you were thirty and almost unknown outside the world of art, to have an exhibition mounted at all was wonderful. To have one mounted in Cheltenham was bliss indeed. The local tradition was that there was far more money available in Cheltenham than in Gloucester. Gloucester was an ancient city with a magnificent cathedral, but Cheltenham was the fashionable spa town which the prosperous English establishment chose to visit and where the affluent middle classes chose to settle. There was money available for fripperies like art in Cheltenham, whereas the Gloucester folk were altogether more down to earth. Ros wasn't at all sure that these distinctions still applied, but she was delighted that her work was going to be on show in a prominent gallery in Cheltenham for three whole weeks.

The owner of the gallery was a hard-headed businessman, with no pretensions to artistic expertise himself. Ros found this reassuring, since she had no idea herself about how best to exploit her gifts to make a living. She needed someone like this man, who would be concerned with the commercial rather than the aesthetic properties of her work. Harry Barnard was that practical presence. His concern was to cover the extensive overheads of his gallery, such as council tax and publicity, and then show a handsome yearly profit. He had already been doing this for twenty years.

Barnard was taking a chance on Ros Barker, though he did not tell her so. It was part of his policy to mount two exhibitions a year by promising but not widely known artists. It helped to keep his gallery in the public eye and secured his position in the artistic press as a patron of the arts, a man who was happy to foster new talent. If he broke even on these two exhibitions, he was content. If he discovered a saleable new painter or sculptor, that was a splendid bonus. He revealed none of this thinking to Ros Barker.

'It's good that you have such variety in your work,' he told her as they discussed the best spots to display particular paintings. 'That always excites interest and makes a tour of your work more interesting for the general public.'

'You mean that I haven't yet found my distinctive vein?' said Ros with a grin, recalling a critic's phrase from his review of an earlier and much more modest display of her work.

Harry Barnard grinned. 'When you do, make sure it's one that sells. I've seen too many clever artists and sculptors who please themselves and almost no one else.'

Ros enjoyed making decisions with him on which of her paintings would look best where. It was good to have a dose of common sense in her life, from someone who knew what he was doing and how to sell. She remembered asking someone years ago why it had taken Lowry so long to become popular. The answer had been that it was only late in life that he acquired a shrewd and successful agent. The preparations for the exhibition occupied most of her day, but she decided that she didn't mind that at all. She would return to her studio with a better perspective and a better grasp of the life led by the sort of people who might buy her paintings.

Kate Merrick was already in the house by the time she got back from Cheltenham. Kate worked for three days a week in the local branch of the Cheltenham and Gloucester Building Society. These were the days when she wasn't, as she put it, 'part-time model and full-time dogsbody' for Ros Barker. Ros called from the front door, 'I'm home from the office, dear. I hope you have the meal ready to serve!' and was greeted with a cheerful selection of colourful obscenities.

She gave an account of her day and an affectionate summary of Harry Barnard, then noticed the envelope with her name on it upon the mantelpiece. 'It was behind the door when I came in,' said Kate. Ros slit the envelope wonderingly and then stared unbelievingly at the single sheet within it.

RESIGN NOW FROM THE FESTIVAL COMMITTEE IF YOU WISH TO REMAIN ALIVE

Sam Hilton pulled the collar of his anorak up around his neck. It was cold by the docks in Gloucester. There was no protection here from the breeze sweeping up the Severn. It had felt quite still as he threaded his way through the older part of the city and down to the ancient quays, but the wind was stronger here, more chilling as the night advanced.

Sam glanced at his watch as he passed under the street light. Ten forty. He had timed it about right. That was the easy part. He flicked again at the collar of his anorak, forgetting that it was already up beneath his ears. It wasn't the cold that prompted the move. It was the need for concealment.

He felt very exposed beside the old docks. No seagoing ships docked here now to unload at the quays, as they had done for six centuries. The old warehouses were antiques centres and museums now, so that this area was busy by day with a more cosmopolitan clientele than it had ever had. But at this hour it was silent and almost deserted. Sam, hurrying along beside the huge, silent mirror of the water, felt very exposed.

He was relieved to turn on to the narrower thoroughfare he

was seeking. He saw the orange lights of the pub windows at the other end of the street, heard the noise growing in volume as he approached. He felt his steps slowing as the sounds increased. It was always like this, he told himself. He always felt nervous at this stage. But it was groundless alarm. Nothing ever happened.

It was easy money, really. You ran a little risk, but you were amply recompensed. He liked to pretend to the world in which he moved by day that he made a living from his poetry. It was a matter of pride, really; people thought you weren't any good if you didn't make money at something. No one except a few people who had tried it realized how difficult it was to make real money from poetry. You could be quite successful; you could publish slim volumes, you could even get favourable reviews, without making a living from verse. You needed something else to support you. If it was something secret, so that people didn't see it and supposed that you were a financial success as a poet, so much the better.

He realized now that he went through these arguments with himself at this stage every time. That was self-knowledge, which was always a good thing for a poet to have. And the next forty minutes would be exciting, with every one of his senses working acutely and every nerve of his body stretched towards breaking point. A thrilling experience, which he would surely be able to incorporate into his verse at some point. The more fully you lived life, the more fully you explored its extreme moments, the more extensive your armoury as a poet became.

Sam Hilton took a deep breath, pushed open the swing door of the pub and slipped into the cavern of noise inside.

Everything was suddenly very bright. Everything was noisy and glaring, when he wanted quiet and obscurity. It was some time before he could get his order accepted at the bar; he felt as if every eye in the room must be upon him in his isolation. Everyone else here seemed to be part of a noisy group, whilst he waited solitary and silent for the barman. Even the raising of his arm to secure the busy man's attention seemed a gesture to excite the interest of every curious eye in this brilliantly lit place.

It was not so, of course. As he was served, he saw that one of the noisiest groups, a set of girls on a hen night, were making their erratic way towards the exit, calling final crude sexual insults to the male group with whom they had been verbally fencing for the last hour. Sam took his pint of lager from the bar and slid gratefully into the alcove the women had lately occupied. The smells of cheap scent and the echoes of cheap language seemed to linger here, but as soon as he sat down he felt much better.

He was less conspicuous, for a start. He realized now that he had never really been the centre of attention, even when he had been standing alone at the bar. The people here were preoccupied with their own concerns, not him. And by this time on a Friday night, many of them had drunk quite a lot. Alcohol didn't improve your perceptions. Moreover, he had chosen the right clothes. There were several others as well as him in dark blue anoraks and well-worn jeans. Not exactly a fashion statement, but that was the last thing you needed if you wanted to be inconspicuous. With his average height and slight frame, he was better fitted to go unnoticed than most men. He had sometimes resented that, when he'd been a teenager, but here it was a decided advantage.

He sipped his beer, tried to look relaxed, and watched the hands of the pub clock creep round towards eleven. Pubs didn't have to close at eleven, or any other set time, now that the licensing laws had been amended. This one was open until eleven thirty on a Friday, but eleven was the time he had agreed. He grinned hastily at the crude invitation to join her group that a girl on her way back from the toilets offered, but didn't otherwise respond. Company might have helped to conceal the purpose of his visit here, but it was the last thing he needed with the time of his meeting approaching.

The pub clock was three minutes fast, as they often were, to encourage people to respond to invitations for last orders and injunctions to drink up. When the fingers on his own watch pointed precisely at the hour, Sam Hilton downed the final half-inch of lager at the bottom of his glass and slipped through the door with the sign above it which read 'Gents' Toilet'. They'd got the apostrophe right, he noted approvingly;

when your life was shaped by words, you became prissier than the most pedantic schoolmarm.

He stood for a moment in the corridor outside, than went past the door clearly marked 'Gentlemen'. He moved on to the last door on the same side of the passage, which he knew led outside. The cool of the air struck immediately through the thinness of his jeans, but the isolation was a relief after the rowdy hilarity he had left. In this enclosed space, he couldn't feel the breeze he had felt on the quay, but he saw it moving the clouds across the patch of sky he could see above him. He caught a glimpse of stars between the clouds, but had no sight of the almost full moon he knew must be present beyond the high wall on his right.

He waited only three minutes, but it felt much longer than that, as he fought to control the tenseness gathering in his limbs. Then the door he had used himself opened briefly, revealing for an instant a shaft of orange light from the crowded world of the pub. His eyes were used to the darkness now, yet he saw no more than the dark shape of a man, appearing bigger and more threatening as it moved nearer to him. He didn't say anything; he'd made that mistake before. You waited until you were spoken to by this man.

The new presence glanced back towards the door he had just used, waited whilst the silence dropped back over them like a blanket in the darkness. Then, 'You shifted what you took last time?' He didn't use names; Sam knew neither the surname nor the forename of this man he had already met four times like this.

'Yes. No bother.'

'You want the same again?'

'No. I want twice the coke and twice the Rohypnol. The horse can stay the same.'

'Coke's no problem. I can only do you the same Rohypnol as last time. Same price for the coke. Rohypnol's up twenty.'

'Can't you do any more? I can move it easily enough.'

'Use it yourself, do you, you randy little sod?' A flash of teeth in the darkness showed the burly man was grinning. He corrected this lapse into the personal as suddenly as it had arrived. 'No can do, my friend. Everyone wants the date-rape drug. Sign of the times, son.'

'All right. I – I thought the coke might be a bit cheaper, if I doubled the order.'

'Preferential rate for the learner-dealer, that was. You now need to double the quantity to keep the rate the same, which is what you're doing. Sellers' market, son. Take your custom elsewhere, if you can. You won't beat our rates and our quality.' He allowed a harder edge to sharpen his words. 'You'd be very foolish to try that, mind you.'

'I've no intention of going anywhere else! I wouldn't know how,' said Sam hastily.

'Wise lad. I've got what you say you want here. You got the money?'

'Yes.' Sam glanced round furtively, but it was no more than an instinctive reaction as he brought out his money in this silent place.

Three hundred pounds. His supplier flashed a pen-torch briefly and expertly over the fifties and twenties on the low wall, 'Another eighty, lad.'

Four more twenties, new and crisp, were slid across. The man felt into the deep pockets of the long coat he wore, produced the packages of coke as though he had had them ready, as though he had anticipated this doubling of the order, though Sam knew he could never have done that. From some other section of that all-concealing garment, he produced the Rohypnol and set it on top of the neatly packaged cocaine. 'Quality as previous: the best. We only supply the best.'

'I know that. I've no complaints.' Sam Hilton wanted to be on his way more fervently than he had wanted anything in his life.

'Glad to hear it son. Remember that and don't sell too cheap. Want you to have a good mark-up. Don't want you to become the sort of dealer who has to sell to feed his habit. They don't last long, that sort.'

It was the nearest thing to advice he ever offered. He looked unhurriedly round at the high wall between them and the outside world, at the cloud scudding across the small patch of sky above them, at the hostelry with its muted noises which they must both re-enter. 'Usual arrangement, son. You go first. I follow in two minutes, unless I hear anything to suggest I shouldn't do that.'

Sam Hilton didn't hesitate. He thrust his new supplies into the pockets of his anorak and slipped without a backwards glance through the door and back into the busy hostelry. The pint and the coldness of the yard were insistent in his bladder. He needed urgently to turn into the gents and discharge its contents into one of the urinals. But he needed even more urgently to be away, to be out of the pub into the darkness outside, and then back to the street in the centre of the city where he had parked the old Focus.

Thirty minutes later, he was back in his flat, peeing at last for what was surely the longest ever time into the lavatory bowl, groaning the exquisite pleasure of his relief. The profits when he sold this stuff on would be good, even ridiculous: almost a forty percent mark-up on even the excessive rates he was sure he had paid. And tomorrow, or at least on the next day or the day after that, the strain of acquiring his supplies would not seem so great.

But at this moment the price of being a poet seemed almost too much to bear.

SIX

Christine Lambert was surprised by the phone call. The caller wasn't unexpected; when you were on committees, it was quite usual for the chairperson to ring you up about committee business. What surprised her was that Marjorie Dooks sounded uncertain, even vulnerable; she had never encountered that before.

'Mrs Lambert? Are you on your own, Christine? Something has come up. I don't quite know what I should do about it. I'd welcome your advice.'

'Of course. I'm happy to say what I think, if you believe it will be any help.'

'Thank you. Not on the phone, though. Could I come round and see you? I think that would be better than you coming here. During the day. Today, if possible.'

The staccato phrases were fired off as if Marjorie was thinking on her feet. That was a shock to Christine Lambert, who was used to the formidable Mrs Dooks being so measured and prepared.

'I'll be happy to give you whatever help I can. Perhaps I should say that although my husband hasn't agreed to appear on the platform with David Knight yet, I'm fairly confident that—'

'What? Oh, it's not about that. It's something quite different, and rather odd.'

Christine was intrigued. It must be something very odd indeed, to throw the formidable Marjorie Dooks so completely out of her stride. 'I have to go out this morning. Would three this afternoon be all right for you?'

'That would suit me admirably. You – you will be alone, won't you?'

'Yes. We won't be disturbed.'

Christine put down the phone and stared at it thoughtfully for a moment. Intriguing. What could be so private that

Marjorie didn't want John Lambert around when it was discussed?

She took her friend for her hospital appointment as arranged, then drove home and snatched a quick sandwich lunch. She left herself time to vacuum and plump the cushions in the sitting room before her visitor arrived. Marjorie Dooks wasn't the sort of woman you ushered into an untidy room. She was flicking a duster over the top of the television when the lady's silver Peugeot swung into her drive.

Marjorie surged through the politenesses of a first visit quickly and abstractedly, as though they were some tiresome rites that had to be observed as a prelude to genuine communication. Christine made a pot of tea, then watched her visitor refuse biscuits and sip abstractedly at her cup, as if it were just another distraction set in front of her to prevent her coming to the point of her visit. 'Something very odd has happened,' she said abruptly.

'Really? And what is that?'

Mrs Dooks looked automatically around the room, as if she thought some hidden listener was there to be discovered. 'I've had a strange letter. I've never received anything like it before.'

'What sort of letter, Marjorie?' Christine Lambert found herself dropping into a role she had never expected, that of comforter and counsellor to this formidable but now clearly shaken woman.

'You'll probably tell me not to be such a fool and to stop over-reacting and go away and get on with my life. Which would be a comfort really.' Marjorie tried a self-deprecating laugh and found herself disturbingly close to tears.

It was her friend who did the smiling. 'Perhaps if you told me what was in the letter it would help us both.'

'Sorry! I'm not usually like this. Well, I've had a note threatening me with violence. Threatening to kill me, in fact.'

'Good heavens! Have you brought it with you?'

'No. I shredded it and threw it away. I was determined not to take it seriously, so I treated it with contempt.'

'And now you think you were rather too hasty.'

Marjorie looked as uncomfortable as she felt. 'I don't know what I feel, and I'm not used to that. Bloody stupid, I suppose.

I just thought I'd like to discuss it with someone. You drew the short straw, I'm afraid.'

'I shall take that as a compliment. I'm afraid I haven't met your husband. Does he know about this?'

'No. We – we haven't been very close, over the last year. I suppose I thought James would just say that it served me right for getting myself so heavily involved with local affairs. He doesn't approve of that.'

Christine wanted to tell her that they weren't old friends, weren't even close enough to be talking like this. Her only contact with Marjorie was through a committee, and though she'd quickly come to like and respect her, she didn't want to begin exchanging secrets with her. She said awkwardly, 'I don't want to pry into your private life, but shouldn't you have discussed this with your husband before anyone else?'

Marjorie didn't answer her directly. She said slowly, 'I suppose like many people who've led a busy public life, I've never developed much of a private one. I haven't got close friends. To tell you the truth, I haven't in the past felt any great need for them. I didn't show the thing to James because he wouldn't have been any use to me.'

Christine suddenly felt very sorry for this woman, who normally exuded confidence and certainty. Twenty years ago, when John and she had been far apart, she had sometimes felt that he too would be no use to her in a personal crisis. It was the children who had drawn them together as the years passed. John had always been good with the girls, had sometimes been able to see things she had not seen for herself. Marjorie Dooks had no children. Christine said, 'When did this message arrive?'

'The day before yesterday. I'd been to a council meeting. It was delivered whilst there was no one in the house. James was home from work before I came in. He brought it into the house but it was addressed to me. I opened it on my own and didn't tell him what was in it.'

'But didn't he ask you about it?'

'No. I think he's forgotten all about it. He's very much concerned with his own affairs.'

It was a brisk, bleak summary of the event and of her own

and her husband's reactions. Once she had been asked to deliver facts, she was almost back in her normal efficient mode.

Christine wondered if Marjorie suspected that it might have been her husband who had perpetrated this strange thing. As she did not know her very well and him not at all, she had no idea whether this was altogether too fanciful an idea. She felt herself being drawn further into something she did not wish to be her concern as she said reluctantly, 'What exactly did this letter say?'

Marjorie smiled wanly. 'Not much. It was short and melodramatic. It said that I should resign from the literature festival committee unless I wished to be killed. It sounds ridiculous, doesn't it, when you hear it stated baldly like that?'

'It does. Nevertheless, I wouldn't like to receive anything like that.'

'That's something I had at the back of my mind. You haven't received anything like this yourself?'

'No. I expect you'd feel better if I had.'

'I suppose I would, if I'm honest. It would feel less personal and I would feel in less danger if I felt some lunatic was firing notes off at all and sundry. Sorry about that.'

Christine said firmly, 'Don't be. I'm sure anyone would feel like that. The question is, what are we going to do about it?' It felt very strange that this normally assured and confident woman should be depending now on her for guidance.

Marjorie felt an enormous relief in just having spoken about it, in having confessed her fear and vulnerability to another human being. 'I shouldn't have shredded it, should I?'

'Probably not. But it's no use our worrying about that now.'

Marjorie found the simple fact that she'd said 'us' rather than 'you' massively comforting. 'I expect I was just trying to convince myself that it was a trivial thing, not something serious. What do you think I should do now?'

Christine frowned. 'I think we've got to let the police know about it. It's probably just a trivial, silly prank, as you thought it was when you shredded the letter, but it should be treated as serious until we know the facts.'

She expected an argument. It was evidence of how shaken her visitor was that she said only, 'I don't think you should bother your husband with this. It's way below his level. And it would expose me to him as a silly woman, who can't even be sensible enough to retain the evidence.'

'John isn't stupid. What he'd see is a competent woman suddenly exposed to an anonymous and alarming threat to her life, to a level of malice she's never had to contend with before. That's a frightening situation for anyone.'

'All the same, I wouldn't want to be seen to be receiving special treatment. If you think this has to be reported, I'd prefer to go through the proper channels, in that phrase beloved of Civil Service mandarins. I think I should just go into the police station at Oldford and tell them what's happened. If that means I deal with PC Plod, then so be it.'

'I'm no expert on police procedures, but I think this would be a CID matter. I take your point that you don't want special treatment. However, I think you should report it as you suggest without further delay.'

Christine went out to the car with Marjorie. The daffodils were over, and she picked a few dead flower heads off them as her friend reversed out of the drive. Perhaps she hoped the resumption of dull everyday tasks could convince her departing visitor that the abnormal was really quite normal. She decided that she would have a quiet word with John about this tonight, despite Marjorie's understandable reservations.

She did not know that her decision would be overtaken by other events.

'I've got the stuff you wanted.' Sam Hilton was surprised how breathy and dramatic he sounded, when he had meant to be businesslike and impersonal. You needed to be more relaxed and in control, when you were selling.

'I told you not to ring me at work.'

The voice was younger and more nervous on the phone than the man he remembered. That gave Sam confidence. 'You also told me not to ring you at home. I had to let you know somehow that the goods had arrived.'

'You could have sent a message to my computer at home. I gave you the e-mail address.'

'I don't put things in writing. Rule of the game, Paul.'

'All right. I'll meet you at the usual spot. The place where I ordered the stuff. After work tonight. Six fifteen.'

You didn't let the punters dictate the terms. 'No. The back room at *The White Hart.* And make it nine thirty. I don't care to operate in daylight.'

'All right. And – and I might be able to take more coke, next time.'

'Got friends who want the best, have you?' Sam smiled at the phone, taking his time, relishing the feeling of power this gave him. 'Good idea to get a little circle organized. Put ten per cent on my price, you can end up getting your own stuff for nothing.' This was the way you built up a dealer network and increased your sales, but he wasn't going to tell the young solicitor that. Let him get in deeper, let him do your work for you. 'I can supply all you need, and you know the quality's right.'

'Yes. And if I can increase my order, I'd expect to get a better deal. Perhaps we could—'

'Nine thirty, then. Don't be late.'

Sam put the phone down immediately on that injunction. That was the best thing about this trade. It was the seller, not the buyer, who called the shots.

'It's probably nothing, but I thought I should be on the safe side.'

Bert Hook nodded seriously. He gave no sign that he had heard this apologetic introduction a hundred times before as he said, 'You did the right thing. It's always as well to be on the safe side.'

'I live on my own, you see, and things tend to get out of proportion when you've no one to discuss them with.'

'I'm sure they do, Ms—?'

'I'm sorry, I should have said. Sue Charles is the name.'

He wrote the name down on the sheet in front of him, then smiled encouragingly and said, 'Not Sue Charles the writer?'

She was absurdly pleased, despite herself. After all these years, it was still a thrill to be recognized. It didn't happen very often. She said, 'Yes, that's me. I'm surprised you know it – especially as a policeman.'

Hook smiled again, his weather-beaten, outdoor features exuding reassurance. 'My wife is an addict of the detective novel. She speaks highly of your work. Library copies of Sue Charles appear regularly on our bedside table. She'll be impressed to hear I've spoken to you.'

Sue tried not to show her almost childish joy in the compliment. 'That's nice to hear. Sometimes when you're wrestling with some writing problem, you wonder if anyone actually reads your books.'

Bert gave no sign of his rising impatience. 'I'm sure you wouldn't be published if they didn't. What can I do for you, Ms Charles?'

'It's Mrs, actually. But I'm a widow now. Well, as I said, this is probably a waste of your time. It's probably nothing more than mischief.'

'Perhaps you should let me be the judge of that, Mrs Charles. It's part of my job to decide what is trivial and what might be more serious.'

'Yes. Well then, I'd be very glad of your opinion on this.' She opened her hand bag and produced the letter she had discovered on the previous evening. 'I put it back into the envelope it was delivered in. My – my fingerprints will be on it from when I first opened it. I've worn gloves to handle it ever since then. I expect you'll think that's very over the top – I suppose it comes from being a crime writer.'

Bert shook his head and said very seriously, 'On the contrary, I wish all members of the public would be so careful when handling what might eventually become evidence. You did exactly the right thing, Mrs Charles, just as you did the right thing in bringing this straight to us.'

'Thank you. I live alone now, you see – well, alone except for Roland, my cat.'

Bert stared at the single sheet on his desk with its stark message and threat. 'When did you receive this?'

'Yesterday. I found it in the early evening, when I was about to have my meal. But it could have been dropped through the letter box at any time during the afternoon. I was working on my latest book in my study, you see.'

'You didn't hear or see anything?'

'No. My study's at the back of the house. I don't even hear the post arriving, unless it contains something particularly heavy. All I can say with certainty is that it must have been dropped through the letter box some time between one p.m. and seven p.m.'

DS Hook went over to the dispenser at the end of the CID section and donned a pair of thin plastic medical gloves. He examined the printing of the words on the sheet of paper and then held it up to the light, holding it gingerly by its bottom corner. 'No watermark on the paper. Standard issue A4 printing paper, sold all over the country for use with home printers, I'm afraid. And it will be difficult if not impossible to pin this with any certainty to a particular computer. The days of typewriters, which were almost as individual as fingerprints, are long gone, I'm afraid.'

Sue Charles gave her first smile since she had come into the room. 'I know. A great boon to crime writers, the old typewriters were. We have to be much more ingenious now than in the good old days, the so-called golden age of the detective novel.'

Bert grinned. 'I grew up with Dorothy L. Sayers and Agatha Christie as a teenager in a Barnardo's home. The library wasn't very up to date. For some reason, the people there thought murder was good safe reading for impressionable adolescents.'

'Perhaps they did make an impression. You became a policeman.'

'Yes. And eventually a detective, of sorts. I never thought there was a connection, though. I think the people who ran the home simply thought that a safe, steady job in the police represented a success for one of their lads.'

'Perhaps they were right. I should think you're much better at handling worried ladies of sixty-eight than most policemen.'

'Two things, Mrs Charles. First, sixty-eight is no great age nowadays and you're obviously in full possession of all your faculties. Secondly, you weren't alarmist in coming to the police station today. You did exactly the right thing. We take threats like this very seriously. This almost certainly came either from some idiot who thinks it's a good joke or from someone with a warped imagination who wants to give you a little scare. Either way, the probability is that the sender intends to do nothing further.'

'That's good to hear. Whoever sent this has already given me a sleepless night.'

'I can imagine that. And although it's statistically unlikely that the sender intends any further malice, we have to take things like this very seriously. We need to follow it up, if only to show the perpetrator of a tasteless joke that he or she can't get away with it. I need to ask you some fairly personal questions.'

That's all right. I'm relieved to have your help. I thought you might tell me I was overreacting.'

'If anyone's going to overreact, it will be us, Mrs Charles. We have to take precautions against even the most unlikely possibility. Have you any idea who sent you this?'

There was a slight hesitation before she said 'No. I've thought about it, inevitably. Thought about it for most of the night, actually.'

To Hook, the hesitation was more significant than the reply. He let it go for the moment. 'What have you been doing in the last few days? Have you offended anyone? Even a minor incident might be significant. People who write stuff like this usually have no sense of proportion.'

She gave a wry smile as she shook her head. 'I lead a rather solitary life, since my husband died. People are very kind in general, but when they're planning social gatherings they tend to think in terms of couples. I'm not a churchgoer – there have been moments in the last couple of years when for the first time in forty years I've wished I was, because any sort of religion puts you in touch with a group of sympathetic people.' She was acutely conscious of not wanting to sound like a moaner with narrowing horizons. 'But most of the time I love my privacy and the time it gives me to work. Writing is a lonely business, as I said, and I need isolation to work on my books.'

Bert Hook pulled her back to his question. 'But you must have upset someone, even if it was to your mind in a very minor way.'

'Not consciously, I'm afraid. Do you think that this could be the work of some schoolchild? Perhaps someone who's been reading Agatha Christie, as you did? Youngsters don't always draw very clear lines between fact and fiction.'

'Not impossible, but unlikely. I think this is the work of someone who knows you and wishes to upset you, even if he or she doesn't intend to do anything further. It may be a longer-standing grudge, of course, but the first thing to do is to check out the people you've seen recently. Let's start with the people you've spoken to in the last week.'

'Apart from phone conversations with my daughter and David Knight, the crime novelist, there aren't many. I attended a meeting of the Oldford Literary Festival Committee five days ago. I'm getting David Knight to speak on crime writing at the festival at the end of May.'

'Yes, I know about that. Chief Superintendent Lambert asked me to be on the platform with you, but I think he's the man you need.'

'Yes. That was the idea of Marjorie Dooks, who chairs our committee, and I think it was a good one.'

Bert stored this up in case he had to argue with Lambert again over the matter. He said with pen poised over his pad, 'I need to know the names of the other people on that committee.'

'Yes.' She realized now that she'd known from the first it would come to this, but she had a curious feeling of sneaking, a notion which came back from her schooldays over half a century ago. 'Well, there's Mr Lambert's wife, of course. But I think we can discount her.'

Bert had a splendid vision of the fun to be had when he warned his wife that her friend Christine was a suspect in this sordid little affair. 'Nevertheless, we won't discount her at the moment. Who else, please?'

'Well, there's young Sam Hilton. He looks about sixteen to me, but I'm told he's twenty-two and a poet of some standing. He's getting the northern poet Bob Crompton to come to the festival. I'm sure this threat wouldn't have come from Sam.'

'Even so, we'll record his name.'

'And then there's Ros Barker.'

'The painter?'

'Yes, she's the one.' Sue could not quite conceal her surprise that a policeman should know who Ros was. 'But again, I like Ros and I think she quite likes me. I can't think she would send anything like that.' For the first time since she had passed it across the desk, she gestured at that sheet with its thick black print.

'We'll add her to the list.' Bert wrote down the name in his large round hand, then looked at her expectantly.

'And of course there's Peter Preston. I expect you've heard of him.'

'Most people who live in this area know Mr Preston,' said DS Hook rather grimly.

'Peter regards himself as an expert on the arts. That's a little unfair; I'm quite prepared to accept that he *is* an expert. The trouble is that he doesn't think that anyone's opinion other than his is worth anything.'

Bert realized that like many people, she had left the person she considered the likeliest suspect until the last. He nodded a couple of times and said, 'Have you had any disagreement with the erudite Mr Preston?'

Sue Charles frowned, trying hard to be fair. 'He might have seen it as that. I would have said that it was no more than a difference of opinion. He doesn't think detective fiction should be part of a literary festival.'

'And his reason for that?'

'He simply doesn't consider crime novels to be what he calls "real literature". He didn't think I and the rest of the committee should have invited David Knight to speak at the festival, even though he's a leader in our field. Marjorie Dooks shut Peter up rather effectively from the chair by reminding him that this had already been discussed at length and the matter decided at a previous meeting.'

'But as you write crime books yourself and were the means of persuading Mr Knight to speak in Oldford, Mr Preston's discontent focussed upon you.'

'I suppose it did, yes. Particularly as he hasn't a high opinion of either Sam Hilton or Ros Barker and I also found myself on their side in the exchanges within the committee.'

'Mrs Charles, I have to ask you formally whether you think Peter Preston might have sent you this note.'

'It's inconceivable, to me. It doesn't seem like the sort of thing he would do. But then it seems even more inconceivable that anyone else would threaten me like this, even as a joke. Unless it was kids, of course, who wouldn't realize the distress they were causing. Peter's the only person I've had any sort of dispute with over the last two or three months.'

'It's important that you don't try to do anything about this yourself. You could accuse entirely the wrong person and end up at best highly embarrassed and at worst losing a friend. Be assured that we shall follow it up. We can be far more impersonal and we have far more resources than you have.'

'That's why I came here, Detective Sergeant Hook. The days of Miss Marple are long gone, if indeed they ever existed!'

'I don't wish to be alarmist, but have you anyone who could move into the house with you for a night or two?'

She smiled wanly. 'I could probably pack up my laptop and go to stay with my daughter for a couple of days. I'm due for a visit.'

'That would probably be best. If you give me the phone number, I'll make sure someone contacts you to let you know the outcome of our enquiries.'

'Thank you again for being so understanding.'

Hook stood up. 'We always treat these things seriously. As I say, it will probably turn out to be some tasteless hoax, but it needs investigation.'

As he prepared to usher her out, a young woman PC appeared in the doorway, looking a little embarrassed. 'Sorry to interrupt you, DS Hook, but I thought from what this lady said at the desk that her complaint might be related to what you're discussing with Mrs Charles.'

Hook saw behind her a diffident young woman, following the officer somewhat reluctantly into the depths of Oldford police station. A fresh-faced woman, with a few freckles still evident in her small, kitten-like features. Older than he'd thought at first; she was probably in her late twenties, he thought. Bert had many years of experience now in assessing ages, a police skill he had found very difficult when he was as young as the officer who had brought in this woman.

He was about to say that he would speak to her after he had seen Sue Charles out when the new entrant spoke, delivering her message hastily and without pause, as if she feared that she might turn tail and flee if she paused for thought. 'My name is Kate Merrick. My partner is Ros Barker. This threat was to her, not to me, but she wouldn't take it seriously. I brought it here because I thought you should see it.'

She stood panting, then thrust an envelope towards him with both hands, like a child anxious to be rid of something that frightened her.

Hook looked at her for a second or two without a word as he donned the plastic gloves he had recently discarded to extract the single sheet from within the envelope.

RESIGN NOW FROM THE FESTIVAL COMMITTEE IF YOU WISH TO REMAIN ALIVE

He said tersely, 'I think Chief Superintendent Lambert should know about this.'

SEVEN

Spring was advancing quickly. The chestnuts were in leaf; even the oak and the ash were swelling their buds. And the daylight was stretching as the year advanced; only eight weeks now until the longest day.

Sam Hilton waited impatiently for the darkness to descend. As usual, his anxiety rose as he prepared himself for the latest episode in this other trade he needed to sustain his status and credibility as a full-time poet. Perhaps he should have accepted the man's suggestion and met him earlier. He wouldn't have had the time to get nervous then. But there was no real need to be nervous, was there? Perhaps he just wasn't a natural lawbreaker. Poets were supposed to make their own rules and go their own way. Yet even at school he hadn't been as happy as the others had been when breaking the stupid little rules.

He felt better as darkness finally crept in over the Gloucestershire countryside and better still once he was in the city. Here the lighting in the streets seemed to bring the night in so much more swiftly than in the fields and the hedgerows outside. He parked the old Focus some streets away from his rendezvous. A vehicle parked regularly in the same place could excite suspicion. That was the advice he had been given when he started to deal. Perhaps he was, after all, a conformist at heart. Philip Larkin had wrestled with thoughts like that, so he was in good poetic company.

The White Hart wasn't near the docks. He didn't like the pub where he met his supplier and he didn't like his journey to and from it. He had chosen to meet his biggest customer in a more central and respectable tavern, much used by the middle classes for a drink after work. At this time in the evening it housed a more cosmopolitan group; the increasing number of tourists was another sign that the year was advancing. This ancient inn was almost in the centre of Gloucester and the streets around it were peopled more thickly than those near the dockside rendezvous where he bought his supplies. Sometimes there was safety in numbers.

The man he was meeting was a young solicitor – older than Sam, but still no more than twenty-five. Paul Martin was his name. You didn't use names more than you had to in this trade, and Sam hoped that the client still didn't know his. Anonymity was a key to safety in this lucrative but dangerous commerce.

The White Hart had numerous small alcoves, which dated from an earlier age. They were much appreciated by lovers and by anyone with a conversation they wished to conceal from a wider public. Sam glanced up at the illuminated sign depicting a young white stag and slipped quickly into the pub. It was nine thirty-five.

He found his man immediately, sipping nervously at a gin and tonic in the same niche they had used last time. Paul Martin said edgily, 'You took your time. I've been here for twenty minutes.'

'Your own choice, that. Nine thirty, I said. I arrived here precisely five minutes after that, as planned. The customer must always be there before his supplier. Rule of the game. You don't hang around any longer than you need to, when you're carrying more than you can claim is for your own use.'

'All right. Let's get this done as quickly as possible, then.' Martin leaned forward to see a little more of the lounge bar of the pub, twisting his face first right and then left, to see if they were being observed.

'You're drawing attention to us. You should be acting as if you'd nothing to fear, as if what we're doing was the most natural thing in the world.' But Sam was secretly reassured. The man was more naïve and unpractised than he was in the situation.

'Let's get it over with quickly then.' The man looked into Sam's face and repeated himself nervously. Though he was in his mid-twenties, he clutched notes in his closed fist, like a small child impatient to buy the sweets he had been promised much earlier. Something for the poet in that image, Sam thought automatically. The material for verse was all around you, in life's rich ironies as abundantly as in its tragedies. But you must keep your senses alive to the richness and the absurdity of the human condition. Everyone used to take drugs, in times past. John Keats might have been a user and a dealer, not a doctor, if he'd been alive now.

He wrenched his attention back from that unlikely image to the sordid facts of the deal in hand. 'Good stuff, this. The best coke you'll get.'

It was the nearest he came to a sales pitch, and it was as successful as it was unnecessary. Paul Martin was too nervous even to register what he was saying. 'Two hundred, we said. You'll find that's correct.'

Sam looked at the whiteness of the finger-joints as they clutched tightly round the twenties. The nails were immaculately clean. They didn't see manual work, these hands, they didn't grub for a living in the soil. Sam forgot for a moment that his own hands hadn't touched the soil for many months. 'I shan't even count this, mate. Shows how much I trust the customer, that, don't it?' He wondered fleetingly why he was dropping into estuary English, when he spent most of his life exploring the richness of language. Role-playing, he supposed. He felt the notes thrust into his palm, felt the fleeting touch of those flawless fingers, leaping away from his flesh as if he had the plague.

Sam Hilton felt a sudden need to assert his power over the gilded young man, to expose the weakness at the heart of this popinjay. He stowed the folded notes in his pocket. 'You said you wanted to double your order.'

Paul Martin made a belated attempt to assert customer rights. 'I said that I might be able to take double the quantity of coke, if the quality remained the same and the price was lowered. That would acknowledge the increase in the order.'

'"Would acknowledge the increase in the order."' Sam parroted the phrase with Martin's inflexion, as if storing it up for his future amusement. Then he deliberately hardened his tone. 'Get real, sunshine! I run the risks, I get the supplies, I call the shots. And the shots I call include price. It will be the same as last time. If I find in the months to come that you're able to increase your order consistently, I'll consider an adjustment to my price in due course. If you don't like my terms, try someone else. But don't think you'll be able to come crawling back to me when you get your coke cut with chalk.'

'There's no need for that. I know you're providing good stuff. The best.' He didn't, because he'd no means of comparison. Like most users, Martin had been drawn into the habit from what he'd thought was a one-off, random use. 'I was just trying to establish a good relationship between client and supplier.'

'This isn't like other trades, mate. The less we know about each other the better. I provide the goods, you pay for them. That's as far as it goes. I'm lucky, because I have quality supplies of a rare commodity. That's why I control the price.'

'All right. I'm not going to argue.' Martin's flimsy resistance fell away and he was back where he had begun, a frightened man who wanted this over with as quickly as possible. 'Did you get the Rohypnol?'

Sam relaxed a little, pressing his back against the shiny leather of the bench seat, savouring the power that he felt. 'Rare stuff, this is. Much in demand. I have to ration it. Might mean you have to ration your shagging, you randy bugger!'

Martin smiled weakly, hating himself for his dependence on this creature. Another hundred pounds changed hands and he thrust his tiny allocation of the date-rape drug deep into the pocket of his jeans. He hated himself as he said, 'Any chance of doubling the quantity of this as well?'

'I shouldn't think so. There's massive demand, as I said. You might just have to keep it in your trousers a bit more. Or get her to sniff a line of the white powder with you. Unless it's a him, of course.'

'It's not a him!' the words were out before Paul Martin could stop them, vehement and indignant. He wondered why he needed to assert his heterosexuality to scum like this, who'd just been talking about the need for anonymity. 'And if you can't supply, it really doesn't matter.'

Sam was tempted to parrot that last phrase again in the lawyer's diffident tone, to assert how unconvincing it sounded. But he'd had his fun. It was time to be on his way and out of this. He glanced at his watch. 'You leave first, as normal. I'll see you here same time, two weeks from now. Anything different, I'll let you know.'

Paul Martin wanted to tell him not to ring him at work again. But he was anxious to end a conversation in which he seemed to have lost every argument. He needed to be away from here. He wanted only to be safely at home with the wife he had told he was meeting a client who couldn't manage a time in office hours. 'Right. No complaints about the quality.' He made a final attempt to assert himself. 'See if you can find a way to adjust your prices and we'll have a lasting relationship!'

Sam responded only with a sour smile. He'd give it ten minutes, as usual. That gave you the chance to check that users weren't stopped and questioned as they left. It was one of the tiny number of precepts volunteered to him by his supplier and he'd always followed it. The idea was that it would at least give you notice of police attention. You would have perhaps three minutes to make your escape by whatever means and whatever route you could devise, if you heard or saw your client being questioned. Not long, but time to ditch your remaining drug stash before they searched you.

But Martin left without any challenge and there was no sound of raised voices in the street outside. All was going to be well, as it always had been previously. Piece of piss, really, this dealing business, as his supplier had assured him from the start that it would be. He sipped his beer and opened the book he had brought with him; he'd found before that immersing yourself in reading was the best defence against the casual company which sometimes offered itself in pubs.

He was conscious after a couple of minutes of another presence in his alcove, of someone sliding themselves on to the bench seat on the other side of the table, where Paul Martin had lately sat. But he didn't acknowledge the new arrival by so much as a raised eyebrow, maintaining an absorbing interest in the print before him, putting up the shutters against any conversational sally from whoever had just arrived. His ploy was successful; there was no word from across the table.

It was perhaps ninety seconds before Sam Hilton stole a glance at the new presence over the top of his book. What he saw startled him so much that he almost dropped his shield. He had no idea what he had expected, but this was certainly not it.

The man now sitting opposite him was perhaps the most strikingly beautiful male Sam had ever seen. He certainly had the blackest skin, smooth and softly shining in the subdued light accorded by the inn to this private niche. He was a little older than Sam; probably late twenties, he decided. He had neat, regular features, with a nose so delicate and perfectly formed that it might have been a woman's. His head was not shaved, but his black hair was cut so close that the perfect shape of his cranium was amply evident beneath it. The whites of his eyes were astonishingly white and healthy against the ebony of his skin, As Sam watched surreptitiously, the man smiled briefly at something or someone on the other side of the room, revealing teeth that were perfectly regular and impossibly white.

As if he was conscious of his exotic appearance and seeking deliberately to accentuate it, the man wore spotless white trainers, light blue jeans which looked as though this was their first outing, and a white cotton shirt, close-fitting and buttoned at the wrists. A being of astounding beauty, Sam Hilton decided. The attraction was increased rather than diminished by the fact that it was completely asexual. Sam had been sure of his sexual orientation many years ago. Indeed, he delighted in the fact that, in the right and perfectly chosen circumstances, poetry drew in the girls. So he could be entirely objective about the attractions of this exotic and unexpected new arrival.

A subject for verse, he decided, as all beauty was; Keats was right about that, as about so many things. Sam's poem about this man would be entitled 'The Black Pearl.' He began immediately to cudgel his brain for an opening line, like a painter who sees a subject and wishes to pin down the moment before the light changes. He must surely begin with the exquisite and perfect blackness of the skin. Or should he save the skin and the gender for the end of the first verse, so as to shock the prejudices of those who thought the subject of a poem about human beauty must inevitably be white and female?

How perfectly formed the man's ears were, as pure and unblemished as a child's. Sam was struggling for the right phrase for them when the newcomer spoke. 'Been here long, have you?'

His voice, like the banality of his opening query, was a disappointment. It had a trace of the local accent, when this exotic presence should surely have produced something much more memorable. But it would be good to speak with him, to watch his lips move, to pin down a lasting impression of this beauty the poet was going to enshrine in words. Sam said, 'Not very long, no. Half an hour or so, I suppose.' He glanced round, seeking for something memorable enough to engage his subject, but finding nothing. 'It's fairly quiet tonight. It gets very busy in here at the weekends.'

'Yes, I expect it does. Come here regularly, do you?'

'Fairly often, once a week or so, I suppose.' For an absurd couple of seconds, Sam wondered if this exquisite man was going to proposition him. It would be embarrassing, but once he'd gently turned him down, he would have the advantage in the conversational exchanges.

But then the dialogue took a very different turn.

'Good place for dealing, I expect.'

Sam was shocked. But, still reeling under the impact of beauty upon his poet's eye, he was not as immediately vigilant as he should have been. 'I suppose it would be, yes.' He looked round what he could see of the lounge slowly, then nodded his head vaguely and tried to look puzzled. 'Dealing in what, exactly?'

The question was ignored. 'I might just be interested in some of the commodities you have on offer. If the price was right, of course.' The black pearl gave Sam a dazzling smile from those sparkling white teeth, as if embarrassed to introduce such a sordid consideration as price.

Sam could hardly believe his ears. This scintillating presence was apparently prepared to become a customer of his. This beauty could be there to admire and to pin down in words at regular intervals, if he handled this right. It was like a unique model offering himself to a painter for as long as he was needed. His right hand strayed automatically towards the deep pocket of his anorak. What a good thing he had brought extra supplies as usual, in case extra opportunity presented itself. 'My prices are as good as anyone's. And the quality is guaranteed.'

That was a worthless statement. Who could guarantee quality, and what was anyone's word worth in a seller's market? But Sam's supplier had been insistent on that when he took him on, and Sam repeated the slogan each time he had a new customer. The black pearl nodded earnestly and said, 'Good quality. I've heard that.'

'Good cocaine, too. As much as you want.'

'Excellent. And horse. What sort of quantities can you do?'

'Whatever you care to order. I might need a bit of notice for the heroin, but you can have as much as you want, so long as you order in advance.' Sam tried to keep his voice steady. This promised to be not only pleasurable but highly lucrative. 'I can do MDMA. And Ecstasy. Even Rohypnol, if you want it. Completely undetectable. Everyone wants Rohypnol, but I can get it. It will cost, but you won't beat my prices.'

'Interesting. And quite enough, for the present.' The man's voice changed a little, became more crisp and businesslike. 'Samuel Hilton, I am arresting you on suspicion of dealing in illicit Class A drugs. You do not need to say anything, but it may harm your defence if you withhold information which you later intend to use in court.'

Sam Hilton had never heard the words before, except on television crime shows. They sounded quite unreal, coming from the fastidious lips of his new acquaintance. But the grip that now closed on his upper arm was firm as polished steel.

The black pearl carried danger as well as beauty.

EIGHT

Peter Preston was doing his great man of letters act. He bustled about his study, taking books from the shelves, spreading letters out over his desk to be dealt with in sequence, affecting to be unconscious of his spouse in the doorway.

Wives are notably impervious to such activity. They have usually seen the signs far too often before to be easily impressed by them. They are often the only audiences available, but in such circumstances it is usually advisable for a man to deny himself a performance. Spouses tend to be stubbornly resistant to exaggerated behaviour that is supposed to impress them. In extreme cases, they may even be heretical enough to view it as posturing.

Edwina Preston watched Peter for some time before she said calmly, 'The lawn needs mowing.'

Although he had known she was there for at least a minute, Peter started extravagantly. 'How many times have I told you not to sneak up on me like that?'

It was the sort of bad acting he deplored in others, she thought contemptuously. 'How am I supposed to make contact with you? I thought you'd have noticed me by now.'

'You know very well that when I'm involved with serious matters, my concentration becomes absolute. I can't help it if I'm a slave to the arts.'

Edwina contemplated this outrageous claim for a moment before deciding against reacting to it. She repeated with deliberate, annoying stolidity, 'The lawn needs mowing.' She glanced at the letters and the books so recently assembled upon his desk. 'The art of horticulture needs your attention. The muse of the garden needs to be propitiated.'

'Denis will be here tomorrow.'

'It's going to rain tonight. He can't mow it when it's wet.'

Peter sighed heavily. People rarely understood the demands

of culture, and wives were the worst of all. 'I don't know why we bother to employ a gardener.'

'Denis comes for two hours a week. He does most of the heavy work, but he can't do everything. You said you liked to do the mowing yourself, now that we have the ride-on and there's no real effort.'

That was another thing about wives. They remembered things you'd said and quoted them back at you. They had a knack of remembering the things that could embarrass you and forgetting the ones that proved far-sighted and justified. Peter gestured with a wide arm over the paper on his desk. 'Can't you see I've got more important things than your damned garden on my mind at the moment, woman!'

Edwina wrinkled her nose to show him how much she disapproved of that form of address, whilst choosing not to trade insults. 'You'll be happy enough to take all the plaudits for the garden when your arty friends are sitting in it with a glass of wine. You've said yourself that gardening isn't a normal hobby; you can't pick and choose when to take it up and put it down, because nature doesn't wait for you.'

Again she was flinging back one of his more high-flown thoughts about horticulture to discomfort him – one which, at the time, he didn't think she'd registered. Peter said impatiently, 'I'll try to get round to it later in the day. No promises.'

Edwina didn't go away as he had expected. She looked at the chaos on his desk, noted that the computer wasn't even switched on, and said calmly, 'What exactly are you doing?'

There had been times in the past, better times, when he'd wanted her to ask that, so that he could show off his latest coup in the world of the arts. Now, when he least expected and least wanted it, she was asking for information. 'A variety of things; I doubt you'd understand them. This damned festival of literature is going to collapse if I don't rescue it. These local nonentities don't realize what they've taken on.'

He'd been much more enthusiastic about the "damned festival" a few years ago when the first one had been mooted, she thought, when he'd expected to take charge of it and make it his private fiefdom. She had an instant of sympathy for him in his isolation, then thrust it away. Peter wouldn't take sympathy, if it meant accepting that he was not the towering figure he pretended to be in the aesthetic world.

The phone in the hall rang as she turned away from him. She looked back expectantly at the phone on his desk, but he said, 'I've unplugged it. I don't wish to be disturbed whilst I'm occupied with important things.'

Edwina had to almost run to the hall phone to prevent the answering machine from cutting in. She gave her number rather breathlessly and a cool, impersonal voice said, 'To whom am I speaking, please?'

'My name is Edwina Preston. I should warn you that we don't buy anything over the phone.'

The woman said with the faintest trace of amusement. 'This isn't a sales call, Mrs Preston. It's Oldford CID here. I'm ringing on behalf of Chief Superintendent Lambert. He needs to have a few words with Mr Peter Preston. Is he at home today?'

'Yes, he is. Would you like me to bring him to the phone?' Let's see if he's as high-handed with the police as he is with his wife, Edwina thought. She quite looked forward to listening in on this.

'No there's no need for that. The chief super wishes to speak to him in person on a private matter. Would one hour from now be convenient?'

'Yes. One hour from now would be fine.' That gives him an hour to decide. An hour to decide whether he tries to shrug off the police in the cavalier fashion he adopts for his wife, Edwina thought waspishly.

Sam Hilton was suffering far more than Peter Preston.

He hadn't really been able to believe what was happening to him on the previous night until he'd found himself sitting between two burly uniformed coppers in the back of a police car. From that moment onwards the exotic beauty of the black officer who had announced his arrest had been denied to him. He'd been kept in the cells, a routine part of the softening-up process. He'd not slept at all until around three and then only fitfully. From six onwards, a drunk and disorderly from the night before had been bellowing from the next cell that he should be released to go fishing with his small son.

You were supposed to be able to see material for poetry in all things, but Sam was finding it impossible in this situation. There was verse of a kind beneath the drawing of an impossibly large male organ on the wall beside his narrow bed and unyielding mattress. But you couldn't call that doggerel poetry. Someone should tell the man who had struggled with 'cock' that not all verse has to rhyme.

He had refused a greasy breakfast and managed only half of the big mug of strong, sweet tea. Sam Hilton didn't know it, but even his status as a criminal was being diminished in the discussions going on among the professionals two floors above him. He was small fry, they decided, not worthy of the attention of the Drug Squad. Wring him dry of any information he had to offer, then dismiss him with a flea in his ear. As a first offender, he was perhaps not even worth bringing to court. But check all of this out in an interview before he was sent on his way.

Sam knew none of this. His immediate concern as he was taken to the interview room was to conceal how frightened he felt. The two men who came there to interrogate him were equally determined to keep him on edge. You were in no condition to conceal information if you were apprehensive. Detective Inspector Rushton and Detective Sergeant Hook, they announced to the microphone as the cassettes began to turn. Rushton was thirty-four and the younger of the two, but to twenty-two-year-old Sam Hilton they both looked immensely experienced. They conferred with each other, then Rushton turned on the camera attached to the ceiling. 'New technology, this,' he explained to the fearful young man on the other side of the square table. 'Enables us to recall how you looked under questioning, as well as what you said and how you sounded. Quite useful, sometimes.'

He didn't explain how, but Sam felt even more like a specimen under a microscope. He folded his arms, but he couldn't keep them still for long, and a moment later he slid them beneath the table and on to his thighs, working them softly against his jeans in an attempt to remove the wetness from his palms. The silence got to him as they watched him and said nothing, as they knew it would. He said, 'This is all a misunderstanding. I really shouldn't be here at all.'

Rushton smiled like a cat which has cornered a particularly stupid mouse. 'Dealing in Class A drugs, Mr Hilton. No misunderstanding there. And the law is very clear, nowadays. A pretty straightforward case, wouldn't you say, DS Hook?'

'I would indeed. And the sentences are pretty straightforward, too. About five years for dealing. Probably in a high security prison initially, with some not very nice characters for company.'

'I – I've been very stupid.'

Hook nodded. 'You're beginning to be more realistic now. That's a good thing, because we don't like wasting our valuable time. I'd say you'd been very stupid indeed.'

Sam nodded, wishing he hadn't got this camera recording how abject his capitulation was. He wondered what would happen to the video after this. Surely they couldn't use it in a court of law? He licked his lips and said, 'Is there no way out of this for me?'

Rushton raised his eyebrows, as if surprised that a man in his position should even suggest such a thing. 'Afraid I can't see one, Mr Hilton. It's so black and white, you see. Actually offering to sell drugs to a police officer. The Crown Prosecution Service likes things to be black and white; not much room for manoeuvre for the defence counsel in court, you see. I should think in this case they wouldn't even contest the guilty verdict; they'd probably confine themselves to a plea for mercy on the grounds of your youth. Unfortunately, though, both judges and juries tend to take a very hard line with drug dealers. I can't see any way for Mr Hilton to help himself. Can you, DS Hook?'

'I'm afraid not, sir. A black and white case, as you say. Plead guilty and beg for mercy will probably be the legal advice. Unless . . .' He let his last word hang in the air, like a fly three inches above a starving trout.

'Unless what?' The trout was hooked in a flash. The young eyes were wide with appeal and a sudden, desperate hope.

'Well, I suppose if Detective Inspector Rushton and I were able to say that you'd given us every assistance, that you'd seen the error of your ways and given clear evidence of your wish to assist the law, that might just count in your favour.

We'd need to be clearly convinced of that before we could offer any such assurance of course. Do you think that might be a possibility, sir?'

Rushton pursed his lips and looked doubtful. 'I think the CPS boys would be very reluctant to abandon such a cast-iron case, you know. Lawyers are like that, I'm afraid, Mr Hilton; they hate letting go of an easy case. DS Hook always wants to help, but he can be something of an optimist. Still, if you're prepared to give clear evidence of remorse, in the form of helpful information, I would certainly be prepared to report as much and put in a plea for you.'

Bert Hook leaned forward, avuncular and concerned. 'It's an evil industry you've got yourself entangled in, Sam. But you're not stupid. You must have realized by now that it's the bigger fish who make the real money out of drugs. And cause the real damage. I don't know how much you've seen of heroin addicts. They first become scarcely human and then die horribly.'

Sam had reached much the same conclusion about the trade he'd been practising through the long hours of a night in the cells. He couldn't agree with them openly, though. At the furthest recess of his mind but increasingly vivid nonetheless, there remained a memory of the final injunction from his supplier, in that briefing which had made it all seem such easy money. "You won't be caught. But if you ever are, you say bugger all. You keep shtum and give the pigs nothing. If you give them anything, anything at all, you'll be dead meat. If you forget everything else, boy, remember that!"

Sam looked into Hook's concerned, experienced face, which was within two feet of his. He wanted to give everything he had, to have this over with and be away, whatever the cost. But that face belonged to a copper; a pig; a piece of shit who would promise you the earth and then laugh in your face once he had what he wanted. Sam tried to summon the worst student and football crowd obscenities about the police to stiffen his resistance. 'Piss off, pig! I don't know anything. And I wouldn't fucking tell you if I did.'

DS Hook was distressingly unshaken. Apparently he rated this performance disappointingly low in the range of opprobrium he had endured over the years. 'You'll please yourself, lad, in the end. We don't beat people up in the cells, whatever colourful tales you've heard. There's nothing we can do to save you, if you won't help yourself.'

DI Rushton nodded and said 'I think it's time we returned Mr Hilton to his cell and got on with preparing the charges against him.'

Sam said desperately, 'I don't know anything. I've got nothing to give to you.'

Bert Hook paused in the process of gathering his papers together. 'Nothing at all, Sam? Not even the tiniest crumb of information that we could cite as evidence of your good intent?'

Sam shook his head miserably. 'They don't tell you anything. That's the way they work. If you ask them anything, you're out on your ear.'

'Which in your case would have been a very good thing, wouldn't it? For a start, you wouldn't have been sitting here facing very serious charges and a prison sentence. You wouldn't have been squirming on that chair and trying to account for yourself to DI Rushton and me.' Hook shook his head sadly.

'I want to help. I can see the sense in what you're saying. But how can I help, when I really don't know anything?'

Hook nodded several times, as if accepting the logic in this. 'Sometimes people know a little more than they realize. When did you begin dealing, Sam?' They watched the young, too-revealing face as Hilton struggled with conflicting emotions. Then Hook added in a low voice, 'I should warn you that if you try to piss us about in this, we'll throw the book at you.'

'January the tenth.'

'That tallies with our information. Carry on.'

Sam had no idea whether they had any information or not. He said desperately, 'I'd snorted a bit of coke at a new year's party. I bought a small amount a day or two after that, in a pub. I remember being appalled by how much it cost.'

Hook nodded. 'What do you do for a living, Sam?'

He wanted to tell them that was irrelevant, wanted to avoid the sniggers and contempt which would be the inevitable reaction of the pigs. But his resistance was exhausted; he wanted only to convince them that he was being honest, when he knew he had so little to give them. 'I'm a poet.' He waited for the uproar of derision, but there was only silence, with perhaps the slightest nod from Hook. 'I've had a few things published and I make a bit from poetry gigs, where I read my stuff and talk about it. But it's not easy to make a living from poetry.'

This time Hook definitely nodded. 'Even T.S. Eliot had to get himself a job with a sympathetic publisher, didn't he? Even Philip Larkin had to be a university librarian in Hull to support his writing. Is that why you started to deal, Sam? To support your poetic career?'

Sam Hilton's mind reeled. A copper talking about two of the men who had made him want to be a poet himself. He said limply, 'Yes. I realize now it was daft, but the man made it seem so easy.'

Hook smiled sadly. 'Tell us about the man, Sam'

'I don't know his name. He had blue eyes, I think, and a flattish nose, which might have been broken at some time. He was burly. Just above average height, but thickset. A bit like your build, but younger.'

The smile this time was from the otherwise immutable DI Rushton. Hook said only, 'What did he wear?'

'Jeans, trainers, a blue quilted anorak. He wore the same every time I saw him afterwards, whatever the weather and the temperature.'

'And who pulled his strings, Sam? Who supplied him?'

'I don't know. I don't even know his name. The first rule he gave me was that I shouldn't ask any questions. No one asked questions if they knew what was good for them, he said.'

The old story. And it wasn't a false threat. Many a dealer who had said a little too much had ended up with a bullet through his head or at the bottom of a river, or simply never been seen again. Hook said quietly, 'It's not much, Sam. What else can you offer us to try to protect you from the law?'

'Nothing. I can see it's not much, but it's all I know. And I'll never deal again. You have to believe me.' The desperation and fear almost oozed through his pores as he strove to convince them.

Rushton said, 'We don't have to believe you, Mr Hilton. You forfeited all credibility when you chose to break the law. However, I am satisfied for the moment that you have told us what little you know. You will be released within the hour and your possessions restored to you by the custody sergeant. The decision as to what charges you will face will be made within the next few days and you will be notified in due course. Interview terminated at five past ten.'

Rushton and Hook remained in the interview room for a moment after Hilton had been returned to his cell. 'Not much there,' said the Inspector dolefully. 'But we didn't expect much, did we? The Drug Squad would have wanted to handle it themselves if they'd thought he'd anything worthwhile to give them.'

Bert Hook nodded. 'From his description, his dealer was Mercer, but we could have guessed that. I think he told us all he knew.'

'Is that a plea for mercy, from hard man Hook?'

Bert grinned. 'I've got boys of my own. That young man we just interviewed is twenty-two, but frighteningly naïve and vulnerable. He saw easy money; I don't think he'll make the same mistake again. As a first-time dealer with a previously spotless record and a good education, he'd get a suspended sentence. Hardly worth the effort of taking him to court.'

'I agree with you that he probably won't re-offend. Fortunately, the decision about whether to prosecute won't be in your hands. But I'm quite prepared to report that we found him both contrite and anxious to help.' For a DI usually anxious to pursue cases where results were guaranteed, it was a notable concession.

Bert Hook believed and hoped that young Sam Hilton had seen the error of his ways. He could not have known at that moment that within a few days he would be interviewing him again, over very different police suspicions.

NINE

The police came at precisely eleven o'clock, the time they had arranged. An hour had given Peter Preston ample time to make his preparations for them.

He watched the tall man climb a little stiffly from the passenger seat of the vehicle. This must be the celebrated Chief Superintendent Lambert, whom the local press seemed determined to make a detective superman. He exchanged a word or two with the burly man who had been driving as they looked at the front elevation of the house; Peter wished he knew what it was they were saying. He was down the stairs and into the hall by the time they knocked. He took a deep breath, then opened the oak door fully and bathed them in his most affable smile.

'Good morning gentlemen. It is a rare and unexpected pleasure to welcome the long arm of the law into our humble abode, and all the more to be savoured on that account.' He turned towards the kitchen behind him. 'Edwina, could we have coffee in the drawing room, please?'

'That will not be necessary, sir. But thank you for the offer. Hopefully this will not take us very long. This is Detective Sergeant Hook and I am Chief Superintendent Lambert.'

'Cancel the coffee, Edwina!' Preston flung imperiously towards the door of the kitchen. He led them into a sun-filled front room and gestured towards a chaise longue, whilst he planted himself in the only comfortable-looking armchair in the room. The two large men perched themselves gingerly on the red velvet of the chaise longue, which proved as uncomfortable as it was elegant.

Peter smiled again to show them how composed he felt. Their slightly ridiculous posture had increased his confidence. He went into the deliberately over-the-top speech he had prepared. 'I am indeed honoured to have in my house the celebrated John Lambert, super-sleuth of our area and acknowledged expert in his field – the man whose excellence has recently been recognized by our beleaguered Home Office with an extension to his service. A rare example of a sensible decision emerging from the echoing towers of bureaucracy, in my view. I welcome this unique opportunity to entertain a distinguished figure, to have in my company the big cheese, in the vulgar modern idiom.'

This was a man who was so over the top that he seemed all the time to be sending up himself, thought Bert Hook. He wished the big cheese hadn't refused coffee. It would have been interesting to witness not only the type of china favoured in this household but how long the central figure in it could sustain his overblown rhetoric. Preston might have been a character from Restoration comedy – Bert's Open University studies had broadened his horizons. It was good to know that the verbose poseurs of those plays usually got their come-uppance in due course.

Lambert said, 'We are investigating some rather strange happenings, Mr Preston. We are looking for a connection between them.'

'This sounds more intriguing by the moment. Do tell me more, Mr Lambert.'

'In a moment. Are you a man with many enemies, Mr Preston?'

Only the abruptness of the question suggested his impatience with the other man's posturings. If he caught that, Preston chose to ignore it. 'What an intriguing question, Mr Lambert! And how pleasingly direct you are! Well, I suppose that if I am being objective, I would have to point out that a man in my position does make enemies. One would have to hope one makes friends as well, of course, by one's staunch defence of standards, and I have pleasing evidence to confirm that. But when one operates in the arts, one inevitably meets opposition as well as approval. That is what one expects, with healthy debate.'

Lambert was rapidly losing patience with this self-serving man. 'Indeed. And one would be inclined to ask for more matter with less art.'

'Ah! A senior policeman who quotes the Bard! All is not

lost for our civilization, after all!' But something in Lambert's features warned Preston against further self-indulgence. 'Yes, I'm sure I have enemies, Chief Superintendent. Indeed, there are people in the arts world of this country whom I should be proud to record as such. It is a guarantee of one's own integrity to have opponents such as—'

'I am thinking locally rather than nationally, Mr Preston.'

'Indeed? Well, at the time of the millennium celebrations, I conducted in the columns of that organ of enlightenment, the *Gloucestershire Citizen,* a prolonged correspondence with some of our local so-called intelligentsia. I can only say that in the last analysis—'

'And recently, as well as locally. If we could concentrate on the last month or two, that might help both of us.'

'I see.' Preston withdrew himself reluctantly from the heights of national aesthetic debate over the last thirty years to a more tawdry and limited local context. 'Recent conflicts seem to have been confined to the deplorable content and conduct of our local literary festival.'

Lambert's sigh of relief was audible and he didn't care if this self-obsessed figure heard it. 'Then I suggest you concentrate your thoughts upon that.'

Preston's answering sigh, if it was meant to be competitive, won hands down. The connoisseurs of melancholy would have treasured its length and its dying fall, but Lambert was not such a devotee. Hook poised his pen over a pristine page of his notebook with renewed hope. But there was still a preliminary. Peter leaned forward and said breathily, 'May I be assured that what passes between us here will not be relayed beyond the walls of this room?'

'No, you may not, Mr Preston. We maintain confidentiality wherever possible, but we sometimes have to take action which demands that we reveal our sources.'

The broad features dropped suddenly into dismay, as if Preston understood at last that his monologue was not suitable for these men. The brown eyes behind the rimless glasses focussed on them for the first time, so that Lambert appreciated that there might be a shrewd man behind the stylized artistic bluster. 'What is it you wish to know?'

Lambert allowed himself a small smile to take the edge off his response. 'I asked you a little while ago whether you had any enemies. Can you please give me some account of the number of people you have offended over the last few months?'

'A number of people have offended me.'

'I see. Well, we should hear about them as well. There may well be some correlation here between the offenders and the offended.'

'There may indeed, Mr Lambert. How prescient of you to see that! I imagine prescience develops with experience in detection, as in so many other aspects of life. I find increasingly that experience is a sadly undervalued quality, nowadays. But to the point, before you begin to see me as Polonius again. I should hate to be stabbed through the arras!' He chuckled lengthily at his cleverness.

Bert Hook hastened to prevent apoplexy in his chief. 'If you could just give us a list of the people concerned, we need not take up any more of your day, Mr Preston.'

Peter studied DS Hook for a moment before deciding to give this representative of honest English yeomanry his approval. 'One has artistic differences with people, which it is one's duty to voice. Unfortunately, an honest difference of opinion is all too often interpreted as hostility, nowadays. The philistines are at our gates, Sergeant Hook.'

'Yes. But I can quite see why a person with a different opinion would take offence, if you called him a philistine. Could we now have some names, please?'

'Yes. Well, I am on the Oldford Literary Festival Committee. I have experienced some hostility there, in response to my sincere but trenchantly expressed views.'

'I expect there has been hostility, yes. Names, please.'

Hook had more success than Lambert in pinning down this exotic linguistic butterfly, perhaps because Preston considered it beneath him to waste his sweetness on the desert air around a mere detective sergeant. 'The committee is chaired by a woman. I have, of course, no quarrel with that.' Everything about him said otherwise.

'So you have no quarrel with Mrs Dooks?'

It disconcerted him a little that they knew the woman's

name. Then he remembered that John Lambert's wife was herself a member of the committee in question. Probably they knew all about the committee members; lists of information were something the pedestrian police mentality could cope with. Perhaps they had even come here equipped with some thoughts of their own. 'Marjorie Dooks is an unimaginative woman who shouldn't be in charge of anything creative. But she has a lot of experience of running committees. I suppose that might have influenced the very predictable people who put her in charge.'

Lambert said irritably, 'Would you say she was an enemy of yours?'

'No I wouldn't, Chief Superintendent. We have our differences of opinion, but we respect each other for our different strengths, I'd say. Of course, if you want to know exactly what she thinks of me, you'd have to ask her.'

Lambert allowed himself a sour smile and Peter realized with a shaft of dismay that they might have already done that. With his first hint of nervousness, he said, 'There are people on that committee who dislike me, I'm sure. The younger ones simply don't understand that one can reject their standards without intending any personal affront.'

Lambert suspected that this man's rejections would be very personal indeed. He said, 'What about the people of your own generation? Sue Charles, for instance; wouldn't she understand your arguments?'

Preston bristled with indignation. 'Sue Charles is hardly my generation, Mr Lambert, She is thirteen years older than me!'

They saw not only his vanity but the emotion it aroused in him; emotion of whatever kind makes people vulnerable, and thus is always of interest to CID men. Lambert said easily, 'But a kindred spirit, would you say?'

'No, I would not! She is a writer, but in a field which by definition rules her out as a serious novelist. She writes what I believe is usually referred to as crime fiction.'

'And you don't think even a much published and well-reviewed writer of detective novels should be regarded as a proper artist?'

'Not as a woman of letters, as we used to say in my youth.

You may not be familiar with the expression. An old-fashioned term, but a useful one, in my view.'

'And you informed Mrs Charles of your views?'

'Indeed I did. I had little choice, if I was to retain my own integrity. Sue Charles is planning to import a well-known practitioner of detective fiction into our festival. I had to tell her that I felt this would lower the tone of the whole enterprise. You may in fact be aware of this, Chief Superintendent.'

'Indeed I am. I have been asked to occupy the platform alongside David Knight and thus further lower the tone.'

Peter decided not to comment on this. He had a feeling that this was not a man to be added to his growing list of enemies. He said, 'I expect Sue Charles has taken offence at my sincerely held views. Women tend to be thin-skinned about these things.'

'On the contrary, it seems that Mrs Charles regards your rather extreme views with what I'd call an amused tolerance, Mr Preston. I gather you have not won the argument within the festival committee.'

'The ignorant and the ill-informed have prevailed, as they tend to do all too often these days.'

In a rare lapse, John Lambert allowed his irritation to get the better of him. 'I shall regard it as an honour to occupy the same platform as Sue Charles and David Knight. Who else have you offended on that committee?'

Peter tried not to show how shaken and isolated he was beginning to feel. He thought of his locked filing cabinet upstairs, but decided it was best not to use the secrets within it when talking to these men. 'The younger members have no standards – and no sympathy with anyone who has. I expect they dislike me; I'm almost prepared to admit it's mutual.'

'Details, please.'

'Well, there's Ros Barker. She's a painter, of sorts. I can't say that I'm familiar with the girl's work.'

'Ms Barker is thirty. You will be able to see an exhibition of her work at the Barnard Art Gallery in Cheltenham next month, if you wish to enlarge your knowledge of her art. You don't consider her a friend of yours?'

'We have little in common. When I chose to question the invitation the committee was offering to a young northern versifier to parade his wares at our festival, she aligned herself with the unenlightened.'

'Bob Crompton.'

'I think that is the young man's name, yes. His work would benefit from discipline, like that of so many of his contemporaries.'

'You are familiar with Crompton's work, then?'

Surely policemen were not in a position to challenge him about poetry, of all things? Peter said uneasily, 'I have a passing acquaintance, that's all.'

'Which you consider is enough to allow you to veto his appearance in Oldford. I see. This no doubt means that you have made an enemy of young Sam Hilton, who, as a friend of Bob Crompton's, has been instrumental in securing his appearance at the festival.'

It was a statement this time, not a question. Peter was disturbed by how much they seemed to know, how much homework they seemed to have done before coming to his house. 'Sam Hilton has little in common with me. I considered it my duty to oppose the appearance of his more celebrated contemporary in Oldford. It was because Ms Barker sprang to his defence that I consider both of them my enemies.' He watched DS Hook making a note in his round, surprisingly rapid hand. 'May I ask what is the purpose of your visit here this morning?'

Lambert said with some relish, 'You may indeed, Mr Preston.'

He nodded to Bert Hook, who delved into his briefcase. He produced a single sheet with a terse message in large black letters, within a transparent plastic sleeve, and passed it across the room to Preston. There was a moment of tense silence before Lambert said calmly, 'That is a letter delivered by hand to Sue Charles. Identical messages have been delivered to Marjorie Dooks and to Ros Barker. Can you tell us anything about them?'

Peter studied the sheet impassively for a moment, feeling the tension building around him in the quiet room. Then he said, 'Excuse me for a moment, please.' He rose and left the room and they heard him climbing the stairs to his study.

He was back within seconds, holding an identical white sheet to the one Hook had just shown him. He set it before his visitors without a word.

RESIGN NOW FROM THE FESTIVAL COMMITTEE IF YOU WISH TO REMAIN ALIVE

Lambert looked into the lined, anxious face, which had now lost all traces of pretension. 'When did you receive this?'

'It was delivered by hand, at about four o'clock yesterday afternoon. Edwina was out, but I was upstairs in my study. I heard the sound of the letter box but I assumed it was just a circular. As a result, I didn't find this for another hour.'

He watched fascinated as Hook inserted the sheet carefully into a plastic sleeve identical to the one around Marjorie Dooks's letter. He started a little as Lambert said quietly, 'What were you intending to do about this, Mr Preston?'

'I didn't take it very seriously. I suppose I considered it preposterous that anyone should be intending real violence towards me.'

Lambert did not give voice to the thought that from what he had seen of Preston he thought it by no means unlikely. Instead, he pointed out, 'Nevertheless, you chose to retain this message rather than to destroy it.'

'Yes. My first concern was to keep it from Edwina, who would probably have been much more disturbed by it than I was. Then, as tends to happen during the dark and silent hours of the night, it began to seem a little more serious. I was wondering exactly what I should do about it when the phone call came this morning, announcing that I was to receive a visit from the district's leading policeman. Dilemma solved, I thought.'

'Have you any thoughts on the origin of these letters?'

'Well, my first reaction is a selfish one. I am happy that I am not alone as a recipient. If all and sundry are receiving them, there can surely be no serious threat intended.'

'That is logical. I think you and the other three people who have received identical letters can take it that this is probably an ill-judged and tasteless prank. But that cannot be the end of the matter for us. You can imagine the impact of this threat on someone like Sue Charles, an elderly lady living alone. She was very disturbed by it. The police cannot allow anyone to threaten people with violence and get away with it.'

'I'm glad to hear it. You asked me where these might have originated. I would think from their content and their recipients that they must have a connection with the literature festival committee. I – I don't think I would care to speculate on the sender. I'd rather leave that matter in your capable hands.'

With this shameless piece of flattery, he released them from their uncomfortable tenure of his chaise longue. Lambert left him with the routine instruction to contact them immediately if he had further thoughts on the issue.

Hook reversed the car out of the drive and drove carefully down the tree-lined avenue beyond it before he spoke. 'I heard you volunteer yourself to be on that platform at the festival, as the representative of real policing.'

'These things are confidential, DS Hook. There is no reason why my moment of weakness in the face of a very annoying man should be taken any further.'

Bert stared ahead at the road and the burgeoning trees as steadily as his chief, but a smile broke steadily over his rugged features. 'I think you did the right thing, John. You are much the best man for the task. It's good to have the matter settled.'

There were long minutes of silence which Hook enjoyed and Lambert did not. Then Hook said, 'Christine's on that committee.'

Lambert nodded. 'And I can confirm first that she has not received one of the notes and secondly that I am confident she is not the sender of them.'

'The local press will be disappointed about that. It would have given them a lurid story.'

'If we rule out Christine, it leaves only one member of the committee who has not received one of these threats.'

'And who thus becomes the leading suspect for the crime of sending them. The man I interrogated about drug offences yesterday. Young Sam Hilton.'

TEN

'It looks like a squalid little side-show, but we've got to follow it up. We can't allow idiots to go round threatening people, if only because the odd idiot might turn out to a psychopath.' John Lambert, sitting in his favourite armchair, delivered this judgement on the anonymous notes to his wife.

Christine smiled. 'Or a paranoid narcissist. That seems to be the latest one for a dangerous man with a firearm.'

'Do you think there's anyone on that literary festival committee of yours who's a potential danger to society?'

'I notice that as soon as there's a problem it's become my committee.' But Christine was secretly rather pleased; it was the first time in the long years of his police career that she'd had a direct involvement in one of his cases. 'For what it's worth, no, I don't. But that view's worth very little; sometimes even wives and husbands know nothing about the secret lives and desires of their spouses, so what can we really know of people we meet once every two or three weeks on a committee? You've much more experience of the criminal mentality than I have.'

'Yes. It's amazing that I remain the relaxed, even-tempered, balanced individual that I am, isn't it?'

'Self-delusion must be one of the dangers of prolonged contact with crime, I suppose.'

'I don't want this business to get out to the press. Peter Preston may not be paranoid, but he's certainly a narcissist. If it suits his purpose, he'll have the local press, and probably radio and television as well, reporting that he's been threatened – probably with an addendum about police incompetence and insensitivity.'

'Is there anyone on that committee apart from me who hasn't received one of these damned notes?' She noted his hesitation and grinned. 'I can easily find out, you know. Once you start questioning people, the word spreads pretty quickly.'

The television news and weather were over. Lambert watched three seconds of a lurid trailer for a programme about Miss Nude Australia and switched the set off decisively. 'Sam Hilton seems to be the only one who hasn't received one.'

'So you think he must have sent them.'

'I don't think anything. I think the situation has to be investigated. What do you think? You know the young man; I've never even met him.'

'I knew him better when he was ten and in my class at school. He was a rather secretive boy, but good with words. And fascinated by them. He loved poetry. And he loved writing bits of verse of his own, even then.'

'So at twenty-two, he might well be a writer of anonymous threatening letters.'

Christine Lambert shrugged, wanting to reject the idea but unable to find any strong argument against it. 'I wouldn't think so, but you'll have to decide for yourself. Who knows what goes on in that secret self that we don't care to show to those around us? I suppose if he wanted to make mischief, words would be the first weapons to suggest themselves to him. I only know that Sam Hilton is now producing some quite interesting poems.'

And supporting his muse by selling illicit drugs, thought her husband. Police work didn't give many grounds for optimism.

Ten hours later, Chief Superintendent Lambert was preparing to make his own judgements on Sam Hilton.

Nine a.m. prompt. Young men who might have a drug habit were rarely at their best in the first part of the morning. Study them at your leisure, learn whatever you could from their actions and words when they were least prepared for you. None of this was voiced; Lambert and Hook knew each other and their strategies far too well for that.

Hilton lived in the least salubrious area of Oldford, but in a small town no street is as squalid or as desperate as those to be found in the great cities of the country. He lived on the ground floor of a late-Victorian semi-detached house, in what had been one of the most prestigious roads of the town when it had been built. The area had descended steadily in status over the last fifty years. The houses here were now divided into much smaller living units, with transient occupiers, who moved in and out of their rented properties with great frequency.

Generally speaking, this rabbit warren of residences was peopled by a motley assembly of life's underdogs: men who had lost wives, families and houses and had to find for themselves the cheapest possible accommodation; European immigrants who picked up whatever work they could and sent home as much money as they could; young men and young women who passed through a variety of jobs because they were feckless or unreliable; petty criminals and others who lived on the edge of the law, who either prospered and moved on or failed and entered prisons.

And then there were sundry others. Would-be poets who wanted to live as cheaply as possible whilst making a reputation were too rare to be a group in themselves. Sam Hilton was bleary-eyed and suspicious, but to the expert eyes now assessing him he did not look like an addict. He had decided after his interview with DI Rushton and DS Hook that it didn't pay to antagonize the pigs, but that didn't now prevent him being cautious, even surly. He addressed Hook rather than the senior man. 'I don't know what you want with me. I told you everything I know when you had me in the nick and grilled me.'

It was Lambert who replied. 'This is about a different matter entirely. You may still face charges for dealing in drugs. We are here this morning about something even more serious.'

'What am I supposed to have done now?'

'That is what we are here to find out, Mr Hilton. It will pay you to be completely frank with us. Obstructing the police in the course of their enquiries can lead to very serious charges.'

They looked round at the place where he lived whilst Sam tried to gather his resources and prepare himself. It was a bedsit rather than a flat. The long, high-ceilinged room, which had once been an elegant Edwardian dining room, had a bed against the wall at one end and a tiny electric cooker beside the scratched steel sink at the other. The wallpaper was at least twenty years old, the light-fitting plastic where once there would have been patterned glass. The single painting of a Scottish Highland scene would have benefited from a good clean. The air smelt stale; the tall sash window did not look as though it had been opened for a long time.

Yet there was no real evidence of squalor in the occupant of the room. Hilton wore a tee-shirt and jeans, both well-worn but clean. His brown hair had been combed, his eyes were alert, and his hands and nails were perfectly clean. The cereal bowl and beaker he had used for his breakfast were washed and draining upon the sink. He was a slight figure, whose nervousness manifested itself in an inability to keep his arms still. Neither the man nor his surroundings were affluent, but Hilton did not look or behave like a druggie. As if he read this thought, he said, 'I shan't be dealing any more and I can't tell you anything more about the people who supplied me. I don't know why else you should be here.'

Lambert nodded at Hook, who produced the letter with its chilling threat. 'What do you know about this, Mr Hilton?'

He stared wide-eyed for long seconds at the large black print with its threat of death. He said through dry lips, 'Nothing. Why should I know anything?'

'It was sent to Sue Charles, a member of the literature festival committee. Have you seen it before?'

'No.'

'Have you seen anything like it before?'

'No. Never in my life. You read about—'

'You haven't received one of these yourself?'

'No. I thought you said it was sent to Sue Charles?'

'This one was. There've been others, as well as this.'

He looked from one to the other of these very different men. Fear began to replace bafflement on his face. 'I've never seen this or anything like it before. I don't know anything about these letters.'

Lambert's grey, steely eyes seemed to be looking into his very soul. After a few seconds he said, 'Then who do you think might have sent them?'

Sam Hilton looked round desperately at the sink with its draining pots, at the radio and the battered television set in the corner, at the black and white drawings of Keats and Tennyson that stood incongruously beside the photograph of his mother on the shelf over the electricity meter. 'Who's received them? You said there were others, as well as Sue Charles.'

Hook glanced at his chief, then leaned forward towards Hilton. 'Normally we'd tell you we're here to ask questions, not to answer them. But I can tell you that these threats have been delivered by hand to several members of the literature festival committee. I'm now asking you to give some thought to who you think might be responsible.'

Sam tried to do as he was bidden, but he was still too shaken to think clearly. 'Mrs Lambert is on that committee. She taught me, years ago, in my last year at primary school. I like her. I've always liked her.' He had no idea why he'd said that. Perhaps he was talking just for the sake of talking, for the sake of trying to convince them that whatever else he'd done, he'd never have sent these letters. Yet this quiet, seemingly friendly man had questioned him only yesterday about dealing in drugs, so he could scarcely have any credit left.

They left him to suffer for another few seconds, which seemed to him more like minutes. Then Hook smiled and repeated his query. 'Who do you think might have sent them, Sam?'

Suddenly, as if someone had turned a switch, his mind began to work again. Not only to work but to race, as if trying to compensate for earlier omissions. His eyes fixed on the twelve black words within the plastic sleeve. 'Am I the only member of that committee who hasn't had one of those?'

'You're asking the questions again, Sam. But all right. Apart from Mrs Lambert, yes, you seem to be the only one who hasn't received one. Does that help you with your thoughts on who might have done this?'

The young poet frowned, then shook his head, seemingly as much in annoyance as puzzlement. 'No. It's difficult to have any idea on the sender, because the whole idea seems so bizarre. I was actually going to say that the only person I know who might be malevolent enough and warped enough to do this is Peter Preston. But if he's been threatened himself, it can't be him, can it?'

Hook didn't respond to that. 'What about someone from outside the committee, Sam? It might be just a coincidence that everyone who's been threatened so far is a member of it.'

'But look at the words. "Resign now from the festival committee if you wish to remain alive." It's very specific, isn't it?'

'It is indeed, Sam. And it's led us to you, as the only member of that committee apart from Mrs Lambert who hasn't received one.'

'But I didn't send them. And now that we've eliminated Mr Preston, I can't think of anyone else who'd have been malicious enough to do anything like this.'

Lambert's eyes had never left Hilton's face, even though it had been Hook who had done all the questioning in the last few minutes. He studied the young man for a few seconds more, then levered himself rather stiffly to his feet. 'Keep thinking, Mr Hilton. It's very much in your own interests as well as ours that you do so.'

They were almost back at the station before he said, 'You think Hilton's innocent of this, don't you, Bert?'

'Yes. But I don't know who else we should suspect.'

'I think you do.'

Hook didn't take his eyes off the road, but allowed a smile to infuse his rugged features. 'You think one of the people who's received a letter could be the perpetrator of this? It would be the obvious thing to do to divert suspicion, wouldn't it?'

'Indeed it would. I think we should pay another visit to the self-regarding Mr Preston.'

It was just eleven o'clock when they drove into the tree-lined avenue where Peter Preston lived.

Building land had been readily available in the nineteen thirties, when these tall, mock-Tudor houses had been built, so that the plots were spacious enough to show each house to its best advantage. The gardens had matured around them over the years, so that each residence had acquired the privacy from its neighbours which had always been envisaged. In May, the foliage and the late spring blossom were at their most abundant, so that the front elevation of the house was not visible until Hook had swung the car between the high gateposts and into the drive.

They had not phoned ahead to arrange a meeting, as was their usual practice. Lambert had preferred to surprise this patronizing self-appointed guardian of culture, in the hope of shaking his self-confidence. There was no reply when Hook pressed the bell, which they could hear ringing faintly in the interior of the big house. He knocked hard on the oak door, but the place sounded very empty. With a habit bred by years of police work, they walked to the side of the house to look for any sign of a human presence. There was a garage at the rear of the house, but the ageing Ford Granada stood outside it. A man's car, almost certainly Preston's; they did not need to voice the thought.

'There's a window open upstairs,' said Lambert. 'He shouldn't be far away.'

They walked to the rear of the house. A long garden, with an unkempt lawn but carefully tended borders with a variety of shrubs and perennials, ran away for forty yards of level ground to a rose bed where the stems were swelling with promising buds. The nearest grass was carpeted with the pink blossom which had fallen from a flowering cherry. A blackbird shrilled its song and blue tits shot in and out of a nesting box in the bole of a tree. There was no sign of a human presence.

They took in this pleasant vista for a moment, then looked up at the rear elevation of the house. There was another window open on the upper storey. 'Some people invite burglary, then complain when we don't catch the culprits,' said Hook. He walked automatically to the back door of the house and turned the handle.

The door opened easily to his touch.

They glanced at each other, then moved softly into the house. Lambert called, 'Mr Preston, are you there? It's Chief Superintendent Lambert.'

There was no reply. He went into the lofty hall and called out again, looking up the stairs. The echoing house sounded very empty. He looked at Hook, who was sniffing the air. 'His study's upstairs somewhere. He went up to it to bring his letter down when we were here yesterday. Probably one of the rooms with a window open. You have a look round down here.' Lambert climbed the stairs. It was obvious which room was the study because its door was wide open. It was empty, with the chair at the desk pushed back as if the occupant had just left it. He went across and shut the window. He was looking at the old-fashioned metal filing cabinet in the corner when Hook called softly up the stairs. 'You'd better come and look at this, John.'

His voice carried easily in the silent house, but his tone was quiet, almost reverential. Lambert descended swiftly and followed him into the room at the front of the house where they had talked to Preston yesterday.

They stopped abruptly just inside the door of the room. You didn't contaminate a crime scene. There was no need to feel for carotid arteries in this case. Peter Preston lay on his back, with his legs slightly apart, in front of the easy chair where he had sat whilst they had perched incongruously upon the elegant chaise longue. His eyes stared sightlessly at the ceiling. His features had relaxed in death into an expression of surprise rather than horror.

The dark crimson patch around the wound in the middle of his chest was almost black at its centre. The lips which had been so active would patronize no more.

ELEVEN

Three hours later, Edwina Preston drove home slowly. It was only thirty miles, thirty-five at the most, so there was no need to hurry. She had no wish to get home quickly; she preferred to reflect on her experiences overnight.

It had been a good time, as usual. Once again it had underlined how inadequate her relationship with Peter was. She hated him again for refusing to talk to her about it. She drove slowly through Oldford. She had always liked the town and the area, but now the very thought of Peter and his airs and graces seemed to be discolouring it for her. She needed time to prepare herself for what she would find at home. She was moving from a new and exciting world to a familiar and depressing one.

Her little Citroen seemed to have a will of its own, however. Every traffic light she slowed for changed obligingly in her favour, every heavy vehicle that might have slowed her pulled obligingly into a parking lay-by to facilitate her progress. All too soon, she was turning into the wide avenue with its tall trees that she had liked so much when they had moved in sixteen years ago.

It was because of the trees that she did not see the policeman until she swung into the drive. He looked very young and quite disconcerted as she indicated and turned. He held up his hand before her like an old-fashioned traffic cop. 'Mrs Preston?'

'I am she, yes.' She cursed herself for adopting the phrase her pedantic husband had always insisted upon.

The young policeman looked even more disturbed. 'I'm afraid I have bad news for you, Mrs Preston.' He looked behind him desperately and she glimpsed blue and white plastic ribbons between hastily erected stakes. His uniform was very new and beautifully pressed; she wondered how long he had been wearing it. He called towards the open door of the big house, 'Would you ask PC Jeffries to come out here, please? Tell her it's urgent.'

Edwina said dully, 'What is going on here? Why are these people in my house?'

He said nothing, but the relief on his face was palpable as a woman police officer, who was only a little older than he was, came reluctantly down the drive. She smiled nervously at Edwina and said, 'I am PC Alison Jeffries. Would you switch your engine off please?' She looked back at the big house and decided that there was no way in which she could allow the woman who was now a widow to breach the scene of crime barriers. 'I'm afraid I'm the bearer of bad news, Mrs Preston. Could you let me into your car for a few minutes, please?'

When you're nineteen, you may not have a clear view of reality. The distinction between the possible and the impossible may be clear to you, but the line between the possible and the unlikely is much less clear. Cloudy judgement leads to bad decisions. Bad decisions can have all kinds of unforeseen repercussions.

Wayne Johnson was nineteen. Last night he had made a bad decision. He was now at Oldford police station, enduring the unforeseen repercussions.

Wayne was one of the young petty criminals who loomed larger by the year in the crime statistics. His school career had been dominated by truancy. He had been designated an under-achiever until he was twelve; from then on his continual absences had determined he should be reclassified as a non-achiever. He had acquired a certain grudging admiration from his peers as a successful shoplifter, the most experienced and gifted amongst his group. He had been absent far more than present in his last year at school, so that the end of his educational career was welcomed by his teachers almost as heartily as it was received by the young man himself.

There was no employment for him, of course. He joined the swelling ranks of those 'on the social' with a weary resignation which should have been alien to a sixteen-year-old. He graduated from shoplifting to petty burglary. Like many adolescents of his background, Wayne had no very clear idea of right and wrong. It was definitely not done to torture babies and old ladies, and young men shouldn't hit women – well, not unless they'd done something really bad to deserve it, anyway. Beyond that, moral distinctions were very hazy. If people were foolish enough to leave things lying around, then they were really very silly; it was only sensible that you should remove such things. It would teach them a lesson; you were rendering them a service, really.

It was a short step from removing things left lying around to searching for such things, and another short step to making your own opportunities. That was the initiative they'd said he didn't have at school, wasn't it? And with the recession deepening and these bloody Poles taking all the jobs round here, you had to do something to survive, didn't you? He had always been quite a nimble lad – could have been a good gymnast, the PE teachers said, if he'd only been at school more often. If people left windows open, they deserved to suffer and Wayne was just the man to ensure they did.

Success made him bolder. He moved on to better streets and bigger houses. He learned what to take and what to ignore. Money was the best, and after that jewellery. Then silver, particularly if it was fairly portable; he learned to distinguish at a glance between the hallmarked article and the EPNS versions which were hardly worth removing. He knew where to dispose of stuff quickly and profitably; you didn't get anything like the retail value, but you had to extract a realistic price from crooked dealers for stolen goods.

Boldness can be a valuable quality for felons. It can also be highly dangerous, if it leads them to overreach themselves. Wayne Johnson had passed his driving test at the first attempt. It was the only examination success he had ever had and for a full day it lifted his spirits. He acquired an old van to carry away his booty and moved on to fresh fields and richer pickings. He could go miles from home now, out to the rich suburbs and the last roads before town finally gave way to country.

The road where he had been last night was simply and grandly called The Avenue. Big gardens, with lots of cover for people doing what he did; big houses, with lots of lovely loot for the deserving and resourceful man like him. But possessions made people suspicious, and success had made Wayne careless.

He had watched the elderly couple leave the first big house at the end of the road. There was no burglar alarm visible on the outside of the house and no bell blared when Wayne gained access. The downstairs windows were the original leaded lights from the thirties. They were certainly picturesque, but no match for a strong young man with the heavy old chisel he had found so effective a tool. You had to force entry without much noise. He was into the room at the rear of the house within three minutes, scarcely able to believe his luck that there should be no effective security in a place this size. No need to hurry; the big Merc had plainly been on its way out for the evening.

He took his time assessing this Aladdin's cave of trophies. His eyes gleamed when his torch flicked over a display cabinet. The silver tea service was solid and a good weight. Regency, probably, his now experienced eye told him. He didn't bother with the china. It was too fragile to travel easily, and you got disappointingly little for it. But there was a collection of gold and silver snuff boxes on the top shelf. Twelve in all; he put them carefully into the shopping bag he had found behind the kitchen door.

The bottom drawer in the bedroom was where he found the money. Tens and twenties, maybe with the odd fifty among them – there must be hundreds here – all beneath several pairs of neatly folded knickers. The woman must have been concealing this from her husband. Naughty old bag! He resisted the urge to count the notes and moved up the drawers to the top one.

That was where he had his real windfall. A jewellery box, with everything neatly assembled for the discriminating intruder to remove. How very obliging! Diamonds, emeralds, what looked to his experienced but uneducated eye like rubies and sapphires. Genuine stones, he was pretty sure of that. Rings and earrings and three or four brooches. Silly old trout! Some people only learned a lesson the hard way, didn't they?

There weren't many dog walkers in the tight little houses

in the centre of the town where Wayne Johnson lived. That was probably what made him omit them from his calculations. But The Avenue was a very different place. It was a man walking his Labrador through the scented spring darkness that saw the battered white van in the drive of the solicitor's house. An odd thing, that, as the house itself seemed to be in darkness. When he heard the sound of the rear door of the van being stealthily opened, the dog walker didn't intervene; he was observant, not foolhardy. He stilled the soft growl of the Labrador and hastened homewards as fast as his ageing legs would carry him.

He was lucky. And Wayne was unlucky. When the 999 call came through to the police at Oldford, there was a patrol car within half a mile. They arrested Johnson as he eased the van out of the driveway of the big detached house. Caught red-handed, with the evidence neatly stowed behind him in the back of van. Charged, relieved of his laces and his belt and the contents of his pockets, and given a night in the cells to meditate upon the error of his ways. A result, in police terms. Something to throw in the faces of those who said burglary wasn't taken seriously, in these days of drugs and terrorism.

Wayne Johnson didn't sleep much. The face of the mother who had warned him against his descent into crime ever since his last days at school kept swimming before him, and his scornful dismissal of her fears kept ringing in his ears. They'd be round to tell her he was in the nick for the night and why. He felt an odd emotion he had not endured since childhood. It took him a little while to recognize it as guilt. In the morning, he managed to down half a piece of bread and most of the mug of strong tea that was brought to him.

The two uniformed cops who interviewed him were truculent. The case was sewn up, whatever attitude this suddenly pitiful creature chose to adopt. Even the cautious boys of the Crown Prosecution Service couldn't reject this. Plead guilty and throw yourself on the magistrate's mercy, lad, there's no other course open to you.

Offer them nothing, Wayne's previous brushes with the law told him. He couldn't see any way out of this, but he'd make it as difficult for them as he could, on principle. He knew he was entitled to a brief, and was disappointed when they announced that. No chance of claiming that he'd been deprived of his rights, then. He knew he was going to plead guilty, but told himself stubbornly that a brief might turn up some mitigating circumstance which he couldn't see for himself. These bloody lawyers cost enough, didn't they? If the state was stupid enough to pay their exorbitant bills, let them earn their bloody money.

They couldn't find a lawyer for him, not immediately. One should be available in a couple of hours. He was returned to his cell until then, wondering darkly about some cunning police ploy. The delay was genuine enough, but it was this chance occurrence that delivered him into the hands of the CID.

When he was taken back to the interview room, a keen-looking dark-haired pig said he was Detective Inspector Rushton. He introduced the burly PC Plod-type beside him as Detective Sergeant Hook. After this, they both looked at Wayne for several seconds without words, as though he were a specimen under a microscope that might reward careful study. It was quite unnerving, especially as he was also wondering why simple burglary should interest top brass like this.

Rushton's opening words did nothing to slow his racing pulses. 'We're not interested in the breaking and entering; that's an open and shut case. You're going to plead guilty once your brief arrives. We're interested in you for something much more serious.' He paused to study Wayne again with that unsmiling, unblinking stare, as if he expected some guilty start to reward him for his attention.

Wayne found it difficult to summon up resistance. 'You might think you have me banged to rights for breaking and entering. Remains to be seen, that. And you'll get me to admit to bugger-all else, so don't think you can build up your clearance figures by pinning some other thing on me.'

'Which you'll claim you know nothing about.'

'Which I've already told you I know nothing about.'

'Correction, Mr Johnson. You denied responsibility for this major crime. You didn't say you knew nothing about it.'

'Well, I'm saying it now.' Again they studied him without comment, letting the silence stretch until he found himself compelled to break it. 'What is this crime you're trying to pin on me, anyway?'

'We're talking about the biggest one of all, Mr Johnson. Capital murder.'

The words had a ring he couldn't escape in this increasingly claustrophobic place. His throat felt very dry as he said, 'I know nothing about that.'

Rushton raised his eyebrows and turned his face towards the older man next to him. DS Hook didn't take his eyes off their subject of study, but took up the questioning. 'Two houses away from the place where you were apprehended last night, on the same side of the road, a man was shot dead. As far as we can tell at the moment, at about the time you were in the area, Mr Johnson. You can see why we're interested in what you have to say about it.'

It was suddenly vitally important to Wayne that he should convince them of his innocence. The pigs would frame you for anything they could. But surely the law wouldn't allow them to pin something like this on him? 'I didn't do it. It's not my style.' He wanted his denial to carry more conviction, but his voice sounded thin and frail. 'I'm a breaker and enterer, if you want, but not a murderer. I wouldn't do that.'

Hook studied the thin, frightened face. 'Do you know, Wayne, I'm almost inclined to believe you about that? Not your style, murder. But as you're a known criminal in the vicinity at the time, you can see why we have to question you about it. You wouldn't be the first young fool to panic when interrupted and resort to violence he never intended.'

'Well I didn't.' As he sought frantically to convince them, a thought that might bring salvation flashed like an exploding firework into his brain. 'I've never carried a weapon. And I wasn't carrying one last night. You can search my van, if you like.'

Hook smiled at his naivety. 'That's already been done, son. Lots of interesting stuff, which will become evidence in due course.'

'But no gun.'

'No firearm, as you say. Which reinforces my view that it probably wasn't you who dispatched the victim. And you've no previous history of violence. The question is, are you able to help us and thereby help yourself?'

Wayne peered at him suspiciously. He'd met pigs before who said you could help yourself. Usually that just meant land yourself deeper in the shit, by telling them everything they wanted to hear. But if what these buggers said was right, he'd been nearer to a killing than he'd ever been before. He didn't like the feeling. 'I didn't shoot anyone and I don't know who did. I'd tell you if I did.'

Bert Hook shook his head sadly. 'Pity, that. I thought you might have been able to do yourself a bit of good. Look, let's accept for the moment that you had nothing to do with this killing, that you were there for other purposes entirely. Criminal purposes, as you're going to admit when your brief gets here, but not capital murder. We haven't got an exact time for it yet, but last night some person or persons unknown killed a man two houses down the road from where you were operating. Think hard, son; it's in your interests to do so. You must have had your ears cocked for any sort of noise all the time you were in that house. Did you hear any activity in The Avenue?'

A few seconds of silence, which this time stretched as long for the CID men as for Johnson. Then he said dully, almost like a man under hypnosis. 'There was a car.'

Hook said quietly, 'Don't make anything up, Wayne, just because you think it might help you. It will do the opposite, in the long run.'

'No. There was a car. In the road, just after I'd got there.'

'Parked there?'

'No. It drove in. I'd reversed my van into the drive at the end house. That's easier for loading, and you can get away quickly if you need to, see. I'd just switched off when this car turned into the road and drove past.'

'What kind of car, Wayne?'

'I don't know. It was dark and I only saw it side-on as it passed.' It was suddenly important to him to convince them of the detail of this. 'Dark colour, I think. Not silver or white, anyway.'

'You must have listened hard when you were about to break and enter. Did the car drive on, until it was out of earshot?'

'No.' Wayne, frowning with concentration, felt a swift wave of excitement sweep over him as he realized what he was going to say. 'No, it stopped quite quickly. Turned into one of the houses further down the road and switched off.'

'How far down the road?'

He shook his head in frustration that he couldn't be precise. Despite his low-key questioning, the PC Plod detective was excited, and Wayne had caught some of that excitement himself. 'I couldn't say. They're big houses, with quite a distance between them.'

'So it could have been two houses away from you?' Hook was leading the witness, but this wasn't a court of law.

Wayne shivered suddenly; it surprised him more than them. 'It could have been, yes. I was just happy that it was well away from me. I listened for a minute, to make sure of that. I suppose I thought it was just someone coming home.'

'Think hard, Wayne. Did you hear that vehicle again? Did you hear it drive away?'

'No. I was doing the house over after that. Perhaps twenty minutes. Maybe even a bit longer. I didn't hear any other vehicle sounds. I didn't hear your blokes drive into the road, but they were waiting for me at the gates.'

Hook glanced at Rushton to convey that he didn't think there was anything more to be had from this wretched, frightened figure. The DI said, 'I hope for your sake that everything you've said is genuine, Mr Johnson. As regards your burglary, you may expect be charged and released within an hour, once your brief arrives. Let us hope that we have made an arrest for the homicide committed close to where you were last night by the time your case is heard. That would enable us to assure the court that you gave us every assistance with a more serious crime.'

In the end, it was Sue Charles who offered comfort to Edwina Preston.

She saw her first in the car park behind the supermarket, when she was preparing to do her weekly shop. Edwina was sitting quietly behind the wheel of her car. She did not appear shocked or even surprised. She simply looked as if her thoughts were elsewhere. Like someone listening to music on the radio or CD, perhaps, thought Sue. She did that herself sometimes, when there was an aria or the movement of a symphony she wanted to hear to its end. Buying for one did not take very long. Sue emerged with her purchases within ten minutes, which included the two when she had been queuing at the till. She would buy vegetables and her first strawberries of the year from Percy at the little greengrocer's on the high street. She liked to support his stubborn resistance to the march of the supermarkets. She'd seen his little notice with its flying apostrophes as she drove past.

Edwina was still sitting in the driving seat of her car, with exactly the same abstracted, unseeing expression. Sue hesitated for a moment, then went over to the little dark green Fiat. She put on a cheerful smile and waved at Edwina from the front of the car. The face behind the wheel started violently, apparently did not recognize her for a moment, then smiled weakly. Sue opened the door of the car. 'Are you all right, Edwina? I saw you before I went into the supermarket.' As if that explained everything, she thought stupidly.

Edwina nodded slowly. Then she shook her head vigorously. 'Peter's dead.'

'Good heavens! Are you sure?' Sue realized how stupid that sounded and took a deep breath. 'Sorry, of course you are. I think you should come home with me for coffee. You shouldn't be on your own at a time like this.'

Edwina said dully, 'I told them I was going to my daughter's. But I suppose I knew I wasn't, really.'

Sue was still stooping awkwardly beside the open window of the car. 'You need someone to talk to. You can come with me in my car, if you like, and I'll drive you back later.'

'No, I can drive. You lead the way and I'll follow you.'

Sue felt relieved about that. She'd be able to send Edwina on her way without the awkward business of driving a distraught woman back to this car park at some unspecified time later in the day.

But Edwina Preston did not seem to be distraught. She drove perfectly competently behind Sue's Fiesta, indicating each turn in good time and keeping just the right distance behind her

Samaritan. She even chose to reverse into the entrance to Sue's bungalow, as if seeking to prove how competent and unshaken she was. Sue waited patiently for her to complete the manoeuvre, then put a motherly arm around the younger woman's shoulders and led her gently into her home.

Edwina stood behind her in the kitchen whilst she boiled the water and made the instant coffee. To Sue's surprise, she picked up the tray with the two china beakers and the biscuits and carried it into the cosy sitting room, careful as a child not to spill the liquid, the tip of her tongue wedged at the corner of her mouth and her eyes firmly upon the task in hand.

She must be around forty-five now, Sue calculated, though she looked understandably older at this moment. She was certainly quite a few years younger than Peter. Edwina had been in the sixth form and at university with her own daughter. That must be a quarter of a century ago now, though it seemed much less to Sue. She hadn't seen much of her over the last few years; she fancied that was because Peter Preston hadn't wanted it, after Sue's successes as a crime novelist and emergence as a minor local celebrity. Peter wasn't the sort of man who rejoiced in other people's successes.

Edwina sipped her coffee and munched a biscuit very slowly. After a few minutes, Sue said awkwardly, 'It must have come very suddenly. Was it a heart attack?'

'What? Oh no, nothing like that. I'd been away overnight, you see.' She spoke as if that explained the whole business, then said nothing more for almost half a minute. Sue was wondering how she could prompt her to reveal more when she said suddenly, 'I believe someone killed him.' She sat with her head on one side for a moment, then added with apparent satisfaction, 'That's what the police think, anyway. They said I couldn't go into the house yet. Said it was a crime scene.'

Sue Charles felt a little thrill of excitement. This would be her first real murder, when she'd created so many fictional ones. And the victim was someone who had derided her skills as a writer; there was something very satisfying about that, however much she might be occupied with ministrations to the sad figure in front of her. 'Did they give you any clear idea of what had happened?'

'No. They spoke as if there might have been an accident, at first. But when I asked questions about it, the young policewoman talked abut a suspicious death. That means they think someone killed him, doesn't it?'

'It does usually, yes.' It would be three o'clock soon. Sue wanted to put the radio station on to see what, if anything, the police had released about this, but she couldn't do that with Preston's widow sitting very upright upon her sofa. 'Sometimes after investigation the police realize there is a more innocent explanation, of course.'

Edwina Preston nodded. 'They won't do that this time, though. Someone killed Peter, I'm sure. I wonder who it could be. He had a lot of enemies, you know.'

Sue Charles would recall those words many times, in the days to come. They should have been chilling, but she found in them a kind of comfort.

TWELVE

It took no more than an hour to set the machinery of a serious crime investigation in place. The house to house trawl of people in this area might throw up nothing, or it might provide the most vital clue of all in establishing who had been in the area at the time of the killing. It was dull, necessary and expensive in terms of manpower. Uniformed officers had to be recruited and put fully in the picture; that was a fact accepted with weary resignation and a few routine groans about the demands of CID by the sections losing staff.

To make sure this expensive team operated with maximum efficiency, the officers, some of them junior and inexperienced, had to be properly briefed. The procedure of house to house and other routine checks was simple enough, but the important thing was to provide officers with the correct questions. The place of the death was obvious and the method was clear, so where and how the victim had died were already evident. When the crime had taken place was now the most pressing question, if the team was to channel its questioning towards the key element in a killing.

Whilst Rushton and Hook were exploiting the windfall that was Wayne Johnson, Lambert received the call he was waiting for, telling him the pathologist was at the scene of the crime. He drove swiftly out again to The Avenue and the big mock-Tudor house. There were already a couple of journalists and a photographer outside the gates of The Willows. He wondered who had told them about this. Possibly one of the neighbouring householders, but in this case far more likely one of the police personnel at Oldford. It was almost impossible to prevent police officers from making easy money by unofficial leaks nowadays. As in other areas of life, professional pride was not what it had been when he joined the service.

He told himself he must behave like a modern chief superintendent and not an old fogey as he went into the house and watched the team at work. They were entirely civilian now, though he recognized a couple of ex-coppers amongst them and knew that the photographer was almost exclusively employed by the police. The 'meat wagon' van was parked discreetly at the side of the house, awaiting the go-ahead to remove its grisly cargo for the post-mortem examination.

Lambert didn't speak to the pathologist until the man had completed his work and finished speaking into the mouthpiece that would record his immediate impressions at the scene as a prelude to the more detailed and scientific dissection to come. Rectal temperatures and the examination of intimate areas always felt like an invasion of privacy to John Lambert, even though a corpse could no longer register such violations. Humanity lost all dignity in death; it was inevitable, but depressing nonetheless. He was pleased that he still found it so after thirty years. A man had to cling to his humanity when he spent his life among such things.

The pathologist was a slight man with red hair and a tightly clipped red beard. He had neat, quick hands and an intensity that reflected his concentration on whatever task was before him at the time. Lambert had once asked him whether with such skills he wouldn't prefer to be a surgeon, and been told that pathology was the most satisfying surgery of all. You could carry your search for answers and the truth to the ultimate, in a way not possible when you had the tiresome issue of preserving human life as your priority.

The pathologist glanced up at the detective's patient, expectant face. 'He was killed at close quarters by a firearm. Shot twice, almost in the same place, so presumably in quick succession. No suicide note?'

'No. And no sign of whatever weapon killed him.'

'Then you must presume that this was murder or manslaughter. Anyone in mind yet?'

'No. His wife was away overnight.'

The medic smiled at the CID presumption that the next of kin must always be considered the first candidate for murder. 'We should find the bullet when we cut him up. Give you a chance to match it with the weapon.'

'Which is probably at the bottom of a river or under tons

of concrete by now.' Lambert grinned sourly. 'You know what I'm going to ask you next.'

The bearded one's grin was as acrid as the policeman's. 'Time of death. And I'm going to tell you that I'll have a better idea after I've cut him up and done my work in the lab.'

Both of them glanced automatically towards what had so lately been a living, breathing man and was now just meat and bone, waiting to be butchered and analysed. 'Give me some idea. You're not going to be held to it in a court of law.'

'I'd say he's been dead fifteen hours at least.'

'Last night, then. Some time during the evening rather than in the small hours of today.'

The thin face winced at such speculation. 'Try to find when he ate his last meal. If you can give me that, I'll give you a more accurate time of death when I analyse the stomach contents. We'll give the autopsy priority. No problem with a suspicious death.'

Lambert thanked him and walked into the hall of the house. The scene of crime team had collected various items, principally from the room where the body had fallen and the study upstairs where Preston had spent most of his time. 'We've got prints from the back door handle,' said the man in charge. 'Probably they're just from the occupants of the house, but we'll need to match up in due course.'

Lambert drove thoughtfully back into Oldford. He was already fairly certain that Preston had been killed at some time on the previous evening or in the early hours of the night. When he entered the CID section, he had his first piece of positive encouragement from DI Rushton. It had come from a man who was about to be charged with breaking and entering. It was the first useful by-product of petty crime that Rushton could recall. A black or dark-coloured car had driven into The Avenue and possibly to the house of the murder at a crucial late evening time.

It should have been exciting, but Ros Barker found herself unable to concentrate upon the work in hand.

She and Kate were deciding which pictures to select for the exhibition in Cheltenham. Ros had already settled on the major ones, which would be in the most eye-catching positions as people entered the gallery. Harry Barnard had been an invaluable guide to commercial considerations in that. But there were still another twenty smaller paintings to be selected for display. The choosing of them should have been a pleasurable task.

But Kate Merrick had done their shopping in Oldford and come back with the news that the high street there was buzzing with rumours. A major crime, apparently, with extra police being mustered to make up the team of investigators. A local sensation in prospect; such dramatic outrages were to be expected in Gloucester and Hereford and Cheltenham, and all kinds of things went on in the major city of Bristol to the south, but they were almost unheard of in sleepy Oldford. It was merely a historical convenience that a major police centre had been established in Oldford, a happy accident that the now nationally famous Detective Chief Superintendent John Lambert should be a local.

To have a gory crime on even the outskirts of the town would be a splendid bonus for most residents of this normally peaceful, even sleepy, rural area. And if the victim at the centre of all this excitement should turn out to be a local celebrity, that would be bliss indeed. There was a good chance of that, for the centre of the investigation was rumoured to be The Avenue.

Kate Merrick was a local, and a very human one. She brought a little of the excitement that was building in Oldford back to the studio with her. Ros Barker, as the older and senior of the partners, tried to pour the appropriate cold water upon such gossip. But she was thirty, not seventy, and the sight of an animated Kate, with her fair skin flushed and her kittenish features so animated beneath her dishevelled fair hair, brought feelings of pleasure rather than irritation to her.

And both of them knew very well who lived in The Avenue, though for some curious reason neither of them chose at this moment to mention it.

Ros listened to the news of the gossip as it poured from her excited partner, made her ritual protest, then settled for running her fingers down the back of the tremulous Kate, feeling the vertebrae and the active muscles around them as Kate said, 'A strangling, that boy in the butcher's said. Someone else came in and said they'd heard it was a whole family. I do hope there aren't any children mixed up in it.'

'Mmmm!'

'And you can stop that maternal stuff immediately.' But she didn't move.

'Mmmm! It isn't maternal.'

'But you can stop it nonetheless. Work first, play later.'

'Mmmm! Promise?'

Kate scrambled hastily away from her partner and on to her feet. 'Why does the young one always have to provide the work ethic round here?'

'I suppose because I've always responded to discipline. When it comes in your shape, it's positively irresistible. The more you accuse me of being an idle old trollop, the more I like it. I suppose I'm just a helpless decadent in my private life, the way all good artists are.'

'Good artists who are idle never became successful ones. And I want you to be successful, Ros. Don't ever have the illusion that I'm with you for your art. You need big money to keep me around and don't you forget it.'

She dodged a half-hearted attempt by Ros to recapture her kitten and they set about selecting which pictures should be among the privileged twenty to be displayed in the Barnard gallery at Cheltenham. Half an hour later it was Kate who said, 'I think this one should go in, Ros. It's different from the others.'

It was a nude of Kate lying on the sofa on which they sat every day, but with a light blue drape beneath her. There was a window frame beside her, with a cat, which was not at all kittenish, looking in with bared fangs. A representative of the dangerous world outside, which always threatens the innocence that blooms in privacy, the blurb for the exhibition would explain.

'You sure?' It was one of Ros's own favourites, but too personal for her to be able to say objectively whether or not it was one of her best. 'People will recognize you, you know.'

'You always said that wasn't a consideration, that art comes first and overrides such petit bourgeois considerations.'

'Did I?' But of course she knew she had; she could almost hear her own voice saying it, in her most sententious vein. 'Well, it seems different when it's personal. It's an invasion of intimacy. At least you should be consulted before being displayed in all your naked glory.'

'How very petit bourgeois! When I was looking forward to all my teachers and the poor sods who used to try to be my boyfriends seeing me tits and all!'

'Don't be coarse, young Kate! Well, we'll put it in if you really think we should. If you aren't just being big and grown up when you don't really feel it.'

'We're putting it in and that's that! Preferably in a spot where it will get maximum attention from your admiring public.'

'I'm not sure I've got a public, admiring or otherwise. And the prime spots have already been agreed with Harry Barnard. But I'm very happy to put it in. I suppose I had reservations partly because I like it myself. I always have reservations about putting what I think is the best of myself on display. It's probably a fear of people being critical of it.'

'Or even worse, of someone buying the painting. I remember you telling me about when you sold your first painting. You felt as though someone was carrying away a part of you and locking it away for ever.'

'You remember far too much, young Kate.'

'I remember that if you're going to make a living you have to sell everything you possibly can, until you're well established.'

'Now you're beginning to sound like Harry Barnard. I shall defer to your sordid money-grabbing instincts in all my selections. Anyway, I seem to remember the experts in these antiques programmes saying that nothing sells as well as an attractive nude lady.'

'Thank you for declaring me an antique. I wonder which pervert's pad I might end up in.'

They selected the rest of the exhibits without argument and with ease, including a couple of extra ones so that Harry Barnard could make the final choice. By four o'clock they were ready for a cup of tea and Ros switched the television on.

They were munching biscuits when the national news finished and the local news began. It did so with a picture of The Avenue and a reporter standing, microphone in hand and with a police car behind him, at the entrance to The Willows. 'In this house last night a man died and foul play is suspected. Police have not yet released the name of the dead man or further details, but the victim is believed to be the well-known radio and television director, Peter Preston.'

Ros Barker had always known it would be so. She looked at Kate Merrick and found her eyes filled with a wild surmise.

Edwina Preston was younger than her husband. Around ten years younger, the experienced eyes of the two senior CID men told them. There was no hint of grey in her light brown hair, but neither of them knew how much of that was due to the hairdresser who had styled it. She looked calm, but so did many people who were riven with grief. Her complexion was good and her only cosmetic seemed to be a rose-pink lipstick. There was no hint of the puffiness that came with weeping around her watchful blue eyes.

The Willows was still a crime scene, and in any case she could not face returning to the big house yet. It was Sue Charles who had convinced her that she needed to inform the police of her whereabouts and her immediate plans; they always spoke to the spouse of the victim as soon as they possibly could, the crime novelist told her confidently. She had rung the station at Oldford from Sue's house. The calm voice of the policewoman had confirmed that they needed to interview her and had then said that the CID officers would meet her wherever she chose. Eventually, to their surprise and perhaps to her own, she had decided that she would come in to the station at Oldford and do it there.

It was half past four on a bright May afternoon, with a gentle breeze and a few high white clouds moving softly across a blue sky that looked so clear that it might have been rinsed by the early morning rain. Lambert opened the window of his office wide, for the first time in the year, and had tea and biscuits brought in for his visitor. Someone must have divined his wish to treat the new widow sensitively, for on the tray there were china cups and saucers he had not known the station possessed. It was surprising what treasures lurked in the deepest recesses of the police canteen.

He asked Edwina to sit in the single easy chair the room possessed. She glanced at his preparations as she took her seat and said, 'Thank you. I don't know what I was expecting.

I suppose one of your tight little interview rooms and a grilling.'

A woman already aware of her surroundings and in control of her emotions. That didn't necessarily mean she wasn't feeling grief. Death, especially sudden death, hit the bereaved in all sorts of ways. A collapse into helpless weeping might be delayed, or it might not occur at all. The mind and the body found all sorts of ways of coping, and in the end most of them worked. It was part of the CID task to study all reactions with ruthless objectivity.

Lambert took in her inspection of the room and the preparations made for her, then watched her listening with her head a little on one side to the unexpected song of a blackbird from the tree below the open window. He said, 'I don't spend much time in here myself. I'm afraid I'm not a modern superintendent, supervising an investigation from my desk. I like to be out and about and meeting people.'

'I don't see why you should apologize for that. It sounds good to me.'

He smiled. 'I should begin by telling you how sorry we are about your loss, and assuring you of our very best efforts to bring to justice the person who killed Mr Preston.'

'Thank you. Perhaps I should respond with an assurance that I was not that person.' He must have looked disconcerted at such directness, because she was driven to add, 'That's why I'm here, isn't it? To clear myself of suspicion.'

Lambert smiled. 'It's part of the reason. You are also here to give us all the information you can about a man who has died. We know very little as yet about Mr Preston, about the way he thought and the way he lived and the sorts of enemies he might have had. Murder victims cannot speak for themselves, as the victims of other crimes usually can.'

She thought about that for a moment, then said with a rueful smile, 'It seems strange, Peter not being able to speak for himself. He always had plenty to say.' She looked up for a reaction, but Lambert was too professional to show how heartily he agreed with that. 'He had rather a lot of enemies, you know.'

She looked at them again. It was Hook who said, 'We didn't know. That's not going to make our job easier, but it's an example of the way we need the thoughts of those closest to him to build up the sort of picture my colleague referred to. If it's not too painful for you at this moment, could you tell us about your own relationship with Mr Preston?'

'We'd been married for twenty-four years. I suppose I knew Peter better than anyone.' She spoke as if the thought came as a surprise to her. 'He was a complex man. I'm sorry – that tells you nothing, does it.'

Hook smiled. 'It tells us how the person closest to him saw him. It would be useful if you could give us some examples of his complexity.'

'Yes.' She paused for so long that it seemed she might say nothing further. But these men were used to silences; they had taught themselves to be unembarrassed by them, to wait as long as it took for people to translate flying thoughts into words. 'He had a self-image which was very important to him. He'd produced programmes for the BBC and the odd one for ITV in the past. One or two important ones. Documentaries on poets and dramatists, things like that. Sometimes, especially with the later ones, they only used snippets of them amid someone else's filming or recording. He didn't like that, but he had to take it. He was quite well paid for his work, in those days.'

'Which would be when, Mrs Preston?'

'When?' She looked for a moment as if Hook had dragged her back from a private reverie. 'Oh, up to about ten years ago, I suppose. I couldn't be precise, but it was about then that the work began to dry up.'

'I see. We have a few press cuttings about him. He usually seems to be described as a freelance producer in the later ones.'

'That's what he took to calling himself, in the last few years. It meant that he wasn't getting the commissions he used to get and didn't have the influence he used to have. The world of the arts is just as cut-throat as any other world, DS Hook. When the people who make the decisions stop thinking of you for work, the work usually ceases. Peter didn't admit that that was what was happening to him, even to me. I think that he was aware of it, but his self-image wouldn't allow him to acknowledge it.'

They had a glimpse in that moment of a more tragic figure lurking beneath the garrulous exterior of the man who had so irritated them a couple of days ago. Hook said, 'Excuse me for probing into private matters at a time like this, but I'm afraid that in a situation such as this privacy is the first casualty. What were the financial effects of this reduction in work for you and Mr Preston?'

She looked shaken for a moment by the question; finance is a far more sensitive area to probe than sex, with most members of the British middle class. Then she said with a tiny shrug of the shoulders, 'Peter refused to confront things like that. We still lived in a big house, still pretended we could carry on as in the palmy days. That was part of his image, you see. But we were living off capital, not income. Peter had inherited money of his own and I got the money from my mother's house plus the rest of her savings when she died. It wouldn't have lasted for ever. We needed to move to a smaller house, but he wouldn't face that. It would have meant a loss of face.' For the first time, she allowed an edge of contempt into this last phrase. She had previously maintained an even, emotionless tone for her account of her husband and the glimpses into her married life.

Lambert let her words hang in the room for a moment before he said quietly, 'Where were you last night, Mrs Preston?'

'I was staying with my daughter. She lives in Oxford.' Her clipped tone showed that she had expected the question.

'You do this regularly?'

'Not in the sense that I go there at set intervals. But yes, I stay with Dell quite often.'

Hook made a note. 'Your daughter's name is Dell? Could you give me a home number for her, please?'

'Her real name is Cordelia. That was Peter, as you might imagine. She doesn't like it. She was Delia for a while, but that was associated with the woman who writes the cookery books, so she calls herself Dell now.' The tone of affection gave them a glimpse of the mother behind the composed, mid-forties face. She had obviously given this explanation many times before, but her eyes lit up for a moment when she repeated it here.

'And what time did you leave home yesterday?'

'About three o'clock yesterday afternoon, I think. The exact time wasn't important to me, at the time.'

Lambert was studying her as she spoke, his grey eyes steady, his head a little on one side. 'I'm sorry you had to find out about your husband's death as you did.'

'There was no way that could have been avoided. You weren't to know where I was.' She spoke evenly again now, as if she were re-living that moment when she had driven up to the gates of The Willows and found the police scene of crime tapes barring her entrance.

Lambert nodded. 'You said a few minutes ago that your husband had a lot of enemies. We obviously need to know about them.'

'Peter gave himself airs and graces, which is irritating. He patronised people, which is worse. People resent that.'

'Indeed they do. But it's a big step, probably several big steps, from resentment to killing a man.'

'Of course it is. And I can't immediately think of anyone who might have taken those steps. He wasn't good with young people – no, that isn't strong enough. He despised most new ideas and most young people. I'm sorry to have to say it, but he did. And they won't take it, these days. They don't just accept it meekly when older people are unfair to them. He knew that, but there were times when it only seemed to make him more determined to insult them.'

'Can you think of any particular young people?'

'It's a long way from feeling insulted to shooting a man, as you said.'

'It is, and we are well aware of that. Nevertheless, we need somewhere to start and at present you are the person who can offer us the most useful initial pointers.'

'I suppose so. But you should bear in mind that I kept away from Peter and what he was up to, particularly in these last few years.' She looked for a moment as if she would enlarge on this, but apparently thought better of it. 'I do know that he's been much occupied with the Oldford festival of literature and that he didn't care for the programme that has been set up.'

'Yes. My wife is on the committee and I gathered that.' Lambert judged that Preston was the sort of man who wouldn't approve of much that he hadn't initiated himself.

Almost as if she read his thoughts, Edwina Preston said,

'Peter hadn't much time for anything he hadn't suggested himself. He liked to be in charge of things. I'm sure he felt he should have been chairman of that committee, controlling the programme for the whole ten days. I would say that he regarded most things which came from younger people to be dumbing down.'

It was said not with real regret but with a sort of relish, as if she enjoyed telling these home truths about him now that he was no longer there to ridicule her thoughts. It was undoubtedly sad, but the men in the room with her were detectives; they considered it significant. This was the woman best placed to plot the removal of a difficult spouse; she was hardly troubling to hide her distaste for him. As she had just almost reminded them, it was a long way from distaste to murder, but marriage wasn't the best environment for fostering a sense of proportion.

Lambert said, 'You are confirming the impression we formed when we spoke to Mr Preston on Monday that he hadn't much time for the younger people on the festival committee.'

'You're right there. I'd almost forgotten that you'd spoken to him so recently. Did you find out who'd sent him that threatening letter?'

'No. And now we've been overtaken by a murder investigation.'

'But surely the two will be connected? Isn't the person who threatened him with death going to be the one most likely to have killed him?'

'Perhaps. And I can assure you that we are still investigating the origin of those letters. I should perhaps tell you that other people on the committee as well as Mr Preston have received identical messages.'

'I see. Then are others also at risk? Are we going to have a series of murders?'

Lambert couldn't be sure of it, but he thought he caught a certain relish in her tone as she made the suggestions. 'I do hope not. I should perhaps point out that such a train of events is far more common in Agatha Christie than in real life. We haven't ruled out the possibility, but we cannot be certain that the person who sent those letters is also the person who shot Mr Preston.'

'Peter would assume that it was one of the youngsters who was threatening him.'

'He did just that. He pointed us towards one of the younger members of the committee. We were still investigating the letters when we discovered his death. Have you any reason yourself to suspect anyone?'

'No. As I say, I kept out of his affairs as much as possible. We didn't talk as much as we used to. I'm afraid I found his ideas rather repetitive and he was aware of that. And he thought that I was such a philistine that I couldn't understand aesthetic matters.'

She sounded as if she had made him aware of her own thoughts in very direct language. But John Lambert sympathized. From his single contact with Peter Preston, he judged that he was the sort of tiresome bore who justified trenchant rejection. 'I must ask you if you have any thoughts yourself on who might have committed this crime. I'm not talking about evidence, just opinion. Your opinions will be treated in the strictest confidence.'

Edwina thought furiously. She would like to suggest someone, to get herself out of their thoughts. Not off the hook; she didn't consider herself their leading suspect. It would have been nice to steer them elsewhere, but she decided that she had nothing strong enough to do that. 'No. I can't conceive of anyone I've met as a being a murderer. I should think it was someone younger, but I couldn't go beyond that.'

They thanked her and asked if she could stay somewhere other than The Willows for a night or two. She considered the matter for a moment, then said. 'I think I shall go back to Dell's flat in Oxford, I'll be better there for the moment.'

They agreed with her on that and showed her out of the station. She rang Dell and arranged to stay immediately. Then she added as casually as she could, 'And just in case anyone should ask, could you say that I was with you last night, dear?'

THIRTEEN

The phone call took Sam Hilton by surprise. It was not at all the sort of voice he was used to hearing on his mobile.

'Sam? This is Marjorie Dooks. I need to speak to you.'

He was so surprised by the cut glass elocution that he missed the urgency in the tone. He said rather desperately, 'I'll see you at the meeting of the festival committee on Friday. I know I said I wanted to resign, but you convinced me that I should stay on.'

'I'm glad about that. We need your input.' Old phrases from her Civil Service days came back to Marjorie when she was nervous. She said hastily, 'I mean, we need to hear what you have to say, Sam. And not just about poetry, but about the other subjects we're including in the festival.'

'Well, I'll be there. We can talk then.' He could hear her breathing, but she did not speak. He made himself say, 'I'll stay behind after the meeting, if you like.'

'It's not really festival business. And it's rather urgent.' She took a deep breath. 'I need to speak to you today, Sam. I'll come to your place, if you like. Or you could come here. My husband's out at work all day, so we won't be disturbed.'

For a moment, he had a nightmare fantasy of the patrician Mrs Dooks luring him to her house and enticing him on to her couch of seduction. He dismissed it hastily. 'No. I'd rather see you here, if that's all right with you. If you don't mind the mess.'

There was a first hint of relaxation in the tense voice as she said, 'No, I don't mind the mess, Sam. I'll be there in half an hour.'

Sam looked round his bedsit desperately. It was like having a visit from your mother. No, it was much worse than that. It was like having a visit from Miss Dagnan. She had been the Senior Mistress in his secondary school, a formidable, large-bosomed dragon who had been responsible for discipline. Sam had made the same jokes about her as his fellows, but he had never lost his secret fear of her.

Surely Marjorie Dooks couldn't be as bad as old Daggers?

'I don't want you here when they come.'

'Why's that? I can give you moral support with the fuzz.' Kate Merrick tried to keep it light, but she felt hurt.

'To tell you the truth, I'm not quite sure why. Perhaps it's because I would be self-conscious. I think I'll find it easier if you're not there, watching my every move.' But Ros Barker found it difficult to look her partner in the face. She couldn't remember when that had last happened.

'You mean I might be like a protective wife, watching your every move?'

Ros did look at her now, hearing the hurt in her voice. 'Don't be silly. It's nothing like that. I just think I'll find it easier to concentrate on what I have to tell them without you or anyone else listening to me,'

'Is it because you don't want them to know that we live together?'

'Don't be silly! I thought both of us got over that a long time ago.'

'Homophobia in the police service. It makes sense, I suppose, especially as this John Lambert is an older bloke.'

'It's nothing to do with that. Honestly it isn't.' She went over and held Kate's shoulders, making her look into her face. She felt the tension in the slim frame, then the relaxation as Kate grinned at her earnestness. 'All right. But wouldn't you rather I was there to back you up with the fuzz? They'll know you didn't like Peter Preston.'

'They'll know because I'll tell them. I shan't make any secret of it. You and I both know that a lot of people didn't like Herr Preston and his assumptions of cultural superiority.'

'You're right there. I don't think you should call him that, though.'

'Now you sound like my mum! But it shows what I mean. I'll find it much easier to talk to them if I don't have you listening. I know you'd be supporting me, but I'd be more self-conscious and less able to concentrate with anyone there – even you.'

Kate nodded, her small, mobile features suddenly very serious. 'All right. I need to pop round to the primary school anyway; apparently there's a possibility of a part-time job in the office there. Go and put your face on for the fuzz and I'll make myself scarce.'

Ros went obediently into their bedroom and noted how neatly the bed was made and how Kate's usual clutter of make-up on the dressing table had been tidied. Ready for the policemen, who would never see it. In many respects, Kate Merrick was a more conventional young woman than she pretended to be, but when you felt tenderly about someone, you loved even their foibles.

She tidied her hair, put on a little lipstick, thought for a moment, then slipped out of her jeans and into the skirt she rarely wore nowadays. Kate wasn't the only one who could be a little conventional; for some reason she could not fathom, Ros thought she might be more convincing to the long arm of the law in a skirt.

She watched the police Mondeo turn into the drive, then skipped quickly down the two flights of stairs to open the big blue front door in the instant that they rang the bell. She thought they looked a little surprised at her promptness as she gave them her prepared smile. 'Do come upstairs. We have the top part of the house, but we don't have a separate entrance.'

She said this as she led them upstairs and into her studio. She had already decided not to speak to them in the rather cramped sitting room on the floor below. The space and light made the studio seem less confining – made it seem as if that would somehow make her answers to them more convincing. She said, 'I'm sorry the place is so untidy – we've been deciding which of my paintings should go to the exhibition of my work in Cheltenham.' She stifled a smile when she noticed that Kate had removed the nude of herself to a position behind the other works they had chosen. So much for her talk about bourgeois reservations.

Lambert and Hook looked round the studio unhurriedly and

with genuine interest. Neither of them could remember being in the workplace of a professional artist before. Then they threw Ros off balance by beginning not with the killing she had geared herself for but with the letter she had almost forgotten in the face of greater events.

Hook said almost accusingly, 'I understand you received a threatening letter two days ago. Don't you think you should have informed us about that?'

'I didn't take it very seriously, I'm afraid. I was still pondering what to do when Kate brought it in to you.'

'Didn't take it seriously? Why was that? Isn't it a serious thing to have your life threatened?'

'Of course it is, if you think it's a genuine threat. But it seemed like the kind of thing that only happens in books. I suppose it was beginning to dawn on me that even if there was an outside chance of it being serious I should report it. Then I heard that Kate Merrick had taken the matter out of my hands.'

'So your initial thought was that it was just a prank?'

How could a man who looked so easy-going be so persistent? She was rattled by his doggedness, particularly as it seemed to imply she was crass or insensitive. 'I was getting round to the idea that it was more than a prank when I heard that Kate had been to see you about it.'

'So initially you thought it might be no more than a joke in bad taste. Who did you think might be the comedian responsible?'

'One of the literature festival committee, I suppose. But I've no real idea.'

'Which one?'

'That would be pure speculation. This really isn't fair, you know.'

Hook's lips twisted a fraction at the edges. 'I know. Nevertheless, we'd be interested to hear who you favoured as the author of these threats.'

'I suppose I thought it might be the kind of stupid thing Peter Preston might do. But it's irrelevant now, because he's been killed himself, hasn't he?'

Lambert took over as smoothly as if the transfer had been

anticipated. 'Indeed he has, Miss Barker. But the threatening messages might not be entirely irrelevant. Did you know that Mr Preston had received a note identical to the one you received yourself?'

'No.' She looked suitably shocked. 'I think DS Hook told Kate that I wasn't the only recipient, but I didn't know that Preston had received one. And now he's dead?'

'Yes.'

He let the simple monosyllable hang in the wide-windowed studio. She breathed deeply and said, 'Do you think whoever sent him the note is the man who killed him?'

Lambert allowed himself a grim smile. 'We don't know yet that it was a man who sent those letters, nor a man who killed Mr Preston. But for what it's worth, I don't think that whoever sent those messages killed Preston. And I don't think you are in any danger because you received one. That doesn't mean that you shouldn't have reported it. We don't encourage foolish bravado in the public. Who do you think killed Mr Preston?'

The question came so abruptly on the end of his reassurance that she wondered if he had done it deliberately in the hope of catching her out. 'I've no idea. Have you?'

'Not yet. We shall know more after we've questioned those who were closest to him in his last few weeks of life – providing of course that they give us their full cooperation.'

'I wasn't close to Peter Preston. We should both have resented that idea.'

'You were physically close, in that you were a member of the literature festival committee. I met him only once myself, but from what I saw and from what I have already heard of his attitude to younger people, I believe you will have crossed swords with him over issues of local culture.' He glanced at the paintings of various sizes that had been assembled for her exhibition. 'And very probably over your own art.'

Ros forced herself to relax physically, remembering the yoga lessons from years ago, which she had almost forgotten. This man – probably both of these men – had played this game many times before, whereas this was her first experience of it. 'You're right. We had very different ideas. I felt it was almost a matter of principle with him to scorn my work, because I'm thirty and he was late fifties.'

'Art is a very personal thing, especially when your living depends on what you produce. It must be very wounding when people criticise it.'

'Criticism is assessment, Chief Superintendent Lambert. It involves praise as well as well as stricture.'

He nodded and gave her a tiny bow of acknowledgement. 'I stand corrected. But I expect Preston's criticism involved much more stricture than approbation.'

She smiled, and in a flash the lean face with the prominent nose became almost beautiful. 'You're right there. And right that it can be very wounding, particularly when you feel the critic does not understand what you are about. But one attempts to develop a thicker skin, over the years. Peter Preston said the things you would have expected of him, once you knew him and his habits. They irritated me a little, because they stemmed from ignorance and prejudice rather than objective analysis, but they didn't upset me.'

'But he clearly upset a lot of people.'

'I'm sure he did. But whilst lots of us might have felt like killing him for a moment or two, we didn't take any such drastic action.'

Lambert shrugged. 'Someone did. Whether it was one of your committee or someone else entirely is yet to be established. Do you know of anyone with a more serious reason than pique to attack Peter Preston?'

'No. I can't think it will be anyone I know who killed him.'

'Where were you on Tuesday night, please?'

'Is that when he was killed?'

'We think so, yes. We would like to eliminate you from the enquiry. It's the way the routine works.'

The routine. She had somehow known that that word would accompany this inevitable enquiry. Ros stared hard at the stained floorboards between them. There was a speck of white paint near Hook's foot, which she and Kate must both have missed when they cleaned up after yesterday's work with her brushes. She was meticulous about cleaning, since they used this room a lot for leisure in the summer months. That ridiculous white spot was occupying her mind, stopping her from thinking about what she must say and how she could best defend herself.

'On Tuesday night I was here. I was alone throughout the evening. Kate Merrick was visiting her mother and her younger brother; Jason is only fourteen.' She wondered why she was giving them these details, when she should have been thinking about how to preserve herself. She watched Hook making a note in his notebook, and felt the image of his child-like concentration would be imprinted on her mind for months.

'Did you take any phone calls during the evening?'

'No. I only have a mobile and it was switched off. I didn't want to be disturbed. I was only watching television, but there was a programme about the Pre-Raphaelites. I'm interested in them and the way they thought.'

She wondered if they would ask her to give details of the programme, to check on her story. But Lambert merely said. 'If you should think of anyone who could confirm this, it would be useful for us to have the name. If you think of anything, even the smallest detail, which you think may be relevant to this murder investigation, please ring this number immediately.'

And then they were gone, leaving her staring at the card he had given her and wondering how much of what she said they had believed.

Sam Hilton tidied his bedsit meticulously for the visit of Marjorie Dooks. He couldn't rid his mind of the image of old Daggers, the Senior Mistress who had so terrified him in his school days. She used to pounce on you if you had even the top button of your shirt undone.

And yet . . . and yet it had been the comprehensive that had developed his love for poetry, which had fanned the flame first kindled by Mrs Lambert in his last year at primary school. He'd never dared to confess that to his male peers at school, of course; they'd have taunted you as a pooftah if you'd even admitted to liking something as unmanly as poetry. Yet he could still remember studying Goldsmith's *Deserted Village* and its portrait of the schoolmaster:

> And still they gazed, and still the wonder grew,
> That one small head could carry all he knew.

He'd looked at the poem afterwards at home, as he was sure no one else in the class had done. He still quoted that couplet when he gave his talk about poetry and read his own work. They were a good example of the proper use of rhyme – how it could reinforce the sense and make the picture more rounded and satisfying – and most people in his audiences seemed to have heard the poem at some time.

Why was he thinking about that? He could hardly lecture Mrs Dooks about poetry, any more than he would have dared to discuss his ideas with old Daggers. He worked the ageing vacuum cleaner more vigorously back and forth over the threadbare carpet, stowed the dishes from the drainer away in the cupboard, even moved the photo-frame and the little pot dog on the window sill and dusted it. He didn't think he'd ever dusted before, but he remembered his mother always talking about needing to do them when she expected visitors.

Marjorie Dooks didn't seem to notice. She glanced round the bedsit as she accepted the easy chair he offered her, but she didn't seem to register how clean and tidy he had made the place to receive her. Perhaps like the queen she just expected these things and didn't see fit to comment upon them.

Then he realized that the formidable Mrs Dooks was nervous.

She said, 'I needed to talk to you in private, Sam. Not in the context of the festival committee.'

'No. You said that on the phone.' Curiously, he found that her unease was giving him confidence. He felt quite adult, where previously her presence had reduced him to a stumbling adolescent. 'I'm sure we can sort out whatever is concerning you.'

'Yes. Well, if you can, I'll be very pleased.'

He said, 'I'll put the kettle on. Tea or coffee?'

'What? Oh, thank you. Either will do. Tea, perhaps.' She

realized as he did that she was being uncharacteristically uncertain and diffident. She sat primly with her knees together and tried to become her normal self as she watched him flick a tea bag into each of two beakers and pour in the boiling water. She couldn't remember when she had last drunk tea with someone who did not use, perhaps did not even possess, a teapot. Sam squashed the bag against the side of the beaker with a spoon and removed it quickly, adding the dash of milk which was all she requested. He brought the beakers and sat down opposite her. She found to her surprise that the beaker was china and spotlessly clean, that the tea tasted surprisingly good.

She took a deep breath and said, 'I wanted to talk to you about these messages. Someone has been threatening people on the committee – telling them that if they don't resign they are likely to be killed.'

It sounded ridiculous when you voiced it in the cold morning light and in a setting like this. It sounded even more so when the young man who was less than half her age said calmly, 'Yes. I've heard about these letters. They sound quite extraordinary. Someone's sense of humour is very misplaced, don't you think?'

'Well, yes, I suppose I do. But perhaps I also think we should take them rather more seriously than that. The police certainly do. Have you had one yourself?'

'No. Is that what you came here to find out?' He was amazed that he should be asking her this, but the words came quite naturally to him.

'No. Well, er, I suppose it's part of the reason, if I'm honest.'

'Much better to be honest, I think. The police convinced me of that, when they talked to me about these letters.'

'The police have already interviewed you about them?'

'I suppose you could call it an interview, yes. I spoke to them about those letters, in this very room.' He looked happily and unhurriedly round the beautifully tidy bedsit. He was positively enjoying himself now. It was almost as if he had old Daggers at a conversational disadvantage. 'I suppose the CID wanted to satisfy themselves that I hadn't sent them. They sent two quite senior people.'

'And did you manage to convince them that those threats hadn't come from you?'

'Well, you'd have to ask them about that. They seemed to accept what I said, but they don't give much away, do they?'

Marjorie said stiffly, 'I expect they don't, no. I haven't much experience of the CID, Sam.'

'Haven't you? No, I suppose you wouldn't have. Well they didn't haul me in for further questioning and throw me into a cell. And no charges have been preferred, so far.'

Marjorie Dooks's lips twisted just a little at the corners. 'I rather think you're making fun of me, Sam. And I rather think I probably deserve it. I can only say that I came here with your best interests at heart.'

'I accept that. And perhaps you were also just a little curious to know whether I had sent those letters.'

'I suppose I was. But my first thought was to warn you that the police might want to speak to you about them, so that you could have time to think what you might want to say to them about the matter. I'm left feeling rather foolish, as I find that they've already done that and you've already satisfied them of your innocence.'

'I hope I have, but only they could tell you whether they believed me. So perhaps I should take this opportunity to assure you that I didn't send them.'

'I never thought you did, Sam.'

'Really? But aren't you now puzzled, when it seems that Christine Lambert and I are the only members of your committee who haven't received one of these written threats?'

She smiled properly now, knowing that he was enjoying her discomfiture but happily prepared to make the best of it. 'I confess that the letter scared me. It doesn't seem anything like as alarming, now that the police have followed it up. I've come round to your idea, that it's someone's misplaced sense of humour.'

'But not mine, I hope.'

'Not yours. Can we now dismiss the matter and talk about happier things?' Perhaps his face showed a certain reluctance to leave behind what he was now thoroughly enjoying, for she added a plaintive, 'Please?'

Sam Hilton grinned, the demons of old Daggers banished for ever with the plea of this pleasant woman from his best easy chair. 'Of course. Bob Crompton is definitely coming. He says he's looking forward to entertaining a different kind of audience from his normal Lancashire and Yorkshire ones.' There was a gleam of devilment in his eye and his tone. 'I presume the literature festival will go ahead, in spite of the death of Peter Preston?'

'Oh, I'm sure it will. We shall take the decision at the meeting, but I'm sure we shall decide to press ahead with the festival. Please don't quote me, but I'm sure Peter's absence will facilitate progress rather than hinder it. Aren't you?'

They grinned at each other like mischievous children. They were conspirators now, rather than mistress of the establishment and rebel child, as he had anticipated before she came. He said, 'It will certainly save time if we don't have to argue fiercely with Peter over anything that is even vaguely modern!'

They hadn't even discussed who might have killed Preston, and it wasn't until an hour after Marjorie Dooks had left that Sam began to ponder how deeply delighted she seemed to be to have Peter off the scene.

At Oldford police station, the post-mortem report had been faxed into CID. Lambert reviewed it in his office with DS Hook and DI Rushton, who was coordinating the collection of data on the case. It did little more than confirm what they already knew.

Preston had been killed approximately fifteen hours before the pathologist made his initial examination at the scene. Two bullets had been fired into the heart of the deceased and death had been instantaneous. The powder burns around the wound indicated that the weapon had been fired from very close quarters. Probably, indeed, it had been held against the chest as it was discharged, a likelihood that accounted for the two shots entering the torso at exactly the same point. The second shot and the absence of the fatal weapon at the scene ruled out any possibility of suicide.

The bullets that had dispatched Peter Eric Preston had been found in the corpse. They were .38 calibre and the likeliest weapon was a now defunct Webley revolver. It was not the most efficient or accurate of weapons, but obviously lethal when employed at such close quarters.

Stomach contents indicated that a meal of minced lamb and potatoes had been consumed by the deceased earlier in the evening. The digestive processes suggested that this had been approximately three hours before death. Obviously if they could ascertain when Preston had last eaten, they would have a pretty accurate time for his death.

The scene of crime and the forensic findings so far reported were more interesting for what was not present than for any vital clue. In Preston's study there were no prints save his, which bore out Mrs Preston's statement that no one save the deceased was normally allowed access to that room. Lambert said thoughtfully, 'Edwina Preston didn't know where the key to his filing cabinet was kept. We now have it; the SOCO team found it on top of the picture rail in the study, which suggests that he secreted it where only he was likely to find it. We'll let the forensic boys have first go, but I may want to examine the contents of that cabinet myself. I've a feeling they might tell us more about the secret thoughts of Peter Preston and his relationships with those around him.'

Prints taken from the external and internal doors of the house were those of the deceased, his wife, and the lady who came in to clean for two hours on Fridays. There were different prints on the side door to the garage and the shed in the garden, but they would no doubt prove to be those of the gardener who came in once a week. There was no sign of a break-in. An intruder would probably have worn gloves, but everything seemed to indicate that the killer had been admitted willingly to the house by the man who had subsequently been shot.

Almost certainly, the killer had been known to his victim.

Something much more revealing came from the computer expert who is now a vital part of any forensic team. Preston's PC had been easy meat to this man. He had discovered the password within twenty minutes and combed the files stored within the memory for anything which might suggest an acquaintance of Preston's who had a score to settle with him. It was routine, boring stuff and it ate up an expensive amount of the professional's time. It revealed nothing of real interest. The implication was that Preston was a novice with computers and their possibilities. This suggested that he preferred not to commit his private thoughts to what he thought of as a new and untrustworthy medium.

There was, however, one highly interesting fact which emerged from the expert's investigation of Preston's computer activities. To most people, computer printouts are identical. Whereas the sheets from typewriters were almost as individual as fingerprints in the hands of an expert, computer print-outs are much more uniform. But not to the modern IT forensic specialist; Rushton was able to relay a most interesting discovery.

The death threats that had excited very different reactions in Marjorie Dooks, Sue Charles and Ros Barker had all been produced on the PC and printer in the study of Peter Preston. He had presented the copy, which he maintained was a threat to his own life, purely in an attempt to divert suspicion from himself as the originator of the letters.

'So Ros Barker was right,' said Bert Hook thoughtfully. 'She thought those letters were the sort of stupid thing Peter Preston might perpetrate.'

FOURTEEN

Policemen make good gardeners. Like many other comfortable assumptions, that has rarely been subjected to the harsh test of statistics. But the idea persists, even though the advance of technology has made modern policing a vastly different task from what it was fifty years ago, when the tradition took root. Perhaps it is the awful things they are compelled to witness during their professional day that makes coppers enjoy something as basic, innocent and consoling as gardening. Perhaps cultivating the soil and following the eternal cycle of the seasons helps to keep things in proportion. It must be instinctive, for few policemen are aware of Voltaire's maxim that, whatever goes on elsewhere, '*Il faut cultiver notre jardin*'. John Lambert knew the quote and embraced it, but then Chief Superintendent Lambert was what is commonly known in police parlance as 'a clever bugger'.

He and Hook gave the garden around Sue Charles's bungalow their cautious approval. Wallflowers offered their scented splendour in the border that ran the length of the front of the building, divided only by the path along which the pair now moved to the front door. The roses at the edge of the well-trimmed lawns were full of swelling buds, reminding them that the glories of late spring and summer were at hand. A cat dozed in the sun beneath the porch. 'Good afternoon, Roland!' said Bert Hook affably. The cat gazed at them disapprovingly for several seconds. He was apparently unimpressed by Bert's recall of his name. Having completed his scrutiny, he disappeared round the side of his home with a quick lash of his tail.

Sue Charles opened the door and instantly recognized DS Hook. She seemed pleased to see him again as he introduced John Lambert. It was an unusual reception for her visitors, who were more used to being received with hostility or a nervous caution. She had tea and homemade cake ready for them, another plus factor in Bert's Hook's assessment. He complimented her on her garden as she poured the tea. Sue said, 'We're lucky here – good Gloucestershire soil, with few stones and only a little clay. I have an old friend who comes in to do some of the heavier jobs when I need him, but I still enjoy doing most of the propagating and planting myself. I did that even when George was alive. He wasn't as interested as I was, and he had a time-consuming job.'

Lambert said, 'Gardeners are like farmers, in my experience. Not many of them admit to having the ideal soil as you do, and the weather is never quite right.' He was watching her closely through the pleasantries. This alert, competent grey-haired woman of sixty-eight was a possible killer, until cleared of suspicion, however unlikely that seemed. Even if she was dismissed as a suspect, they still needed to know how reliable she was, both as a witness of events leading up to Preston's death and as a judge of character where other people were involved. Initial impressions were favourable. He could see her impressing judge and jury in court with her maturity, intelligence and precision.

As if she were reading his thoughts, she said, 'I'm sure you'll find who killed poor old Peter Preston pretty quickly.'

Lambert smiled and moved eagerly into the main purpose of their visit. 'You speak of him with some affection. We've been told that you had good reason to dislike him.'

'I suppose I had. But I had a soft spot for old Peter and his posturings. I felt sorry for him, in many ways. He was one of those people who've done good work in their youth but seem unable to move on. He was irritating at times, even insulting, but I couldn't take him seriously enough to be really offended.'

'Even when he denigrated your own work?'

She smiled at him, an unexpected hint of mischief in the blue eyes beneath the grey hair. 'You have an eye for human weakness, Mr Lambert. Few of us are completely objective about our own work. If you want to hurt someone who writes or paints or plays music, the thing to go for is their work.'

'Which we hear Preston did with your detective novels.'

'Do you, indeed? Well, I suppose Peter never made any secret of his prejudices. He enjoyed parading them in public.

I disliked him when he did that – but dislike isn't an emotion which translates into hatred and murder.'

'I agree. But I expect we shall find a lot of people who disliked Mr Preston and very few who moved on from that to a murderous hatred.'

'I shall be interested in the details of your investigation. I have what I suppose you could call a professional interest in this. I write about murder all the time, but I've never been even remotely connected with a serious crime before.'

'Most murders are either gangland killings or domestic incidents among the victim's family, as you probably know.'

'I do, yes. I study the statistics. But one of the rules of writing is to deal with what you know, and I've no experience of gangland criminals, drugs, or prostitution.' Sue was rather enjoying her exchanges with a real chief superintendent. This man didn't seem to have much in common with the tortured psyches of most fictional creations. 'Speaking of domestics, I do hope poor Edwina is coping with Peter's death. She was very shocked when she was here yesterday morning, but that was only to be expected.'

'Mrs Preston came here yesterday morning?'

'Yes. I found her looking quite distracted in the supermarket car park. That's how I heard about Peter's death. I brought her back here for coffee and sympathy.'

It was curious that Edwina Preston hadn't mentioned that when they'd talked to her later in the day. But no doubt she'd been confused by the speed of events after arriving home to hear of Peter's death. Lambert transferred his attention swiftly back to the crime novelist and decided that it was time to test this likeable woman's composure. 'Where were you yourself on Tuesday night, Mrs Charles?'

'I was here. Alone, as I am on most evenings.'

'Is there anyone who could confirm this for us?'

'I'm afraid there isn't.' She looked affectionately at her cat, who had just strolled into the room with tail erect, glaring resentfully at the two large men on the sofa. 'I can hardly invoke Roland to attest my alibi, can I?' She watched Hook making a note, glanced at Lambert's long, grave face, and said, 'I'm sorry, I know this is serious stuff for you. And I'd obviously like to absolve myself as a candidate for murder, but I can only report the truth. The fact is that I venture out very little in the evenings. People tend to invite their visitors in pairs, so my social life has become constricted in the ten years since my husband died.'

'We seem to be agreed that Preston was a man with many enemies. It's almost material for one of your whodunits, Mrs Charles.'

'Indeed. Except that I never put real people into my books. The other difference is that this situation is not imaginary but deadly serious. I still find it difficult to believe that Peter is dead, and even more so to imagine that someone took a pistol to his house and shot him. I believe that is what happened.'

'It is indeed. And you summarize our major problem. We have to find someone who didn't just dislike the man but who hated or feared him enough to kill him. Who do you think that someone might be, Mrs Charles?'

She tried not to be shocked by the suddenness of the question. It was a query she had expected, after all, so she shouldn't be put out by the manner of its arrival. 'I've given it some thought, as you no doubt would expect me to, but I haven't solved that conundrum. Everyone on the literature festival committee found Peter irritating, because he so patently wanted to be in charge of things and wasn't. I'm sure all of us rejoiced when his pretensions were exposed and he was put in his place, usually by Marjorie Dooks from the chair. But I can't think that any of us could have killed the man, annoying as he was.'

'Everyone we've seen so far has said something similar. But as yet we haven't found any recent contacts with people who might have been enemies of his in the past.'

'I'm sure he made some very serious enemies when he was producing for the BBC and ITV. Rich and powerful people, some of them – people with the money and the contacts to employ a hitman to do their work for them.'

She tried to make the suggestion without a smile. She had used the term occasionally in her books, but she was not sure she had ever produced the word in conversation before. Lambert didn't smile. He said, 'It's a possibility we have to explore. We are checking on the activities of known professional killers. So far we have not been able to establish the presence of any of them in our area on Tuesday evening. What car do you drive, Mrs Charles?'

Again the question was thrown in suddenly, almost brutally, on the back of a completely different train of thought. It was as if they were trying to catch her out. Sue found it was quite exciting, really, being involved in a real murder enquiry. 'It's a Fiesta. Two years old.'

'Colour?'

'Dark blue.' She watched Hook recording this in his notebook and then reeled off the registration number with a mischievous ease. Her husband had never known the numbers of his cars; she had made a point of learning hers, as a small assertion of female competence.

Lambert stood and said, 'I accept that your experience of crime is largely or wholly fictional, Mrs Charles. But please do not let that inhibit you from making suggestions. If you think of even the smallest detail which you think might have a bearing on this death, please ring this number.'

Sue Charles looked at the card and nodded. Then she looked up into the long, grave face and smiled. 'I think you should call me Sue, Chief Superintendent. Particularly as I understand from Marjorie Dooks that I am to share the pleasure of your company on a platform at the literary festival in ten days time.'

Hook contained his merriment until they were safely out of the presence of Sue Charles. He gazed solemnly at the road ahead of him as he said, 'You've accepted the role of real-life crime authority at the festival, then.'

'Not accepted. It was somehow conferred upon me. I don't quite understand how it happened,' said Lambert sourly.

Poetry worked well with girls. It gave you an exotic appeal; it offered something outside the normal range of a young man's attractions. It was, let's face it, a powerful aid in getting girls into bed.

Sam Hilton was quite prepared to face it. He was in bed with a girl by nine o'clock in the evening. The last of the daylight still showed beyond the threadbare curtains he had drawn before leaping eagerly between the sheets. He lay comfortably in that post-coital tristesse, which was still quite novel to him, and considered serious issues. The most disturbing and powerful things were the feelings stirring within his breast. Poetry was all very well as a means to an end, but what did you do if the unforeseen happened?

Sam thought he was getting serious about Amy Proctor. But he had no idea how serious she was about him.

They had been at school together, but they had been just mates in the sixth form then, members of a group that went around together. Since then, Amy had spent three years at Cambridge and he had spent three years acquiring experience in the university of life. Time seemed to have altered things; everything between them was more personal and serious now, rather than part of that glorious fun of their last year at school, when everything had been a laugh and the whole world had been there to amuse them and their peers. Sam gazed up at the high ceiling of his bedsit and reflected on the mysteries of love and life. Beside him, Amy Proctor stretched her delightful limbs and yawned luxuriously. She stroked Sam's thigh to show that her yawn was a symptom not of boredom but of delicious content. She said, 'Have you any readings lined up?'

For once, Sam Hilton did not want to talk about poetry and its important position in the scheme of life. But you couldn't let yourself down when you feared that the only reason this delectable girl was lying beside you was because of your verse. He said, 'One in Hereford at the end of the month. One in Oxford early in June. And of course, there's the literature festival in Oldford coming up.'

'Yes. You're on the organising committee for that, aren't you?'

The assignment he had tried hard to be rid off suddenly seemed important. Men of twenty-two lack gravitas, so that anything which seems to offer it must be seized. 'Yes. They seemed to think I had something to offer, that my views on poetry and literature in general might be worth having. Just as part of a larger whole, of course.' It was difficult to balance gravitas with modesty, but you had to try. In his so far limited experience, girls didn't like blokes who took themselves too seriously.

'Will you be reading your own poetry?'

'Not at the festival, no. I'll be chairing one of the sessions. My friend Bob Crompton is coming down from Lancashire. I expect we'll have a bit of fun stirring up the Oldford middle classes.'

'I mustn't miss that.' Amy put her arms above her head and stretched again, touching the impressionable young man beside her from shoulder to calf, twitching her hip in a movement he was not sure was reflex or invitation.

'Would you like a cup of tea?' He wasn't quite sure why he had said that. It came from some vague, unformulated compulsion to detach himself, to look at his relationship with Amy Proctor from beyond the limits of her highly desirable flesh.

She shifted her position and looked at him, her very blue eyes no more than six inches from his. 'Tea was the last thing I had in mind, Sam Hilton. What happened to the view that

"In the spring a young man's fancy
Lightly turns to thoughts of love"?'

Sam smiled back into the pretty, amused face. How red and moist her lips were, how wonderful her mouth was, when it rose at the corners like that. He said, 'Old Browning knew a thing or two, didn't he?'

She giggled outright now, a movement which made her body tremble against his at all the important points and caused him to forget about tea. Then she said, 'It's Tennyson, actually. *Locksley Hall*, I think.'

'Just testing.' Then they both dissolved into brief, helpless laughter and moved seamlessly into a renewal of their passion, which was intense enough to drive out all thoughts save gratification.

They had been lying sated and soundless for perhaps ten minutes and he was thinking that she might have fallen into a doze when she said, 'Did you know this Peter Preston who's been killed?'

Sam was suddenly wide awake, though he tried to keep his body motionless to disguise it. 'Yes. He was on the festival committee with me. Annoying man, but I didn't think anyone would want to bump him off.' That curious, dated phrase seemed somehow to detach him from this death.

'Suspicious death, the police say. That means he was murdered, doesn't it?'

'Yes, I think so.' He was silent for a long time before he nerved himself to say, 'You couldn't say you were here with me on Tuesday night, could you?'

He regretted it as soon as he'd said it. The silence that followed his request seemed to him to stretch for a long time. It was broken unexpectedly by the shrilling of his mobile phone on the bedside cabinet beside him. He picked it up and gave his name. A cool, impersonal voice said that Chief Superintendent Lambert, who was conducting the investigation into the death of Peter Preston, would like to speak to him in the morning at Oldford police station.

'It's good of you to see us as late in the day as this.'

Marjorie Dooks looked at the clock. It was just after eight o'clock. 'As a former public servant myself, I should say that it's noble of you to be working as late as this.'

Lambert gave her a thin smile, hoping it masked the fatigue he would once never have felt. 'Murder overrides most of the rules. We try to push our enquiries forward as quickly as possible.'

'Before the scents get cold? Before the people who were nearest to the victim have time to cover their tracks?'

This time it was DS Hook whose weather-beaten face creased into an understanding smile. 'We find it best to gather as much of the routine information as quickly as we can. People's memories are usually at their sharpest and most reliable when they are still close to the crime. Once we have assembled that information, we are in a better position to proceed. It is easier then to spot those areas which warrant further investigation.'

Marjorie nodded thoughtfully. 'Assuming, of course, that everyone is telling you the truth.'

Lambert quickly forgot his tiredness as he studied the demeanour of this composed woman. They were in her sitting room, which exuded a quiet opulence. Nothing here was assertive, but nothing jarred with its surroundings. The green leather of the three-piece suite was echoed in the paler green of the walls, which were almost white but with the faint hint of colour which the seats and carpet demanded. The original painting of the view from the Worcester Beacon in the Malverns was by a respected local artist. The prints of the Alps and the Grampians were in matching expensive frames on the other walls. The Bang & Olufsen hi-fi and the flat-screen television in the corner were as muted as these modern necessities to the civilized life could ever be. They had already refused drinks from the discreet walnut cabinet in the opposite corner of the room.

He said, 'Assuming that people are telling us the truth, as you say Mrs Dooks. Most people do, and when someone does not, it often becomes clear who that person is when we put everyone's impressions together. That is another reason for seeing everyone who was close to the deceased as quickly as possible.'

'I wouldn't say I was close to Peter Preston, Mr Lambert. But that may well be why I was not one of your immediate priorities.'

So she'd been checking on whom they'd seen so far. Mere curiosity, or the self-interest of someone involved in this crime? Perhaps just the natural inclination of a woman who had got used to being in control during her professional life in the Civil Service and had since then carried that control into a more local setting. He said, 'We usually see the widow first in cases like this, for the obvious reason that she should be the person who knew the victim best. She is also usually able to help us compile a list of other people we should see.'

'So it was Edwina Preston who suggested you should quiz me about Peter.'

'Your position as chair of the literature festival committee ensured that we would want to hear what you had to say about Mr Preston. In connection with which, I'm happy to be able to tell you that the matter of these threatening letters has now been resolved. There is no reason for you to have any fears on that score.'

'I'm glad to hear it. I hope you didn't think I was over-reacting when I contacted your wife about the one I received. I had no means of knowing at that time that I wasn't the only recipient.'

He had the impression that she was enjoying this civilized, controlled verbal fencing. The thought irritated him, coming at the end of a day that had already been too long. 'You didn't over-react. It would have been better, indeed, if you had gone directly to the police at Oldford.'

'Perhaps. My training induced me to try informal contacts before setting hares running. Have you arrested the culprit?'

'I can't see any reason why you should not know this: the culprit was Mr Preston himself. It was presumably some sort of tasteless joke on his part.'

'Or a more malicious attempt to scare people like Sue Charles out of their wits.'

'Possibly. It seems that now we shall never know. And we have to concern ourselves with the infinitely more serious matter of murder.'

'Yes. One hears of people who make friends easily – I've even met one or two of them. Peter Preston was a man who made enemies easily. He seemed at times to go out of his way to do just that.'

Lambert smiled. 'That is the impression DS Hook and I formed in our single twenty-minute meeting with him. Perhaps you could now give us some names from your more prolonged contact.'

'I didn't see him socially. Peter regarded most people round here as his cultural inferiors.' For an instant, there was a hint of real resentment. Then she recovered herself and went on, 'My experience of him was almost entirely confined to our exchanges within the literary committee. He did speak to me on the phone fairly frequently, but exclusively on matters that had been raised there. Frankly, he resented the fact that I was in the chair. He'd like to have been directing matters himself, preferably without a committee at all.'

'Who do you think killed him?'

If he expected her to be shocked by his directness, he was disappointed. She sat back in her chair and took her time. 'I've thought about that a lot in the last twenty-four hours. No one that I know, is my conclusion. I can't think that anyone on that committee would have done it. He'd been unpardonably rude to most of us, over the last few months, in different ways. I suspect Peter hadn't read Sam Hilton's poems, but he despised him on principle because he was twenty-two and "lacked discipline" in his verse, as Peter put it. Strangely enough, he insulted Ros Barker's art because it wasn't avant-garde and abstract enough for him – I suspect he simply wouldn't entertain her as a serious artist because she was only thirty and had her own ideas. Sue Charles is older than he was and could hardly have been more friendly or cooperative; but he derided her because she was a crime writer rather than what he considered a serious novelist. I doubt whether he'd read her books. I suspect he was just jealous of her because she was a success. He seemed to get more annoyed when she refused to take offence at his barbs. But you can hardly consider Sue as a candidate for murderer. Which leaves me, I suppose. I'd probably crossed swords with Peter more often than anyone.'

She stopped, breathless after this summary of her thoughts, rather surprised that they'd listened so carefully and hadn't interrupted her. Lambert said quietly, 'But I don't suppose you killed him, Mrs Dooks?'

She wondered if he was trying to provoke her by the question, but she didn't hurry her reply. 'There were times when I would cheerfully have dispensed with Peter's services and opinions for ever. But I never thought of killing him. I hope you will believe that I have far more sense than to consider such an idea.'

Lambert's long, lined face had the trace of a smile as he said, 'Where were you on Tuesday night, Mrs Dooks?'

'I was here throughout the evening with my husband. Dull, but helpful, I suppose.' She watched Bert Hook making a note in his swift, round hand and looked slightly smug.

'What car do you drive?'

'A blue Honda Civic.' She waited for Hook to record it,

then reeled off the number as if it were further proof of her innocence.

Lambert rose and said, 'Any further thoughts you have on this crime will be treated in the strictest confidence. Please contact us on this number if you think of anything, however trivial. Sometimes small details can be very significant when we put them together with data being collected from other people.'

She nodded as she led them across the big room. She turned to Lambert in the doorway. 'Good luck with your enquiries. If I don't see you before then, I'll look forward to hearing your views on crime writing at the literary festival.'

A second reminder. Hook kept his face studiously straight until he had turned the police Mondeo and driven out of the Dooks' drive. Then he said, 'Perhaps I'd better come along to that session at the festival. It sounds more interesting each time I hear it mentioned.'

FIFTEEN

DI Rushton was eager to see the chief. He checked that Lambert was to interview Sam Hilton at nine thirty on Friday morning. He was waiting for the chief superintendent when he came into the CID section. 'There's stuff from forensics.'

'What sort of stuff?'

'Stuff from the filing cabinet in Preston's study. He was an old-fashioned man. He stored things away in files in a cabinet, rather than use his computer.'

Lambert grinned. 'Such people do exist, Chris. What did Preston record in such an outdated way? Anything more than gossip?'

'Much more than gossip, from the little I've seen so far. Things about people you've already seen. I can summarize it and put it on the computer, but that will take time. It's more than we expected. I think you might want to look at it yourself.'

Lambert tried not to be too optimistic. He failed. This might be the thing that answered the question everyone, including himself, had been asking: how could dislike and irritation transform itself into the sort of hate that led to murder? He said as evenly as he could, 'I'll look at it as soon as we've finished with young Mr Hilton.'

Sam Hilton looked rather bleary-eyed as he gazed around interview room number one in Oldford police station. The delights of Amy Proctor had been numerous and prolonged, but they hadn't left a lot of time for sleep. He was also beginning to think he was in love, which was causing confusion in his mind when it most needed to be clear.

The small, square, windowless room did not offer him much relief. The walls were painted in a bilious green, frequently renewed to conceal the coarse graffiti of the army of the unfortunate who had waited here to be grilled. There was a single white light in the ceiling above him; Sam gazed up at its harshness for a few seconds and then wished that he hadn't. He could feel the blood hammering in his head. And the police hadn't even put in an appearance yet.

He was left on his own in the room for precisely ten minutes after DI Rushton had shut the door upon him. Ten minutes to muse upon the unfairness of life, and himself at the centre of that unfairness. It seemed much longer. He tried hard to think about the poem about his grandfather he was working on. *Die Happy*, it was called – a sort of reaction to Dylan Thomas's 'Do not go gentle into that good night'. He wanted to say that when Alzheimer's was taking over, there was no real life left, so that you should welcome death whilst you could still remember the real person who had lived. But this was not the place to make a poem.

Bert Hook studied him coolly for a moment when he arrived before he said, 'I'm Detective Sergeant Hook and this is Detective Chief Superintendent Lambert. You'll remember us from two days ago.'

The big cheese again. Bloody John Lambert, the man the press had endowed with an almost mythical capacity for solving violent crimes. He and Sam eyed each other cautiously, wonderingly. It didn't seem to Sam as if this was going to be an equal contest. He felt as if he were about twelve; as if this grave, unsmiling elder could see everything he had done wrong in the whole of his young life.

Before the thought had properly formulated itself in his mind, he was saying desperately to Hook, 'I've given up dealing. I've taken notice of what you and that inspector told me about the drugs.'

'Good for you, lad. We'll be watching you in the coming months, to make sure you keep to that. That's unless you're banged up for murder, of course.'

'That won't happen. Unless you lot frame me for it.' Sam tried a flash of defiance – and found that it didn't work. His words sounded ridiculous in his own ears, as if he were spouting clichés in a television scene, rather than being up to his neck in the real thing.

Lambert had been studying the young man as dispassionately as if he were a specimen in a laboratory. He now said with quiet menace, 'You didn't like Peter Preston, did you, Mr Hilton?'

'He didn't like me.'

Lambert nodded slowly, as if that were entirely understandable. 'Not what I asked you, is it? Would you answer my question, please?'

Sam wondered whether the man was biased against his youth or whether he was like this with everyone. 'All right, I didn't like Preston. In fact, I found him insufferable.' Take that, you bastard! You might have caught me dealing drugs, but I can do the big words. 'But that isn't significant. Lots of people found Preston insufferable.'

Lambert nodded even more slowly. 'Interesting choice of word, that. If you found him insufferable, you had to do something about it. Perhaps you couldn't go on suffering his insults any longer.'

'No. Well, yes, in a way, I suppose. But I didn't kill him.'

'Where were you on Tuesday night, Mr Hilton?'

He hated that iteration of his name and title. It made all this sound as if it was merely a preliminary to charging him. 'I was at home in my flat. In the bedsit where you saw me on Wednesday morning.'

'Yes. You were rather disturbed then. Was that because you'd shot Mr Preston on the previous night?'

'No! Of course it wasn't!' He tried to make the idea sound ridiculous, but all he could hear in his voice was fear. 'I was at home on Tuesday night. I didn't go out at all. I rang Bob Crompton and had a talk with him about his visit to the literary festival at Oldford.' He and Bob had enjoyed a few laughs, said some pretty insulting things about the old fogies who were likely to attend the Manchester poet's readings in Oldford. For no reason he could think of, it seemed to Sam Hilton that the game would be up if he revealed any of this to the men in front of him.

It was DS Hook who now looked up from his notebook and said, 'What time was this phone call made, Sam?'

His first name, at last. Even a measure of sympathy in the tone from this man – or had he imagined that? He wanted to say he had spoken to Bob later in the evening, but they could trace the time on mobiles, couldn't they? 'About half past seven, I think.'

Hook shook his head sadly. 'Too early to help you, I'm afraid. Is there anyone who can confirm to us that you were at home throughout the evening?'

Sam's mind was racing as fast as the pulse in his temple. 'My girlfriend was with me.'

Hook studied him for a moment before he said, 'Name?'

'Amy Proctor.' Sam watched Hook record that in his notebook. Time seemed to be suspended in that claustrophobic room; the squat hand clutching the ball-pen seemed to move with impossible deliberation. Next Hook wrote down Amy's address with equal care. Sam said he couldn't remember her phone number. He couldn't think what had made him volunteer the name; panic, he supposed. Amy hadn't agreed to his request to say she had been with him on Tuesday. Passion had prevented that and he'd not asked her a second time. But she hadn't refused, had she? He wasn't even sure that she'd agree to being described as his girlfriend.

As if from a long way away, he heard Hook saying, 'Was she with you overnight, Sam?'

'No. She left at about midnight, I suppose. Maybe just before.' He wondered why he hadn't claimed she'd been with him all night, as she had last night. Perhaps because it made the lie seem a little less complete. He'd have to get back to Amy, to check that she was prepared to support him. He'd do it for her.

But then he was sure now that he was in love with her.

Just when it seemed that this more sympathetic man was going to handle things, it was Lambert who now took up the questioning again. 'Do I take it that you're denying any connection with the killing of Peter Preston?'

'Yes. Denying it emphatically.' But again the adverb emerged as ridiculous, when he had meant it to sound indignant.

'I see. Then who did kill him, Mr Hilton?'

'I don't know, do I?'

'Don't you? You may well know things related to this death that we don't. It is our duty to discover these things. It is your duty to reveal to us anything which might have the smallest connection with this killing. This is murder, Mr Hilton. Not shoplifting, not breaking and entering, not even dealing in drugs. This is the most serious crime of all. Concealing the smallest detail which might have a bearing on this death could make you an accessory to murder. I advise you very strongly to conceal nothing from us.'

Sam licked his lips. 'Ros Barker didn't like him any more than I did. Perhaps he was more of a threat to her art than he was to mine, but you should ask her about that. Marjorie Dooks didn't like him, because he wanted her job and was very rude about the way she was doing it. Even Sue Charles couldn't have had much time for him, because he liked to pretend that her writing was trivial rubbish. I can't see any of us killing him, though.'

The now familiar dilemma, which they shared themselves, but couldn't admit, especially to this talented, dangerous young man. Lambert said evenly, 'Then who did kill him?'

'Someone from outside the festival committee. Perhaps it was someone from his family, or from his past.'

'Perhaps. What car do you drive, Mr Hilton?'

'A black Ford Focus. It used to be my uncle's car. It's fourteen years old now, but it runs well enough. It's taxed and insured and MOT'd.'

Hook noted the details and the registration number, with a small smile at these unnecessary additions. He thought the nervousness was a good sign; he didn't really want this raw, gifted young man to receive a life sentence, though he wouldn't voice that unprofessional thought to Lambert. He said, 'We've charged you with the serious crime of dealing in illegal drugs, Sam. That doesn't mean you will be treated with any more suspicion than anyone else who is involved in this murder investigation. But you should heed the Chief Superintendent Lambert's advice. If you think of anything at all which might be relevant in the next few days, you must demonstrate your innocence by bringing it to us immediately.'

Sam Hilton emerged blinking into the sunlight outside the station and breathed deeply of the warm spring air. He felt as though he had received a physical battering. But with a young man's resilience, he decided within half an hour that it had gone reasonably well. They didn't seem to be aware of the serious motive he'd had to be rid of Preston.

Long let it remain so.

The contents of Peter Preston's filing cabinet were interesting indeed. They were voluminous and detailed. They were the collections of a natural gossip. But this was a gossip with a malevolent streak, material assembled by a man who had sought to turn the weaknesses of humanity to maximum account for himself.

Peter Preston might have been old-fashioned in his storage methods for information, but within his own terms he had been methodical. There was an almost priggish rectitude in his organization of the material he had gathered. Each dark green file carried the name of an individual. The thickest files were the oldest ones, presumably devoted to the people who had been acquaintances of his, or more probably rivals, in his more active and successful days. Most of the names Lambert did not know, though he recognized one or two BBC and ITV luminaries from a previous generation. He flicked open a couple of these files; much of the material was bitchy gossip picked up from others, but occasionally there was the date of some action that Preston had obviously thought might be of use to him. The last entries in all of these were several years old.

Lambert turned with quickening interest to the more recent compilations, which included files on every member of the Oldford Literary festival committee. He couldn't resist turning first to the one on his wife, headed grandiloquently, 'Christine Evelyn Lambert.' Disappointingly, it was confined to a single sheet in Preston's small, neat hand. It included, 'Husband is Detective Chief Inspector John Lambert, who has been lionized by the media as a modern Sherlock Holmes. No doubt much less bright than he thinks he is. Difficult to get beyond the police mafia to discover the skeletons in his cupboard. Might contact Alexander Bryden to see what dirt he can offer on this Lambert fellow.'

Bryden was a Cheltenham-based con man who had taken a succession of rich widows and divorcées for the bulk of their savings. He had eventually been trapped and sent down by

Lambert, who was intrigued to know what connection he had enjoyed with Peter Preston. Perhaps the dead man had not known that Bryden was currently in prison, though the case had been well covered in the press at the time.

The only entry on Christine herself was, 'Likely to support the Dooks woman in the chair, unless I can find some means of putting pressure upon her. But she seems a moderately intelligent woman, who could be convinced in time of the excellence I have to offer.' Lambert decided from the other material in the cabinet that 'moderately intelligent' was in Preston's terms a high compliment. He thought it might be difficult to convince Christine of that.

He had seen enough to realize that the material in these files needed to be thoroughly checked. He told Chris Rushton that and gave instructions that he was not to be disturbed for the next few hours. Then he carried the files on the literature festival committee away to his office and shut the door firmly.

Amy Proctor was finding hormones a troublesome thing. Her own seemed to be raging out of control and now there was a young man standing on the doorstep who looked as if he was having trouble with his.

She said, 'I suppose you'd better come in.'

It was hardly the most welcoming of greetings for a man who had lately decided that he was in love. Sam Hilton said as much.

She gave him a smile which sent the aforementioned hormones into vigorous action. 'Sorry. I was preoccupied with other things. I've got application forms for jobs, which I have to complete today.'

'This shouldn't take long. It can't, really – I've to be at Morrisons in two hours myself to take up my gainful employment. Stacking shelves leaves my brain free to work on other things.' He didn't choose to confess to many people that he couldn't exist on his poetry earnings alone. That he should do so to this bright, animated, enchanting creature was really a declaration of trust and love, but he didn't suppose she recognized it as that.

Amy said with a touch of affectionate mockery, 'I like the

idea of the poetic muse being at work amidst the machinery of life in the supermarket. Collecting trolleys from the car park and contemplating the eternal verities of life at the same time.'

'The muses don't seem to pay much attention to me. If I wait for inspiration, I produce nothing. I have to batter my brain into activity and bully my mind into looking beyond the bread and the eggs and the baked beans.' Writing, whether in prose or in verse, was a serious activity to Sam; he was prepared to outline the mechanics of it to anyone who offered him the opportunity.

'Student stand-by, the tin of baked beans. I expect I shall have to move on to more adult sustenance, once I get a full-time job. Do you want a cup of coffee?'

'Yes, if you've time.' He should have been in and out in a couple of minutes, as he'd promised, but he couldn't resist spending time with this delectable girl with the glossy black hair and the lissom, mobile figure. He followed her into the kitchen and watched the rear of her jeans dreamily as she boiled the kettle and spooned instant coffee into two beakers. He was filled with a spiritual attraction that went far beyond the coarsely physical; but you couldn't simply ignore the flesh, if love was to be complete.

She sat him down opposite her at the round white melamine-topped kitchen table and glanced at the wall-clock behind him. 'What can I do for you, my wondrous wordsmith, before you depart to worship the glory of honest physical toil?'

That's what he was, a wordsmith, Sam Hilton thought. It was an honourable term, not a derogatory one. Especially when this fascinating faun prefaced it with 'wondrous'. But he was suddenly bereft of the words needed to introduce a delicate and urgent subject. He stirred sugar into his coffee, watching the whirling surface of it as if he were noticing it for the first time. 'It's about this death. Peter Preston's death.'

'This aficionado of the arts, who was fostering the flame of creativity in the young poet. About his murder, you mean.'

'Yes.' Sam wished she hadn't immediately switched to that brutal, inescapable word. And he wished she would vary the affectionate, half-mocking tone which she was adopting towards him and his poetry. 'He was murdered. That's why the police are talking to everyone who was in touch with him at the time of his death.'

'Including my poet-lover.'

'Yes. And Preston wasn't fostering the flame of creativity. He was as rude as he could be about my poetry and my membership of the literature festival committee. So the pigs have me down as an enemy of his.'

'Not surprisingly. And as a man with a criminal record, you must be centre-frame.'

He wondered now whether he was right to have told her about his arrest for drug-dealing. It was the kind of honesty that came upon you between the sheets, when the body was deliciously exhausted with love-making and the mind was easily swayed. You surely shouldn't have any secrets from your loved one, that mind had said. Now the same mind was telling him that perhaps it hadn't been such a splendid idea. 'I'm hoping I'm not their prime suspect. But it would help if I could prove that I wasn't around at the time Preston was killed.'

Her bantering tone fell away and she was suddenly serious. 'What is it you want, Sam?'

What had seemed a simple request was abruptly very difficult. He was silent for a moment and then said quickly, 'I asked you last night, actually. I want you to say that you were with me on Tuesday night.'

There was a pause before Amy said quietly, 'Where were you, Sam?'

'I was in my flat. All night. But I need a witness.' He made himself look up from the coffee beaker and into those large, dark, wonderful eyes. 'The police had me in this morning and grilled me about it. I told them you were there with me until midnight.'

There was a long pause, which was agony to him. He wanted to break it, but he sensed there was nothing he could say to improve things. Eventually Amy Proctor said slowly. 'I'll say I was with you, Sam. But don't ever do anything like this again without asking me first.'

SIXTEEN

Within two days of her husband's death, Edwina Preston was back in the big house with the mock-Tudor frontage where Peter had died. Her daughter had made her welcome enough in the small flat in Oxford. But Dell had been grieving for her father, whereas her mother had found it difficult to conceal her elation.

Edwina walked slowly round every room of The Willows when she returned on Thursday afternoon, as if it were a new residence waiting to be explored. She lingered for a moment in the room at the front of the house where Peter had fallen, but there was nothing now to remind her of the death. The drawing room seemed to her quite impersonal, despite that elegant but uncomfortable chaise longue, which Peter had insisted upon keeping. Even the room upstairs which he had used as his study looked quite anonymous now. The police had removed both his computer and the filing cabinet about which he had been so protective, and with them had departed the things which had once made this room distinctively his.

Life without Peter was going to be very different, she thought with satisfaction.

She was not as nervous during the night as she had feared. She remembered how she had welcomed Peter's overnight absences, even in his younger and more successful days. She couldn't understand now why she had endured her loveless marriage for so long. She should have ended it years ago.

In the morning, Denis the gardener arrived. He offered his condolences, which she accepted with a solemn face. Then she doubled his weekly hours. They discussed their aims for the summer, which was now at hand. Outside the kitchen, these were the first domestic decisions she had taken for herself in years. To Denis's surprise and satisfaction, the mistress of the house controlled her grief and worked with him in the garden for the last hour of the morning. When he had gone, Edwina ate a solitary lunch in great content.

She was to have a CID visit during the afternoon. The police had rung Dell's number in Oxford, found that her mother had returned home, and arranged to call at four o'clock. She was pleased about that. Once she had cleared the final hurdle of their visit, she could get on with the rest of her life. She decided that she would make some scones for her professional visitors. And she would entertain them in the conservatory – that's the sort of thing Sue Charles would do, and you surely couldn't have a better role model for this situation. She must assume a suitably sombre face for them, as she had for Denis. She wasn't going to pretend to any great grief at her husband's passing, but a sober attitude was suitable for a new widow. At quarter to four, she donned the expensive dark blue woollen dress which was the nearest garb she had to formal mourning wear.

She was surprised how difficult it was to maintain a solemn mien when her visitors arrived. She felt that she was playing a part, particularly when the older man, Lambert, seemed to study her with unceasing intensity. She was glad she had made the scones, for the serving of tea gave her plenty to do with her hands; she was sure she would have been self-conscious about her movements without it. DS Hook carried the big tray with the scones and the plates into the conservatory, whilst she went before him with the silver teapot and the cups and saucers. She poured the tea carefully and handed round the scones, noting with pleasure how steady her hands were. Chief Superintendent Lambert seemed anxious to begin, but she made him wait through the ceremony of the tea and the scones.

Hook had barely time to compliment their hostess on the excellence of her baking before his chief said, 'We now have a fuller picture of your husband and the people around him at his death. We are following up certain discrepancies in what people have told us over the last couple of days.'

'That's good. I'm impressed by how quick and thorough you've been. I trust the things your colleagues removed from Peter's study proved interesting?'

'They did, yes. We are still digesting and reacting to that

information. But no doubt you will be more interested in accounting for the deficiencies in your own statements.'

Edwina kept her clasped hands scrupulously steady. It was gratifying to hear how steady her voice was as she said, 'I can't think what they would be. But I'm glad to have the opportunity to clear up any misunderstanding immediately.'

'This is a matter of fact rather than a misunderstanding, Mrs Preston. You told us you stayed with your daughter Cordelia on Tuesday night. She was not able to confirm that.'

Bloody Dell! Sue told herself she should have known her daughter hadn't the nerve for this. Perhaps she hadn't had the will either, the wretched girl. Dell had never been able to understand the full extent of her father's cruelty to her mother.

As if he read these thoughts in her face, DS Hook said suddenly, 'She tried to support you. She said at first that you'd been with her, but the officer taking her statement sensed that she was lying, I'm afraid.'

Before she could react to this apparent sympathy from his junior, Lambert said, 'So where were you when you claimed to be in Oxford, Mrs Preston?'

It was all going to come out. Edwina told herself that she had been prepared for this, that she had half-expected that this would happen, sooner or later. She took a sip of tea before she said in a low voice, 'I was with a man.'

'We shall need details. The man's identity, and exactly where you were on Tuesday night.'

'Of course you will. I can see that. But it's important to me that you understand why I asked Dell to say I was with her. I wanted to keep Hugh out of this. And I also wanted to preserve my own privacy.' Then she added with a touch of self-contempt, 'I suppose I also wanted to avoid my own embarrassment.'

'Privacy is always a casualty in murder investigations. We cannot even consider issues as trivial as embarrassment. The raw facts are that your husband was murdered on Tuesday night and you chose to lie about where you were at the time.'

She said dully, 'The man's name is Hugh Whitfield. We were at a hotel in Broadway, near Stratford-on-Avon. He is married but separated. I would appreciate it if his connection with this could be kept confidential.'

'We shall need to check this out with Mr Whitfield and the hotel. We shall not reveal it unless it becomes part of a case in court, but there can be no guarantees of confidentiality. You will probably appreciate that you forfeited our goodwill when you chose to lie to the officer in charge of a murder investigation.'

'Yes. I suppose I can see that now. My first instinct was to protect Hugh. I didn't want him involved in this business.'

'Which he now is.'

'Yes. I can see things more clearly now.'

'What was your husband's attitude to this liaison?'

'Peter didn't know about it. He was far too occupied with his own concerns to give any thought to me and what I might be doing.'

'What did he think you were doing when you were away from home overnight?'

'I told him I was visiting Dell – that's my daughter – or old friends. There weren't so many occasions. More often than not, Hugh and I met during the day.'

'What would you say if we told you that your husband was aware of this relationship? If we told you that he had recorded the dates of your overnight meetings and some of the venues involved?'

Edwina felt the shock running through her limbs like an electric charge. She told herself that she must deal with this, must offer them some sort of response. Her voice seemed to come from a long way away. 'I didn't know about that. It doesn't surprise me. Peter was a very secretive man. He was very sensitive about that filing cabinet.'

'He had Mr Whitfield's name and address recorded. He seems to have been compiling some sort of dossier.'

'That's what he liked to do. He needed to feel he had control of people. I didn't think he'd do it with his wife. I didn't know he knew about Hugh. I should have known better. Finding people's weaknesses was an obsession with him.'

'Blackmail?' It seemed an unlikely crime for one of Peter Preston's background and pretensions.

'No. He wasn't interested in money.' She said it not with admiration but contempt. 'All he was interested in was having a hold over people. Power, if you like, but a particular sort of power. He didn't always use his information, but he liked to feel it was there if he needed it.' She repeated like one in a trance, 'I didn't think he'd do it to me.'

'What car do you drive, Mrs Preston?'

'A Fiat C3.'

'Colour?'

'Dark green. You think I did this, don't you?' She glanced automatically back from the conservatory towards the house behind them and the place where Peter had fallen.

Lambert did not attempt to reassure her. He stated the bald, inescapable facts. 'We have to consider the possibility. You lied to us about your whereabouts at the time of your husband's death. You were conducting an affair, which he was documenting for his own purposes. You had ample reason to want him out of your life.'

'But I didn't know he was spying on me until you told me just now.'

Hook looked up from his notes. 'We only have your word for that, Mrs Preston. As far as money and property are concerned, I presume you are the main beneficiary of your husband's death?'

'Yes. Unless he revised his will, as well as spying on me.'

'He wasn't expecting to die. He's unlikely to have done that.'

'No. Are you going to say that I killed him to avoid it?'

Lambert put his crockery back on the low table between them and stood up. 'We shan't accuse you of anything, Mrs Preston, until we have more evidence. What do you know of the contents of your husband's filing cabinet?'

'Nothing. I told you, he was a very secretive man.' This time the adjective hissed with contempt.

'Please don't leave the area without giving us your new address. We'll need to speak to you again.'

They drove back to the station in Oldford without exchanging many words. Each was preoccupied with the paradox of this quiet, unremarkable-looking woman in her mid-forties, who had conducted an affair and might well have dispatched an unlovable and increasingly inconvenient husband.

Marjorie Dooks found that she was having to work hard. She was used to dealing with people, to taking account of their backgrounds and reading their feelings. Usually she was very good at achieving whatever she wanted.

It was more difficult with a husband. The domestic setting was very different from a committee one, for a start. And both of you carried the baggage of many years together. You could hardly know too much about anyone, she had decided a long time ago. But there were times when they could definitely know too much about you.

She wanted James to introduce the topic of this murder, which must surely be in his mind as it seemed to be in everyone else's in Gloucestershire. She talked about plans for the festival and the way the programme was now complete and looking very promising. He complimented her politely on that, as a stranger might have done. But he did not take up the issue of how the sudden death of the most prominent member of that committee was going to affect the programme. Was he uninterested in her affairs, as was usual, or was he deliberately refusing to talk about the topic that dominated her thinking?

In the end, she had to introduce it herself, which she felt put her at a disadvantage. 'The police were here yesterday, about Peter Preston's death.'

'You didn't tell me.' He made it sound like an accusation.

'No. You were late home last night and I didn't want to bother you with it. It was no big deal – just part of their routine, in cases like this.'

'Have they got a prime suspect yet?'

'I don't know. I don't suppose they'd tell me, even if they had.'

She wanted him to ask about what they'd said to her, to be at least a little anxious on her behalf, however bizarre the idea that she might be treated as a suspect. But he merely nodded deeply and went back to the *Telegraph*. She had to say, 'They asked me if I knew anything about who might have killed him, which of course I didn't.'

'Of course not.'

'They wrote down the details of where I was at the time he died. Just routine, they said.'

'Yes. It would be.' James turned over the page and began to read about the prospects for the weekend's rugby internationals.

'Tuesday night it was. I told them I was here with you.'

Now at last he looked up at her, his eyebrows raised elaborately in that movement she found so irritating. 'Was that wise, old girl?'

She hated it when he called her that. She'd told him so; she wondered whether he was now using it as some kind of taunt. 'I thought it was, at the time. I was anxious to complete their routine for them, to let them remove me from their thinking so that they could get on with arresting the real killer.'

'Not like you, that. Lying to the police, I mean – well, not telling them the complete truth, anyway. I've always thought of you as a classic conformist. You've been quite short with me when I've tried to cut the odd corner, as is necessary in business.'

She was sure now that he was enjoying himself. His puzzled, slightly pained tone told her that. 'Anyway, you'll need to confirm it, if they ask you.'

'Need to confirm it.' He pursed his lips, as if weighing it as a proposition. 'I see, old girl. You're trying to cut a few corners. Whatever you say, then.' James Dooks returned to the sports pages with a small, enigmatic smile.

Saturday the fourteenth of May. A bright morning, with the sun high in the sky by nine o'clock and a gentle breeze moving the few high white clouds very slowly across a very clear blue sky.

Lambert picked Hook up in his big old Vauxhall. The lanes were quiet and they enjoyed the journey through the burgeoning Gloucestershire countryside. The hawthorn hedges were full of new pale green leaves and the rich red soil was disappearing beneath neat rows of spreading corn and barley. The large eyes of Herefordshire cattle gazed curiously at them as the car breasted the slope beside their pasture. Then the Vauxhall ran into the valley and into the deep shade between long, straight rows of newly foliaged beeches, arching over them like the nave of a great natural cathedral. Bert thought of the boys he had left at home, dearly loved but full of energy and increasingly fractious, as they moved towards adolescence. There were compensations for having to work at weekends.

They were surprised to see Sue Charles in gardening trousers and gloves when they arrived at her bungalow. She stood up and put her trowel down on the barrow beside her, which was full of discarded wallflowers after their short and glorious blaze of colour and scent. Lambert said, 'I'm sorry. Were you not expecting us?'

'Yes, of course I was. But I was up early and it was such a lovely morning that I thought I'd do a little weeding before you came. But I don't wear my watch in the garden and I lose track of the time. Come in and I'll put the kettle on. It will only be instant, I'm afraid, but it won't take long. That's what the name implies, I suppose.'

Lambert said that there was really no need, that it wasn't long since they'd breakfasted, but Sue insisted. They sat for a couple of minutes on the sofa in the sitting room, trying to regard Roland with as much disdain as the cat accorded them. Hook apologized for disturbing the crime novelist's weekend and her gardening, but she said, 'Don't be ridiculous, I'm glad to see you. I have a few old friends, but I don't get many visitors, nowadays.'

Every action and reaction made it seem more ridiculous that this friendly, competent woman should be involved in a murder enquiry. They were served with coffee and home-made biscuits before Lambert could say, 'We know a lot more about Mr Preston than when we spoke to you on Thursday. He seemed to us then a rather petty man with annoying pretensions. He has now proved to be much more vicious that that.'

Sue sat down carefully with her own cup of coffee. 'I'm sorry to hear that. He was no friend of mine, but one doesn't like to hear such things about the dead. One would rather they could be left in peace, but I quite understand that in the case of a murder victim you need to unearth every fact you can.'

'You write about murder, Mrs Charles. You must study

people, as I'm told all writers do. Did Mr Preston strike you as a man who would excite the hate that seems to have motivated this killing?'

'Goodness me, Mr Lambert! I'm an amateur in these things. One has perforce to acquire a little knowledge about police procedures, and I suppose you're right about studying people, but you must have far more experience of murderers than I have!'

'Nevertheless, we should like to have your views, since you had much more contact with this victim than most people we have spoken to.'

'I suppose that's true, though I hadn't thought about it before. To put it crudely, Peter had been discourteous to me for a number of years. I think I told you yesterday that he took care to let me know how little he thought of my writing. He was also dismissive of crime writers in general. "Practitioners of trivial ephemera," he called us. I rather enjoyed asking him if that wasn't a tautology.' She chuckled at the reminiscence and took a large and unladylike bite of ginger biscuit. 'I'm sorry. I realize this is a very serious business. Did I see Peter as a candidate for murder victim? I never really thought of him as that. I couldn't take him very seriously, but I suppose if I had done I'd have seen him as malicious, perhaps even dangerous. I certainly shouldn't have liked to live with him! Poor Edwina had to do that, of course. She must have seen something attractive in Peter, at one time. I suppose he was handsome, as a younger man.'

She spoke as if she was considering that idea for the first time. Lambert said quietly, 'How close was Preston to his wife at the time of his death?'

Sue furrowed her brow as she gave due consideration to that. 'I didn't mix with them socially as a couple, but I've met Edwina in other settings. I'd say they were growing steadily further apart, that she had devised methods of coping with his tiresome pretensions. I think she'd developed a life of her own which did not involve Peter.'

There was a shrewd writer's brain behind the ageing, wordy woman whom he sensed she was enjoying playing. Lambert acknowledged that by asking simply, 'You saw Preston many times with Marjorie Dooks. Would you tell us about that, please?'

'I only saw them in committee, though just occasionally he tried to pursue his ideas more informally after the meetings were over. I confess I rather enjoyed their confrontations – probably because Marjorie had the measure of Peter. She was fair but firm, in a way which I could never have been. Of course, she held most of the cards, in that she was chair of the committee, but she was as tactful as it was possible to be.'

'Thank you. What about the younger members of that committee?'

'Ros Barker and Sam Hilton? I've thought about them as candidates for homicide, of course, since this happened – that's inevitable, I suppose, when you're involved in a real murder and have a background of writing about it. Peter was very insulting and dismissive about Ros's paintings and Sam's poetry, and when your work is attacked you're more deeply hurt than you like to admit. And in so far as one can generalize, young people seem to react more violently to insults than my generation. George, my husband, used to say that if young men still had National Service to endure, they'd have a better sense of discipline, but I've never been sure about that.'

'Peter Preston's sense of grievance went much deeper than most people realized, Mrs Charles. Were you aware of that yourself?'

'No.' She paused for a moment, her face filling with the interest of a new idea, then nodded. 'It doesn't surprise me, though. What evidence do you have for saying that?'

'The contents of the filing cabinet in his study. He kept detailed files on everyone he regarded as an enemy.'

'How very interesting. Peter never struck me as a blackmailer.'

'We have no evidence that he ever tried to extract money from anyone. His wife thinks that he used what he gathered to manipulate people rather than to exert financial pressure.'

'How intriguing!' The head with its neat grey hair was a little on one side; the clear blue eyes alight with mischief. 'Did he have a file on me, Mr Lambert?'

Lambert was as serious as she was amused. 'He did indeed.'

'And are you able to tell me about it?'

He paused to glance at Hook. He was struck as strongly as he had ever been in his life by the incongruity of people like Sue Charles being involved in the grim business of murder. 'There were several rather trivial and petty entries about yourself. There were also some rather more serious allegations about your husband.'

Her face clouded as quickly as it had grown amused. 'About George? What sort of allegations?'

'About his business dealings. About some of the people he had employed and some of the things he had done during his working life. About the methods he had used to achieve his success. Bribery was mentioned, or "bungs", to use Preston's word.'

The lines around her mouth were suddenly deeper as it set into a determined line. 'I wish I'd known about this. Peter Preston would have had me to contend with. It doesn't happen often, but I can be very direct, when I am upset.'

Lambert was as grave as she was. 'Are you saying that you had no knowledge of this material Preston had gathered?'

Her detached, slightly amused air had gone completely. 'I am. If I had known anything about this, I should certainly have confronted Mr Proud Peter Preston.'

Sue Charles still looked shaken as she showed them out. They had little doubt that this elderly, gracious woman would make a formidable opponent if anyone gave her reason.

Sue came slowly back into the room and stared unseeingly for many minutes at the empty coffee cups on the low table. The cat, which was her sole domestic companion, eventually sprang from his chair, came across the room and rubbed himself against his mistress's calves, breaking the spell of her meditation.

Sue smiled as she bent to fondle his ears. 'You didn't like those nice men, did you, Roland? Well, you can relax now. I don't think they'll be coming here again.'

SEVENTEEN

Like many doting fathers, Walter Merrick still chose to think of his daughter as a vulnerable child. He ruffled her short fair hair as she came into his house and kissed him, just as he had done her much longer blonde locks when she had been four years old.

He was seventy now; he had been ten years older than his wife and forty-eight years old when Kate was born. She sometimes wondered whether living alone had made him more conservative. He seemed to her older than his years, not so much in body as in mind. Her mother and he had always argued; their angry raised voices had been the recurrent chorus of her childhood. Kate hadn't really been surprised when her mother had gone off to live in Durham with a younger man six years ago; Dad and Mum had been chalk and cheese. With all the accumulated wisdom of her twenty-two years, Kate had pronounced it a good thing. Now she was not quite so sure. Dad seemed to be ageing more rapidly than he should be.

He gave her coffee in a cup and saucer, then vigorously stirred his own in the beaker he had used for as long as she could remember. They talked a little about her infancy and the small, precocious things she had done. Kate smiled and answered a little absently, but he was too occupied with his delighted reminiscences to notice that. She was wondering how she could broach the subject she had come here to introduce. She couldn't leave him in the dark for ever, whatever his reaction. That would be behaving as if she was somehow ashamed of herself.

She talked at some length about the exhibition in Cheltenham, about how good it was for Ros Barker, and how it proved that she was a serious artist, who was going to make a good living out of her painting.

Walter said, 'She's a talented girl, your friend. I've heard that from other people as well as you. I don't understand much about art myself. I like a good Constable or Turner, but I don't pretend to know much. I'll go to that exhibition, though. Be good if you were able to come with me and guide me around it.'

'Of course I will. I'll be in there a lot of the time. I said I'd be in the gallery as much as I could.'

She hoped he'd take that up, or at least raise an eyebrow, but he merely smiled at his coffee. She was compelled to say as lightly as she could, 'You might be a little shocked by some of the paintings, Dad. Well, by one of them in particular. One of them with me in it.'

He looked up eagerly. 'Ros has done a painting of you? That's a nice thing, isn't it? Quite a compliment, I'd have thought.'

'Several of them have me in. One might shock you, though, Dad.'

'Take a bit to do that, girl.'

'It's a nude, Dad.' She looked out of the window at the familiar small, neat garden, watching him out of the corner of her eye.

He didn't say anything for several seconds. 'I'm glad you told me, Kate. I need to be prepared. I suppose I haven't seen you like that since you were about eight.'

'It's not highly realistic – it's part of a larger painting. You might not even recognize me, but I thought I should tell you.'

'Yes. Yes, I'm glad you did. You said you'd acted as a model for your friend, but I didn't really think that she might want to paint you in the altogether. I suppose I should have done.'

'No reason why you should. But no reason why I shouldn't do it, is there?'

'No reason at all. You need to spread your wings, as you told me when you moved out of here.' He looked out of the window and she sensed that he was going to change the subject and talk about his vegetables. Sure enough, before she could think of what to say, he said, 'You must take some of those carrots with you when you go. They're young and tender. And I'll get you a cauliflower and a lettuce. There's far too much for me – I give most of the stuff away.'

He was moving the talk steadily away from her, as if he understood her purpose and was out to frustrate it. She said desperately, 'The thing is, Dad, Ros and I live together.'

'I know that. Very sensible to share; you don't earn enough to rent a place of your own.'

'I mean we really live together. We're partners. Like man and wife, if you like. We love each other, Dad.'

He gazed at her very seriously for what seemed to her a very long time. Then his face cracked into the broad, familiar smile she remembered so well. 'I wondered when you'd get round to telling me.'

The mouth beneath the pert little nose he loved dropped open. Then she gulped and said, 'You knew about it? About Ros and me?'

'Of course I did. I was born in the twentieth century, not the nineteenth, you twerp. I saw the way you were with boyfriends and I wondered then. But you had to make your own way, find these things out for yourself.'

'And you're all right with it?'

He stood up and held out his arms to her. She flung herself delightedly against his chest and he kissed her, then held her as tightly as he ever had in his life. He looked fondly down at the familiar head with its short blonde hair, then away down his garden to the rows of vegetables at the end. 'Not many people find happiness in love, girl. You grab it and hold on to it. I was never much for grandchildren, anyway. It's women who want them.'

She was weeping softly with her joy. He held her more gently for a few seconds, then sat her down again and resumed his own seat. Eventually she leaned across and punched his knee. 'You old fraud! You knew all the time! And I've been so worried about telling you.'

'We people with bus passes know a lot more about life than you give us credit for. Experience, we generally call it.'

They took a chance on Sam Hilton being at home. It was possible that he wouldn't be there at eleven thirty on a Saturday morning, but Lambert wanted to surprise him.

Sam wasn't bleary-eyed or half dressed, as they had half-expected he would be. He had been working on the poem prompted by his grandfather's decline into Alzheimer's, trying to force his ideas into some sort of framework.

> 'Die happy, old man. Go content into
> The welcoming darkness. The slow limbs

Struggle. The brain is fractured, faltering
Towards death. Remember him as laughing,
Young limbs flying fast in games . . .'

There was something here, something he thought was worth developing. He'd bring in the lasses from the old man's youth – he always called them that, rather than girls. Perhaps he could work in a reference to the curls he'd had as a young man, because that might be both touching and a little humorous. He might close with a reference to Dylan Thomas's dying of the light. This poem needed a lot of work yet, but he felt it might repay the effort. He'd been very fond of his granddad and it would be nice to salute him, to pin his memory down for others in print.

The sharp rapping at his door made him almost leap in the air with shock; he had been concentrating hard.

Sam looked carefully around the familiar room, as if that would restore him to the real world, then opened the door. The surprise they saw in his eyes turning quickly to fear. He made his ritual, unthinking gesture towards resistance as he led them into the bedsit. 'It's only yesterday that you dragged me into the station for a grilling. This is police harassment.'

It wasn't worthy of a reply and Lambert didn't give it one. He looked unhurriedly round the very tidy room and at the small table with the single sheet where Sam had been wrestling with the elegy for his granddad. 'New information has come to light since yesterday, Mr Hilton. You are not yet under caution, but I would advise you to think very carefully about what you say to us this morning. You would be most unwise to lie or to attempt to conceal information.'

Sam wanted to scream at them, to deny what they were implying and challenge them to prove it. But it was too vague to challenge. And when it came to it he didn't fancy demanding a specific accusation from a chief superintendent who clearly meant business. Instead and to his dismay, his voice became a whine, which sounded even in his own too-intelligent ears like that of the habitual cornered offender. 'It's once a criminal always a criminal, for you lot, isn't it? Pinch a bloke for a bit of dealing and you think you can pin a bloody murder on him next! Typical bloody pigs!'

'Mr Preston kept a filing cabinet in his study. What do you know about the contents?'

'I've never been in Preston's bloody study.'

'That's not an answer to my question, Mr Hilton.'

Very few people had addressed Sam as 'Mr' so far in his young life. He was again finding Lambert's repetition of the formal title disconcerting. Was it a prelude to the formal charges this grave elder of the CID had already hinted at? He said sullenly, 'I knew the bastard kept notes on people. What does it matter where he kept them?'

'It matters to us, now, because that cabinet has preserved a record not only of his thoughts about other people but of things in their past they wouldn't wish us to be aware of.'

Sam needed to know how much they knew, but he could hardly ask them that. He said obliquely, 'I'm not surprised he put everything down in writing. I can see him poring over things and hugging himself, the prissy bastard!'

The last phrase rasped with hate. Lambert recalled Sue Charles's thought that writers and artists were most wounded when you attacked their work, however bravely they tried to shrug such things off. He nodded to Hook, who said immediately, 'Preston emerges from what we've read in his files as a most unpleasant man, Sam. There are several people as well as you with ample reason to dislike him. However, he is now a murder victim. I think we shall discover within the next day or two who killed him.'

Sam hadn't thought it was going to be as rapid as this. He wondered how much they knew and found himself fighting against a rising panic. 'Preston deserved to die. But I don't know who killed him.'

Hook carried on as if he hadn't heard the pointless words. 'He had a file on you, Sam. You'd be surprised how much he'd managed to gather on you.'

'Like you lot! Like the bloody police.'

'Oh, much worse than the police, Sam. We're only allowed to retain what's been proved, even when you've got a record. Peter Preston had no scruples and no rules.'

'So what he wrote about me might all have been lies.'

'He did write things down, Sam, yes. Very malicious things.

His writing gives us an insight into the man himself which we wouldn't have had otherwise. He didn't think much of you.'

'I know that. He called one of my poems an undisciplined rant. He said I should get myself a job and forget about writing poetry. He said what wasn't doggerel was second-hand ideas from a second-rate mind.' He reeled off phrases which had obviously hit him hard, however much he had pretended otherwise.

'You'd be surprised how much he knew about you. We don't know who he used to help him discover things, but he gleefully recorded whatever he learned.'

'Knew things? What sort of things?' Sam felt the question drawn from him, even though he then knew immediately that he shouldn't have asked it.

'He knew all about your dealing, for a start. Well before it was drawn to our attention. He's got times and places where you dealt coke and horse. Shortly after you became a regular user, he reckoned.'

'You can't use this. Even you bloody pigs can't call a dead man into court.'

Hook smiled into the defiant young face. 'We could offer the evidence, if we chose to. Or we could use the dates and names he has noted as starting points for further investigations of our own. The Drug Squad may well find some of the names useful, though I fancy they're already well aware of them. We have not the slightest interest in that today; today we're going to arrest someone for murder, Sam.'

'Not me you're bloody not.'

'Remains to be seen, that does, Sam. You've not done yourself many favours, so far. We'll come to that in a minute.' Hook watched fear replace defiance in the young features. 'Preston's been quite useful to us, in your case. We didn't know about your use of firearms in the past, until we found it documented with date and victim in his notes.'

'It wasn't a firearm. It was only a bloody air pistol.' His fury meant that the denial flashed out before he realized that he should not have spoken.

'An air pistol waved six inches from the face of an enemy by a sixteen-year-old. Might not have killed him, but might well have cost him an eye. Not very reliable, sixteen-year-olds, when driven beyond endurance.'

Hook's last phrase was an invitation, and Hilton accepted it eagerly. 'I was being bullied by four of them. I had to stop it.'

Hook frowned and nodded thoughtfully. 'Possibly. Maybe that's why the boy's father agreed not to involve the police. You showed a tendency to react violently, though, which has to interest us. You showed panic when driven into a corner; the same sort of panic which might have overcome the person who shot Peter Preston.'

'I didn't kill him. I was at home when he died.'

He didn't see any sign pass between the experienced pair, but it was Lambert who said ominously. 'So you say. You've admitted he was your enemy and a very serious one. That's the other thing we need to talk to you about: your whereabouts at the time of his death.'

'I was at home. Nothing more to be said.'

'Lots more to be said, Mr Hilton. Perhaps lots more to be said in court, in due course.'

'You'll never make Preston's stuff stand up in court.'

'Maybe not. But we probably won't even try. When we can prove that you told lies about the night of the crime, other evidence will be of minor importance.'

'I don't know what you're talking about.' But the energy he had been trying to maintain had left his voice when he most needed it.

'I think you do, Mr Hilton. You have tried to get a young woman to lie on your behalf. To make her an accessory after the fact.'

That formal title again. And what sounded like a formal charge. Sam stared dully at the threadbare carpet between them, noting that the rug he had used to cover the worst patch when Amy had been here had moved itself sideways again. 'Amy can't be that. I didn't commit any crime.'

They waited to see if he would say more, but he remained silent, staring at the carpet, as dull and expressionless as a punch-drunk boxer. It was Hook who said with the gentle firmness he had used throughout, 'You'll need to convince us of that, Sam. Amy Proctor did her best to support you, but the officer who was taking her statement could see she wasn't happy so he got her to tell the truth. I'd say she's a girl who isn't used to lying.'

He'd found Hilton's weak spot. The young man who spent his days trying to force words to do his bidding, to find new language for old, profound ideas, now said with abject simplicity, 'I shouldn't have asked her to lie for me.'

'Indeed you shouldn't, Sam. From your point of view, as well as from hers. You'd better put that right with us, if you can. Then you can think about what you're going to say to her.'

'I was here that night. Amy wasn't.'

'Then why tell us she was? Why try to get her to lie for you?'

'Because otherwise you were going to get me for this. I've admitted I was dealing drugs and you've got me banged to rights for that. And you've dug up all this stuff that Peter Preston had on me. When you pin murder on me, what court is going to listen to me?'

Lambert's irritation was barely under control as he snapped, 'We've never pinned a crime on anyone, Mr Hilton. You're an intelligent man. Come out of your cheap fantasies and confront reality. If you killed Preston, we'll be back very shortly to arrest you and charge you. If you didn't, stick to what you know about and don't try to manufacture evidence. And if you didn't kill the man, give us any thoughts you have on who else might have gone to his house and shot him.'

'I don't know who did it.' And I'm too shaken to give you my thoughts on any other possibility, was the sub-text of that. Sam often delighted in suggesting sub-texts, beneath the compressed phrases of his verse, but he wished now that there wasn't one here.

Lambert studied him hard for another long moment, then rose and said, 'Don't leave the area without informing us of your intended destination, Mr Hilton.'

Sam Hilton stayed very still in his chair for a long time after they had left. He wished as deeply as he had ever wished anything in his life that he'd never laid eyes on Peter Preston.

The last match of the season at Hereford United. A big crowd on a breezy day of blue sky and high, racing clouds. Big crowd for Hereford, that is. The ancient town is not one of the great citadels of British football like the Theatre of Dreams at Old Trafford or the luxurious new Emirates stadium where Arsenal weave their complex patterns over perfect turf. Six thousand is a big gate at Hereford.

But at least you could arrive at ten to three and still be in your seat for kick off. And to a ten-year-old attending his first match, the wonder of it all was enough to make his blue eyes widen and his breath catch in his throat as his team strode out and the crowd roared. A small and eminently civilized roar – this was Hereford – and the crowd today little more than five thousand.

Detective Inspector Chris Rushton was not a regular supporter of the Bulls. It was seven years since he had last attended a match. That had been at the Bulls' old ground by the river, prone to flooding and a mudheap through most of the winter. He was impressed by the green sward of the new ground at Edgar Street, but he was only here today because he was fulfilling a promise to his fiancée to bring her youngest brother to a match. Anne was ten years younger than Chris, and in his view intensely beautiful; he could scarcely believe his luck that she was willing to take on a divorced man whom she must surely see as very dull. Chris had willingly volunteered to bring young Thomas here. He was pleasantly surprised by how much he was enjoying the experience.

One of the advantages of a small, tight ground is that you are very close to the players. You may even hear the odd frustrated expletive from them, which is not good for young ears. But the young men on the pitch positively glowed with health and fitness, even at the end of a long season where they had played forty-six league matches and various other ties in the knock-out cups. There were one or two grizzled veterans, shaven of head and stern of visage, who guided and occasionally rebuked their younger colleagues. But a team like Hereford United cannot afford huge wages, so that nine of today's team were under twenty-two. They showed the bright, fierce effort as well as the occasional naivety which was appropriate to their youth.

It was an even and well-contested match, and Chris's young companion became thoroughly involved, as healthy ten-year-olds should. It was one goal each at half time, and in the first ten minutes of the second half, each side scored again. Thomas shrilled his high-pitched encouragement as the locals equalised for the second time in the match. Thereafter, there were many thrilling goalmouth incidents, but no further goals. As the end of the match approached, it seemed certain to be a draw.

Then the home left winger took a fine pass in his stride and was away down his wing, his young feet flying over the turf no more than twenty yards from Thomas's excited eyes. He was too fast for the ageing full back and he knew it. With eyes fiercely on the ball, the winger sped ever further in front of his despairing opponent, cut in towards the goal, and then rolled an inviting pass back across the penalty area. Time seemed to stand still for Chris and for Thomas. Then Hereford's experienced striker, toiling manfully behind his young star, arrived to smash the ball high into the corner of the net, leaving the goalkeeper pawing frantically at the empty air, then beating the ground in frustration as he lay prone upon it.

Thomas shrieked his approval of this wholly appropriate conclusion to his first match. He was so excited that his eyes brimmed with tears and he could not trust himself to speak in the wonder of it all. Two minutes after the goal, the referee's whistle shrilled the three long blasts which marked the end of the match and he was able to join for the first time in the crowd's long, wailing cheer for a win achieved.

Chris let him wait in his seat until the players had left the field, so that he could savour the heady draught of his first match to the last dregs. They filed out of the small stand and through the big gates on to the busy Edgar Street outside, with the boy still chattering animatedly about the performances of his favourite players. Chris was too occupied with his young charge and the traffic to notice the man who followed them cautiously down the side street towards his parked car.

A slight figure with an unfashionable mackintosh over his arm, he moved about ten yards behind the excited boy and his tall, dark-haired guardian. Chris was opening the door of the car to stow his passenger safely within it when he became aware of the man. He could hardly fail to register him, since his pursuer now stopped abruptly at his side.

'You're a police officer.' It was a statement, not a question.

Chris stood upright and looked into a sallow, grey-white face beneath lank hair with wisps of grey in it. Five feet seven; between ten and eleven stones; Age probably between forty-five and fifty. The policeman's swift, automatic calculations were concluded almost without his realizing it. 'I am. What is it you want?'

'I need to talk to you. I might have information.'

A nutter, in all probability. They usually were, when they accosted you in the street like this. Chris wondered how the man had spotted him as a police officer when he was in jeans and a sweater. He glanced quickly at Thomas's open, inquisitive face within the car. 'You should go to your nearest police station on Monday morning. Tell the duty sergeant at the desk whatever it is you want to report.' Neighbour trouble, probably, he thought; that was the most common source of complaint and supposed 'information'.

'It's more urgent than that. Least I think it is. You can make up your mind for yourself.'

A hint of defiance in the last words, an attempt perhaps to arouse CID curiosity. Chris said, 'I can't talk here. I have a boy to get home, as you can see.'

The man hesitated, then produced a card and handed it to the taller man.

CLIVE BOND. Private Investigator.

All commissions undertaken. Divorce work a speciality.

Chris looked at the card, then back into the thin, crafty face. 'This isn't the place for this. If you think you have important information, you should go to Oldford police station.' He climbed into the car and shut the door.

Thomas wanted to know what this encounter might be about, but he was easily diverted to talk of the match, which was still bright in his mind. Chris kept up his end of the conversation with brief contributions, his curiosity excited despite himself by the unprepossessing figure they had left behind them.

EIGHTEEN

Marjorie Dooks said that four o'clock would be the most convenient time to see them on a Saturday. Over many years in the Civil Service, she had become accustomed to having her requests accepted as orders, so that she was not surprised when it was immediately agreed that Lambert and Hook would come to the house at that time. She did not realize as she put down the phone that the time was almost exactly the one they would have suggested.

Her assumption that she was in control of matters dissipated swiftly with their arrival. She took them into the dining room, which was nowadays infrequently used, and said, 'I don't suppose this will take long. My husband's out playing golf, so we shan't be disturbed.' She offered them tea, which was promptly refused. She said, 'I do hope you're making progress with this. I wasn't close to Peter Preston – indeed, we crossed swords on a few occasions – but we can't allow anyone to get away with murder, can we?'

Lambert studied the strong, composed face beneath the auburn hair for a moment before he said evenly, 'Indeed we can't, Mrs Dooks. That is why we would expect and demand the full cooperation of all innocent parties in our investigation.'

'I appreciate that. I trust you've been receiving it.'

'In some cases, yes. In others no. There are implications in that. One of the people who hasn't cooperated fully is probably our murderer.'

Marjorie had been perfectly relaxed. She now felt that she was involved in some preliminary fencing. She usually enjoyed verbal bouts, but she sensed that she wasn't going to come out on top in this one. In the past, and particularly during her working life, her diligent preparation had meant that she was normally better informed than her opponents. That was plainly not the case with this tall, grave figure who was studying her every reaction so intently. She said with uncharacteristic uncertainty, 'I'm sure I wish to give you all the information I can, but I'm afraid that won't—'

'Did you know that Mr Preston kept detailed notes on all the people he regarded as enemies?'

'No. But it doesn't surprise me. It's the sort of thing he would have done.' She wondered now what was coming, but she kept her mask of affability.

'We now have access to his files. There is a fairly detailed one on you.'

'I confess I'm surprised at that. Perhaps I should be flattered that Peter thought me worthy of such attention.'

'He kept his ear very much to the ground and picked up a surprising amount of local gossip. He also made regular use of a private detective. He seems to have been well aware of the state of your marriage.'

'I regard that as gross impertinence! I can hardly pursue him for his prying now. I understand that you had to read whatever he had left behind. However, it seems to me an ill-mannered intrusion on your part to raise this now.' She glanced at Hook, who had his notebook on his knee; he was watching her as closely as his colleague.

Lambert smiled mirthlessly, feeling a small quickening of his pulse as he saw her losing the coolness she had been determined to retain. 'Had you not concealed matter which has a bearing on a murder inquiry, there would have been no reason to see you today. As it is, I must point out that you clearly had a motive for wishing Peter Preston out of your life.'

'I agree with that, but I would argue that you're putting it too strongly. I cannot think that in my case Peter had more than a little malicious gossip on his files.'

'He had more than that, as you know. Perhaps you should know that he also recorded his conversation when he confronted you with his knowledge, which was less than a week before he was killed.'

For the first time they saw real fear in the strong-boned face. She said in a strange, tightly controlled voice, 'He knew things that I thought no one knew. Things my husband didn't know. He said he would make them public unless I chose to "play things his way" on the literature festival committee.'

'And how did you react to that?'

She paused for so long that Lambert was driven to add, 'In view of your previous concealments, you would be most unwise to hold anything back from us today.'

Marjorie stared at him for a moment, then nodded slowly. 'I agree with that. Please do bear in mind that I have never been in a situation like this before. I've never been questioned as a murder suspect, and I've never been the target of the kind of prurient pressure to which Peter Preston was subjecting me.'

Lambert nodded. 'It's high time you gave us a full account of what took place.'

Marjorie took a very deep breath. She was a private person. She hadn't been pressurized to reveal intimate things like this since she had been a child. And she couldn't come to terms with it. She had no idea how to begin and she showed her uncertainty by opening with a question. 'You know about my association with Mr Forshaw?'

Lambert was deliberately brutal in his attempt to ruffle her. A disturbed subject almost always revealed more about herself than she wished to. 'We have considerable detail about what Mr Preston described as a full-blown affair with Ronald Forshaw. Including the dates and times of several of your meetings.'

How strange to hear that name 'Ronald' for her Ron. She'd never heard him called that before. She looked past her unwelcome visitors, stared at the wall behind them with its familiar prints without registering anything. She spoke more to herself than to them. 'It's the first liaison I've ever had. Perhaps it began as a blow against James. My husband has strayed outside our marriage many times. But this quickly became much more than a mere affair. I've known Ron for a long time. We even worked together for a year in our Civil Service days. Nothing improper ever occurred then. It was when I met him at a reunion last August. He had a wife who no longer cared for him, I had a perennially straying husband. I suppose we'd always been attracted to each other, but we'd done nothing about it until that point.'

Hook made a note that the affair had been going on for the last nine months, according to Marjorie Dooks. Then he spoke more gently than Lambert. 'We're not here to make any moral judgements, Mrs Dooks. We're interested in your private life only in so far as it impinges upon a murder investigation. You say Mr Preston confronted you with his information. Would you tell us a little more about that meeting, please?'

'He said I should give up any connection with the literary festival and recommend him as my successor in the chair. Provided I did that and supported his plans in the appropriate committees, he would reveal nothing and I could remain on the local council.'

Bert wondered if she realized how her obvious contempt and bitterness was making her a stronger candidate as the man's killer. He said gently, almost sympathetically, 'And how did you react to this?'

'Not well, I suppose. I'm not used to being bullied or threatened. My first reaction was "publish and be damned". Then he pointed out that if he went public the news would be certain to affect Ron's future. Ron Forshaw is planning to stand as a parliamentary candidate in the next general election. He has been a local councillor and party worker for the Liberal Democrats for years. He hopes the present coalition government will make the country take them more seriously as a political force. I know he's a bit long in the tooth to be planning a parliamentary career, but he doesn't want to be anything more than an MP. He's always wanted to change the way things work for people and he's excited by the idea of being involved in policy making. And I'm excited with him; I think Ron will make a brilliant constituency MP.'

She was really animated now. It was important to her to convince them about the merits of this man they had never seen and might never see. Hook brought her gently back to the matter in hand. 'And Peter Preston thought he could damage his prospects?'

'Oh, he was quite certain that he could. He said when he'd released the details of an extra-marital affair to the country's tabloid press, Ron wouldn't even be nominated as a candidate to contest the election. I had no doubt that he was right. There are always plenty of candidates on offer and appointing committees tend to play safe. They hate any whiff of scandal.'

'Did you believe this?'

'I did. He had dates and times. He said the right papers would run it over several days and make a big thing of it. When I told Peter he surely wouldn't be so cruel, he laughed in my face. He said I should consider how cruel I'd been to him. I think he really believed that. He couldn't accept that we'd had an honest difference of opinion. He equated his discomfort in losing an argument to the real suffering he proposed to cause to an able and innocent man.'

'So did you agree to his demands?'

'No. I could never have done that. Peter was in the wrong.' Then, as if she saw that as stubbornly didactic as it sounded, she added much more quietly, 'I don't really know what would have happened. I played for time. I pointed out that even if I acceded to his desire to direct the literary festival, people would want to know the reason why I'd resigned. I'd need time to devise some convincing reason for withdrawing from work I believed in and enjoyed.'

'And did you set about doing that?'

She looked at Hook's caring, enquiring face and at Lambert's grimmer one beside it. 'No. I suppose it was no more than a delaying tactic, to give me time to think.' For the first time since Lambert had told her about the contents of Preston's filing cabinet, a small smile flitted briefly across her strong features. 'It's an old Civil Service strategy. When something is sprung upon you unexpectedly, you go away, gather all the information you didn't have earlier, and come back with better arguments to a meeting a couple of weeks later.'

'And what arguments were you able to muster?' This was Lambert, acerbic and sceptical, resuming the questioning.

'None. I don't think there was a solution. If a man is warped, unreasonable and unscrupulous, he doesn't listen to arguments.' She produced the adjectives with a surprising relish; they sensed that she had rehearsed them many times for her own benefit but never expected to produce them for others.

'And five days later, Mr Preston was dead.'

'Yes. I don't think the world has lost much with his demise. Rather the reverse, in fact.'

'Did you kill him, Mrs Dooks?'

'No. I don't approve of murder, even though on this occasion I shall not be sorry if your investigation is unsuccessful.'

'You have just given us a vivid account of the desperate situation in which you found yourself. You are a woman who prefers decisive action to indirect resistance. Didn't you see murder as a logical step?'

She stared at him steadily for a moment before she replied. 'Mr Lambert, you're beginning to sound like a lawyer in court. I've told you I didn't kill Peter Preston. Any discussion of the logic of such a course is irrelevant.'

'Where were you last Tuesday evening?'

'I think I told you this on Thursday. I was at home throughout the evening. I understood that my husband had confirmed that.'

Lambert nodded to Hook, who flicked to a different page of his notebook and studied a note he knew perfectly well, allowing the tension to stretch even tighter in the silent room. 'Your husband confirmed that you were in the house together at the beginning of the evening. He said that he retired to his own quarters to do some work and that you were at the other end of the house. He says he did not see you between seven forty-five and ten thirty. He pointed out that the television was on in your section of the house throughout the evening, but we have to be aware, of course, that you could easily have left it on when you vacated the house for a time. Do you dispute any of this?'

Damn James and his petty vindictiveness! Typical of him to call that small study 'his own quarters'. Marjorie could see him now, pretending priggishly that he had to be honest, allowing them to persuade the information in driblets from his reluctant lips. She and he had existed in an atmosphere that had varied between carefully distanced and unspoken hostility for months now. For the first time, she wondered how much James knew about her and Ron. She said, as if the words had been wrung from her, 'No. This is a big house, as you imply. And as you might deduce from what you've heard from me today, our marriage is no longer close. It's probably almost over, to be honest. We often choose to spend our evenings apart.'

'So it would have been perfectly possible for you to leave the house without his being aware of it.'

'I suppose it would. As James has no doubt already told you – very reluctantly, of course.'

The bitter sarcasm of the last phrase made them wonder about the depth of her feeling for the unexpected new man in her life. She'd left them in no doubt that she would be capable of extreme measures to prevent the disclosure of Ronald Forshaw's affair with her to the public at large. Hook said quietly, as if confronting a sad truth, 'This house is less than three miles from the spot where Preston was killed. You could have been there and back within twenty minutes, with Preston removed from your life for ever.'

Marjorie managed a smile. 'You're very persuasive. You make it sound an attractive option. And indeed it would have been – if it hadn't involved murder. I don't think in those terms, DS Hook. I never left the house.'

Lambert stood up, made as if to leave, then paused on what might have been an afterthought. 'Do you or your husband possess a pistol, Mrs Dooks?'

'No. I wouldn't willingly have one in the house and James has never had any interest in such things.' She seemed for a moment as if she was about to say more, then glanced up into his face and decided against it.

Lambert said, 'I believe you supervised the collection of arms during your final Civil Service years.'

A small smile flitted briefly across the strong features, as if in brief recognition of a point scored by an opponent. 'Yes. I had overall responsibility for the collection of IRA and Ulster Volunteer arms surrendered after the resolution of the Irish conflict. I suppose it might have been possible for me to acquire a pistol then, had I been so inclined. I did not in fact do so. I directed the staff involved, but I had no direct contact with the collection and disposal of the weapons involved.'

He studied her for a final moment, then said abruptly, 'If you have anything further to tell us about yourself or others, please ring Oldford CID immediately.'

She watched their car turn slowly out of her drive and out of vision, standing at the window until the last sound of it was gone. Then she moved back through the silent house and turned her thoughts to what she was going to say to James when he returned from golf.

The unprepossessing figure who had accosted Chris Rushton as he left the football ground in Hereford waited until Sunday morning to present himself at the police station in Oldford. He reckoned correctly that the CID people he needed to speak with would not be in the station on Saturday night.

This man knew his way round police stations and police procedures. It was a bright May morning and spring was advancing rapidly, so he took the major sartorial step of relinquishing the long gabardine overcoat he regarded as his winter uniform. For the first time in the year, he wore the shabby blue anorak, which was his normal summer garb. He shrugged aside the efforts of the station sergeant to make him reveal the subject of his visit. 'It's CID stuff, this.' When the stolid face remained doubtful, he added solemnly, 'It has to do with the murder your CID people are investigating. I need to speak to the chief superintendent in charge of the Preston case.'

The uniformed man had his doubts, but with his pension less than a year away, he wasn't going to risk a rocket from that bugger Lambert or any other senior officer. He directed the man through to the CID section. Three minutes later, after a moment studying the board with its photographs of locations and people in the investigation and scrawled questions from the investigating officers, he was in Lambert's office.

'Mr Clive Bond, sir,' the young woman DC announced to her chief. She kept her voice studiously formal, as if to protect some private joke.

The detective shook the stranger's hand, installed him in a chair, studied him politely but unhurriedly. The man said with a short, nervous laugh, 'So I meet the illustrious Chief Superintendent Lambert at last. I never thought I'd do this.' He tried to settle and take in the details of the tight, disappointingly anonymous little office, with its small desk, its computer, its rather ancient filing cabinet.

Lambert afforded him a brief smile. 'The reality is much less exciting than the fevered creation of the media, I'm afraid. I'm fully occupied with a murder case at the moment, or you wouldn't find me here on a Sunday morning. I'm told that you've come here as a member of the public anxious to help in an enquiry; we are of course grateful for that. But neither of us wishes to waste more of our Sunday than we have to. Please state your business.'

The small figure took an impressively deep breath, produced a card and deposited it on Lambert's desk. '**CLIVE BOND. Private Investigator'**. He waited for Lambert to study the card and show the first glimmer of amusement. 'I state that baldly on my cards because I find it's best to get the hilarity over my name out of the way at the outset.'

Lambert controlled all thoughts of Miss Moneypenny directing this diminutive figure against the forces of world evil. 'It could have been worse, Mr Bond. You mother could have opted for "James" at the christening.'

'In which case I should have adopted a different name entirely. I sometimes think that would have been the best way, but I started with my own name and I'm stuck with it.'

Lambert studied the thin-faced, undernourished-looking figure and controlled the smile which threatened the solemnity of his reception. 'What can I do for you, Mr Bond? Or should I rather ask, what you can do for us?'

'Mr Peter Preston, your murder victim. I worked for him.'

'In which case, many thanks for taking the initiative and coming here. We should certainly have unearthed your name and contacted you in the next few days. That is one task less for Detective Inspector Rushton.'

'He's the man who told me to come here. I approached him when he was leaving the football ground at Hereford yesterday afternoon. He had a young boy with him, so he didn't want to speak to me then.' He volunteered each fact grudgingly. Bond was a man who did not yield information easily; he was used to being paid for each fact he disgorged.

'How fully and how often did Mr Preston employ your services, Mr Bond?'

The small man glanced at Lambert sharply with the repetition of his name; plainly he was sensitive about what others saw as its comic possibilities. This time he saw no such intent. 'I did quite a lot of work for him – at times I was almost his full-time employee. But the work was intermittent and there was no real pattern to it. He kept coming back to me, so he must have been satisfied with the way I worked and the things I produced for him.'

Lambert understood the man's urge to advertise himself. His was a calling in which successes could not be openly proclaimed and the only one who could prove your efficiency was yourself. 'No doubt you were working on something for him at the time of his death, or you wouldn't be here now.'

'Yes.' Clive Bond looked unhappy; he wasn't used to his revelations being anticipated. He liked to reveal a morsel at a time, to emphasize the value of what he was being paid for. But then he'd never been questioned by a chief superintendent before; that must surely confirm that his work was important. 'Mr Preston asked me to watch his wife and to document her movements for him on certain occasions. He let me know in advance when these excursions were to take place.'

'That means you wouldn't usually have had much notice.'

'I was prepared to drop other assignments for Mr Preston; he was a good client who made regular use of my services. Sometimes you can pass less important work on to other people in the profession. We have agreements among ourselves. If you haven't much on at the time, you're glad to take on the work.'

Lambert knew enough of the strange, hand-to-mouth existence of the private detective to know that such transfers would be eagerly received by the less successful and less established practitioners of the trade. 'So you've come here to tell us about the movements of Mrs Edwina Preston on the night of her husband's death.'

'Yes.' Again he had intended to reveal this in stages. He was being hurried along and it spoilt his rhythm. 'She was with another man on the night of his death.'

'A Mr Hugh Whitfield.' Lambert told himself he was being petty, but he couldn't suppress his amusement in anticipating what Bond had planned as a startling revelation.

Clive frowned at the leather-backed notebook he had produced and opened with such ceremony. He drew a mental line through the name he had meant to produce so proudly.

He looked so crestfallen that Lambert was moved to say, 'We have questioned Mrs Preston very closely on two occasions since her husband's death, as you would no doubt anticipate. But I'm sure you can add to what we have learned from her.'

Bond nodded, returned to his notebook and announced with diminishing confidence, 'Mr Whitfield and Mrs Preston spent that night in a hotel.'

'In Broadway, Worcestershire, yes. I'm afraid she revealed both the location and her companion to us.'

'I see.' Clive paused again, running his eye down the page, hoping that he still had material which would surprise this grave-faced, seemingly omniscient interrogator. 'Did you know that Mr Whitfield was late arriving?'

Now at last he had Lambert's full and eager attention. 'When did he get there?'

'Not until ten thirty-four p.m.'

'I see.' Lambert made a note on the pad in front of him.

Clive recovered a little of his poise. He said ponderously, 'Mrs Preston went out during the evening. She left in her green Fiat C3 at ten past eight p.m. and did not return until ten twenty-seven p.m.'

Lambert made a note of the times. 'I compliment you on your precision, Mr Bond. And where did Mrs Preston journey to in that period?'

Just when he had recovered his equilibrium and told them things they did not know, Clive was deflated. This was the one section of the evening where his detective skills had proved inadequate. 'I don't know, I'm afraid. I tailed her as far as the B4632, where she turned south, but I had to wait for a stream of traffic at the junction and I was well behind her before I could follow her. I never picked her up again.'

'Pity, that. It would have been interesting to know where she went in those two and a quarter hours.'

'It's not easy to tail someone at night, you know. Particularly when you don't want them to realize they're being followed.'

'Indeed I do know, Mr Bond. Even professional police drivers on surveillance have great problems during darkness.'

'All you can see is rear lights. One small car looks very like another. It's much easier in daylight.'

'Of course it is. And we're very grateful for the new information you have brought to us. It will be added immediately to our other material from the enquiry and be the subject of our further investigation. What did you do when you decided that you'd lost contact with Mrs Preston's car?'

'I went back to the hotel in Broadway to check whether my subject was going to reappear there. She did, but not until ten twenty-seven. Mr Whitfield arrived in his own car, a Volkswagen Sirocco, exactly seven minutes later.'

'Thank you. We shall use this material in questioning the parties involved in due course. You did the right thing in coming forward. Unfortunately the law regards you as merely a good citizen doing his duty and there is no obvious means of rewarding you. However, I will see if we can make you some sort of payment from the money we use for police informers.'

'I've never been a police snout.' Bond spoke instinctively and indignantly, for once unmindful of his own interests.

Lambert gave him a mirthless smile. 'I understand that. But you should not be too proud to accept a payment if it can be engineered. Obviously the person employing your services on that night is not in a position to pay you. I would think that a claim on his estate would not be well received.'

Clive Bond relaxed for the first time. 'Thank you for your consideration, Chief Superintendent Lambert. It is much appreciated. A regular income is not one of the benefits of private detection.'

Lambert was still smiling at the stiff formality of this a minute after the man had left. Then he buzzed DI Rushton, whom he had seen twenty minutes earlier organizing the mass of information that had come in from house to house enquiries and team interviews into a more coherent whole on his computer. 'I think you'd better come in here, Chris. I have a new development to report.'

NINETEEN

The Ros Barker exhibition in Cheltenham was going well. Harry Barnard's gallery was spacious and well-sited, near the centre of the town. He might have no artistic pretensions himself, but he knew his business and knew how to display the work of those he chose to favour with their own exhibitions. He had taken pains to advertise this relatively unknown protégée in the most telling places and he had produced a brief but impressive brochure to introduce her paintings and what they were about.

There was a photograph of Ros on the front, earnest but smiling shyly, an expression that took the severity out of the strong, aquiline nose. It had been taken two years ago and selected from those available by Kate Merrick, who thought it suggested the humour as well as the essential seriousness of her partner and her art. The account of her work and her budding career inside the brochure was followed by a quotation from the eminent television art critic, Arthur Jackson: 'Rosemary Barker's work is original without being merely fashionably avant-garde. It is comprehensible without ever being trite, strikingly intelligent without attempting to confuse.' There were small but well-printed reproductions of the paintings which had been accepted by the Royal Academy for its last two summer exhibitions.

Barnard had decided that the exhibition should be attended by the artist herself for three hours on the opening Sunday afternoon, divining correctly that serious art lovers were likely to visit when the rest of the town was quiet and parking was easy. Ros and Kate Merrick had enjoyed staffing the gallery for an unusually busy session. There were now three more paintings carrying red 'Sold' stickers than at the beginning of the afternoon, two of them major works, with price tags which only Harry Barnard had thought realistic.

An altogether satisfactory day. Thus far.

Ros had scarcely had time to think about the CID visit, which had been arranged for five o'clock, the advertised closing time for the gallery. In the event, she quietly locked the doors and put up the 'Closed' signs whilst allowing the three potential patrons who were examining her work an extra quarter of an hour – you didn't wish to hurry people who might be prepared to spend hundreds of pounds. Lambert and Hook arrived at their appointed hour, but seemed perfectly happy to examine the various paintings until she was ready to talk to them. 'Enlightened policemen,' Kate muttered at her from the side of her mouth. 'Civilization is really beginning to advance.'

Ros grinned at the comment, but was surprised by the awareness both men seemed to exhibit when they moved briefly into the small room behind the gallery that Barnard had allotted to her for private conversations with people interested in buying. Hook actually suggested a Pre-Raphaelite influence in her work; she found herself disproportionately pleased by that. She made a conventional remark about hoping their Sunday's work had been as fruitful as hers, whereupon Lambert moved briskly into the reason for their visit here.

'You must wish Peter Preston was here today to see the number of red discs on your paintings.'

She smiled. 'He wouldn't have acknowledged it meant anything. "Philistine money pursuing philistine art." I can almost hear him saying that. In a curious, masochistic sort of way, I shall almost miss him.'

'That is a generous thought. I doubt if he was ever so generous towards you.'

'No. Perhaps he was good for me, though. It's salutary for you to have to justify your approach to art every now and then – not that I was ever going to convince Peter. He was harmless enough, I suppose, if you didn't allow yourself to be upset by his barbs.'

'Which you were, on occasions.'

How precise the man was, how ready to pick you up on what you said unthinkingly. She remembered now that she'd told him on Tuesday that most serious artists were easily wounded when you attacked their work. She'd probably been talking about Sam Hilton and his verse, but it was equally applicable to her own art. And these men had been talking to others for days now; probably someone else had told them how aggressive Preston had been towards her. She would take it as a warning to weigh carefully what she disclosed to them in the next few minutes. She said quietly, 'Preston had done good work himself in the past. He no doubt realized that although you try to develop a carapace around yourself against criticism, you remain vulnerable to attacks on your work.'

Lambert smiled. 'Which includes praise as well as negative comment, as you reminded me on Thursday.'

How accurately he remembered things she had tossed out so lightly at the time! Ros smiled back at him and said, 'Mr Barnard has selected extracts from the critics which reflect well on me. Perhaps I should take care to remember that there are other and less flattering judgements.' She felt perfectly relaxed, buoyed by her successes of the afternoon, cocooned for the moment from the more sordid realities of life outside her art.

'You are very charitable towards Mr Preston. He was far more vindictive than you suggest.'

The first warning bells rang in her head, recalling her abruptly from the successes of the day. She said thoughtfully, 'I suppose he was the kind of man who treasured a grievance.'

'Not only treasured it but documented it fully. The sort of man who would build up detailed dossiers on people he came to regard as enemies.'

Ros was conscious of both men studying her intently, watching her reactions to this, trying to decide whether it was news to her or whether she was already aware of it. 'Are you saying that he compiled such a dossier about me?'

'Yes. Are you telling us that you were not aware of that?'

She did not answer them directly. 'It's the sort of thing he would have done, I suppose. He couldn't let anything go. If he thought you were being favoured at his expense, he took it very personally.' She forced a smile. 'It's flattering, in a way, to think that he thought I was worthy of that sort of attention.'

'He had a lot of practice. By the time of his death, he had

become an expert at delving into people's pasts. He employed a private detective to build up his knowledge, whenever he thought that was worthwhile. He had people followed and kept careful notes of dates, times and other details.'

Ros made herself pause and think. 'Preston would hardly have found that sort of attention worth his while, in my case. I have made no secret of my association with Kate Merrick – rather the reverse, if you wish to know. I've been proud enough of it to proclaim it at times. Everyone knows we're partners. A generation ago, that might still have been mildly interesting, though hardly scandalous, except to a few old fogies. Nowadays, I don't think anyone turns a hair.'

Lambert still knew a few who would, in rural and highly conservative Gloucestershire. 'I think Peter Preston realized that. He'd moved in circles where being gay was common and accepted, even thirty years ago. But he took care to inform himself about your earlier history. He didn't name his sources in his files, but I suspect he knew former police officers and sounded them out about you. Information like that should remain confidential, but we have little control over people in the police service once they retire. For the unscrupulous, it can be a way of supplementing a pension. I suspect Preston paid people for information revealed, though in your case there are no names attached.'

Ros's mouth was suddenly very dry. 'What sort of information?'

'He went back ten or twelve years. To your last days at school and your years at the art college.'

'I got in with the wrong set.' For the first time in her life, she found herself mouthing the phrase she had heard so often from her mother.

'Very much the wrong set. You probably know that several of your former associates are now in prison. Two of them serving five-year sentences for GBH.'

'I cut myself off from them. I haven't followed their careers since then.' She tried to be firm, even dismissive, but it sounded a weak denial even in her own ears.

'You were guilty of some pretty wild things yourself, when you were nineteen and twenty.'

'I was never charged with any offence.'

'You came very near to it, even with the good lawyer your mother called in for you.'

'It's ten years since I was in any trouble. It's no longer relevant.'

Bert Hook said gently, 'It wouldn't be, Ros, if this wasn't a murder enquiry. We have to take into account any previous tendency to see violence as a solution to problems.'

She could think only of going into the tired clichés about once a villain always a villain and innocent until proved guilty. From being on a high from the sale of her paintings, she felt abruptly deflated and exhausted. She was back in the world of reality, which was presenting its harshest aspect to her. She repeated the same futile argument in a flat voice. 'My life now is totally different from my life ten years ago. What I did then has no bearing on my life today.'

'Unless your behaviour then shows character traits that persist, Ros. It doesn't make you guilty of the crime committed last Tuesday night, but we have to take these things into account. Past experience tells us that we need to do this. The records show that people who've been violent once tend to be violent again, when they're put under pressure.'

She tried to muster some sort of denial, but he made it all sound distressingly logical. And her mind was weary, too weary to resist. She nodded dumbly, not trusting her tongue. Hook spoke with a gentleness which mitigated the harshness of his message. 'Ten years ago, you stabbed a man, Ros. By all accounts, you were lucky that he didn't die.'

She found a voice, low but steady, resisting the instinct deep within her that her case was hopeless. 'I was threatened. We were in a gang, fighting a rival gang. It all happened very fast. The situation was much more confused than you're making it.'

'You were the only woman there. Didn't that warn you that there might be violence?'

She was silent for so long that they wondered whether she would answer. Then, with a voice that seemed to come from a long way away, she heard herself say, 'My mum thought for years I was just a tomboy and at the time I bought into that.

Drug fixes and breaking the law seemed normal, once you were in the gang. Rumbles were part of the excitement. You didn't think much about it, until it got out of hand and everything went wrong.'

'But wasn't it the prospect of violence which drew you into the group? You were an intelligent girl, an intelligent young woman by then. You must have known that there were violent, aggressive men in that gang, that there was a war going on over territory at the time.'

'I was naïve. I was very young for my age.' Again she could hear these plaintive, futile pleas in her mother's voice. She sought for some more genuine reason of her own. 'I hadn't found my own sexual identity at the time. I didn't want boys for sex, but I wanted the other excitements of being in a gang. Perhaps I was attracted to violence – I certainly found it exciting.'

Hook switched to the present, so deftly that she did not realize at first what he was about. 'We have the file that Peter Preston compiled on you, with the details of this and other incidents. Did he threaten you with what he had found? Did he say he would reveal these things about you?'

She wanted to deny it all, to say that she'd known nothing and been completely unaware of what Preston could do to her. But her brain was working again now. There was no way she could know what other people had told them. If they caught her out in a lie, it would make what they already knew even more damning to her. 'Yes. I knew Peter wanted to speak to me after the last literature festival committee, but I stayed with other people, then left without speaking to him. But he rang me up at our flat. He seemed to know that Kate was out and I was on my own, but I don't know how.'

'When was this?'

A long pause, which seemed to her only to make her reply more damning when she produced it. 'Last Tuesday morning.'

The day of the murder. Hook let the thought hang between them for a moment before he said quietly, 'What did he say, Ros?'

'He'd heard about this exhibition – seen the advanced publicity, he said. He told me that he knew about the fight and the knifing and one or two other things. He said I should resign from the festival committee and everything connected with it. Or I could stay on it, if I changed my attitude and supported him. Then he would reveal nothing of what he knew about my past and the criminals I had associated with.'

'And if you didn't accede to this?'

'Then he'd turn up at a time of his choosing during this exhibition and make a public denouncement of me. He mentioned the arts correspondent of Radio Gloucester and a couple of national journalists he knew. He said he could ruin my reputation over three or four days by gradually revealing what he knew.'

'Perhaps you should have told him there was no such thing as bad publicity, Ros.'

She smiled weakly, looked him briefly in the face before glancing down at her hands again. 'Perhaps I should. I didn't come up with anything like that. I couldn't think straight – couldn't think at all. I was so shocked that he should know these things about me that I was completely floored.'

Hook nodded, full of understanding, even regret. 'So you couldn't see any way out of it. You thought you had to shut him up at all costs. You went to his house on Tuesday evening and decided to silence him once and for all. Maybe you didn't even intend to kill him when you went there. Maybe there was an argument and you reacted instinctively to his threats.'

'No. I probably felt like killing him, when I found what he'd been doing. But in fact I did nothing. The next day, I heard that he was dead.'

Hook nodded slowly. 'Where were you on Tuesday night, Ros?'

Now at last she spoke with a flash of spirit. 'I told you that on Thursday. I was at home on my own. Kate was visiting her mother and her young brother. Why do you ask me again?'

Hook smiled at her in the avuncular manner he had adopted throughout. 'I just thought I'd give you the opportunity to revise that if you wished to.'

'And why should I do that?'

'No reason, if it's true.'

'It's true. And it's also true that I still haven't found anyone to prove it to you; nor have I any further ideas on who rid the world of Peter Preston.'

Hook glanced at Lambert, who plainly thought they were done here. Bert stood up beside his chief. As he followed him out, he stopped and turned round, almost treading on the toes of Ros Barker as she followed them across the small room. 'So long as you are innocent, I shouldn't worry too much about an alibi. It's often the guilty who take care to have something lined up for us.'

Sue Charles worked the hoe steadily and systematically over the soil she was preparing for the antirrhinums. 'I love the spring and the blossom all around us, but you have to keep up with it in the garden or nature will take over. George used to say that gardening wasn't a hobby like other hobbies, because you couldn't pick it up and put it down as you pleased. If you neglected it at certain times, it could overwhelm you.'

'That's very true, I suppose, Mrs Charles,' said Brian, 'And as you say, spring is one of those times. The weeds soon take advantage, if you're not around.' The gardener dumped his final batch of weeds into the wheelbarrow and prepared to wheel it away towards the larger of the two compost barrels. He stopped to fondle Roland's ears and smiled as the cat stretched his body indulgently and began to purr.

Sue looked at the pair fondly. 'He used to run away from you, when you first came. He gets used to people quite quickly, really. It's four o'clock and time you were packing up, Brian. Have you got time for a cup of tea?'

He sensed that she wanted company. It must be lonely being a widow at times, even though she had her writing to keep her busy. And she made the best flapjacks he had ever tasted. 'I'd love to, Mrs Charles. I've finished for the day when I'm done here.'

He sat in the neat sitting room in the bungalow. She brought in flapjacks on a plate as he'd hoped and he leapt forward and said, 'I'll pour the tea, Mrs C.' That was the most informal address he used for her, and it seemed quite daring to take the initiative with the teapot. But his wife said men should be prepared to do these things, even old-fashioned pensioner men like him; he had found over the years that Margaret usually knew what was best for him. He munched happily at his flapjack and said gallantly, 'There's no need for you to work with me in the garden, you know.'

'I enjoy it, when I can muster the time. I expect the proofs of my latest book will be here for checking tomorrow; that will take all my time up for a few days. It was good of you to come on a Sunday.'

'Makes no difference to me, Mrs C. Be able to take the missus out somewhere during the week.' Brian didn't speak of the project with any great eagerness. He accepted the direction to take a second flapjack and said, 'Have they got anyone for this murder yet, Mrs Charles?'

'I don't think so. Perhaps they never will.'

'I should think you might be able to help them, writing about such things all the time.'

Sue laughed. 'The last thing the CID would want is my help, Brian. It's a very different thing writing tales which people might enjoy reading from the real thing. I realize that and I can assure you the police do.'

'I bet you still have your own ideas, all the same, Mrs C.,' he said loyally.

'They wouldn't want me bothering them Brian. They have a big team on a murder case and they gather all sorts of information. For all I know, they may be preparing to make an arrest at this very moment.'

'Anyway, you make the best flapjacks in Europe. No one's going to dispute that,' said Brian, licking his lips after the last delicious mouthful.

Whilst Sue Charles was entertaining her gardener, the woman she had comforted in this room on the morning after the murder was seated in her sitting room with very different visitors. Edwina was attempting to explain her conduct to the CID.

She said, 'I've told you where I was when my husband died: in a hotel at Broadway. And I've explained why I was less than honest about that at first. I should like to have kept Hugh Whitfield and my relationship out of this, had that been at all possible. He has a wife who is dying of an incurable disease; surely you can see why I wouldn't want her to know about Hugh and me?'

Lambert had refused tea. He sat beside Hook on Edwina's sofa looking large and threatening. 'That attempt to deceive us was understandable, though ill-advised, as was your attempt to persuade your daughter to lie on your behalf about your whereabouts on that night. Now we find that you have still not been completely honest with us. Find, indeed, that you have lied to us about what happened on that evening.'

She stared past them across the big room, looking through the window to the border beyond thirty yards of lawn, where peonies were opening to their full brief grandeur. 'You've been talking to the hotel staff.'

'We know more than that.'

She looked at them now and the grey-blue eyes beneath the neat hair widened with fear. 'More than they can tell you? How can you?'

'I told you that your husband was aware of your affair, that he had employed a private detective to furnish him with the details of it. He followed you out of the hotel that night. So we know that you left at eight ten p.m. and did not return until ten twenty-seven p.m. He recorded also that Mr Whitfield drove into the hotel car park at Broadway exactly seven minutes after you, at ten thirty-four.'

'I see. No doubt Peter employed someone very efficient to do his snooping.'

'You were away from the hotel for two and a quarter hours on that night. Where did you spend that time, Mrs Preston?'

Edwina said acidly, 'I'm sure your very efficient private detective has given you a complete account of my movements on that night.'

'We should like to hear from you where you went, please.'

Maybe he'd lost her after he'd followed her out of the hotel. She would surely have been aware of someone watching her at some point if he'd followed her throughout the evening. She said carefully, 'I had a message at the hotel that Hugh wouldn't be able to join me for dinner. The carer he'd arranged for his wife had let him down. He'd got a replacement to stay overnight, but she wouldn't arrive until around nine thirty.

That meant he wouldn't be with me until some time between ten and eleven. I decided I couldn't face dinner on my own in the hotel. I had a sandwich sent up to our room and then drove out. Needless to say, I didn't realize I was being followed.'

It seemed for a moment as if she would say no more. Hook prompted her gently, 'You turned south on to the B4632, towards your home and your husband. What happened then?'

The implication was clear. She had driven to Oldford, despatched a husband who stood between her and a happy future, and been back in Broadway in time to greet her lover. Edwina fought against the panic that seemed to be coursing through her veins. She heard herself saying, 'I wanted time to think. I drove south to Winchcombe and turned off towards Sudeley Castle and stopped in a lay-by with the valley below me. I wanted to consider my future. Hugh and I aren't going to marry whilst his wife is alive. But I needed to work out how I was going to – was going to divest myself of Peter.' She smiled a little at the last phrase and the way she had fumbled for it, but did not look at her questioners. 'I've no idea how long I was there, but it must have been quite a long time. I was cold by the time I started the car and got the heat back on. I had the radio tuned to Classic FM; I think most of a concert passed whilst I was up there.'

She looked at Lambert now, wondering how convincing these last details were to him. His face was as grave and unrevealing as it had been from the outset. He said only, 'Did you kill your husband on that evening, Mrs Preston?'

'No. I don't deny that his death is convenient for me, but I could have got rid of him without such an extreme solution.'

TWENTY

Sam Hilton was trying to concentrate on his art. If poetry was to be your *raison d'être*, you should be able to concentrate, whatever was going on around you. Keats had managed it, with his girlfriend buggering him about and consumption taking over his body, so surely you should be able to cope with being a murder suspect.

He sat down resolutely with ball-pen in hand to work on 'Die Happy'. Rather too soon for his comfort – as soon, in fact, as he had one new phrase for the third line – there was a knock at the door of his bedsit. He glanced round at the neat, functional room, at his notes on the battered table, his attempt to make a poem. That was the old word for a poet, a 'maker', and it was an appropriate one. People thought you just sat and waited to be inspired but you worked very hard, word by word, phrase by phrase, line by line, to make a poem. There were false starts, rejected ideas, fierce wrestlings with language to force original ideas into a framework which would make the most of them. And usually many, many rewrites before you were satisfied that it was the finished article, or at least the very best of which you were capable.

His first instinct had been to cover up work that was so personal and incomplete. On second thoughts, he left his jottings exposed. Why be ashamed of them? Let the bloody pigs see the creative process for the tortuous, agonizing thing it was.

But it was not the police at his door. It was Amy Proctor. She was not the confident, affectionately mocking, young woman she had been when she had last been with him, when she had seemed to Sam so much more mature and experienced than he was himself. She stood hesitantly in the doorway for a moment, as if fearful that she might not be welcome here. Then she moved uncertainly to the dining chair beside the one he had been using at the table and sat down. She did not look at him. When he came and sat down before his half-finished poem, she stared at the table and said, 'I've let you down, Sam. What you wanted me to tell the police, I mean. I let you down.'

'I know. It doesn't matter.'

'You know?'

'The coppers came round here again – the bigwig, Chief Superintendent Lambert and his sidekick.' It was an absurd assertion of his status as a leading suspect.

'I'm sorry. I wanted to let you know that they'd seen through me and broken me down, but I couldn't get here yesterday because of the family party I told you about. I picked up the phone to ring you and tell you twice, but I couldn't explain it on the phone. I'm not sure I can explain it now that I'm here.'

'There's no need. I shouldn't have asked you to lie.'

'I'm not much good as a liar, Sam. I tried, but the fuzz could see what I was about.'

'That's to your credit, Amy.' He was glad to get her name out at last. He realized now that it was that DS Hook, the one who did the soft-cop routine, who'd said that about his girl, that it was to her credit that she couldn't lie. Because Amy was his girl. He could feel that now. He could see it in her every embarrassed, uncertain move. The strings fell away from his tongue and he said wonderingly, 'I love you, Amy Proctor.'

She smiled at him as if she had known it all along. But only for a moment. The notion which had crept into her mind two days ago had taken it over until she could think of nothing else. It could now be denied no longer. Her forehead twisted into the frown which in other circumstances he had found so attractive. She said as if the words caused her physical pain, 'Why did you want me to say I was with you when I wasn't, Sam? Was it you who shot Peter Preston?'

Monday morning was the time to bring everyone up to date. Lambert had already briefed the large team working on the Preston case about the events of Saturday and Sunday. Most of the DCs and the uniformed men had been off duty at the weekend; the house to house enquiries and the routine checks were complete. The newer officers in the enquiry were secretly surprised at the amount of work Lambert, Hook and Rushton had conducted on Saturday and Sunday. The experienced ones knew all about Lambert's habit of worrying at a case until it released its secrets. And every police officer was aware of the statistic that success rates in murder crimes declined sharply after the first week of investigation.

Later in the morning, John Lambert exchanged thoughts with DI Rushton and DS Hook in the chief superintendent's office. He opened the discussion by saying, 'I'm satisfied now that the killer is going to come from the immediate circle of Preston's acquaintances, that is to say his wife and the people who were on the literature festival committee with him. These are the people on whom he has compiled his most recent and most vitriolic files – the information and opinions we found in that innocent-looking filing cabinet.'

Chris Rushton was encouraged. Experience told him that this case was moving fast towards a conclusion. That old fox Lambert usually emphasized the need to consider every possible solution and not to exclude even the most unlikely; this time he was narrowing the field. Rushton felt the quickening of the pulse which is natural for a CID man as a serious crime is cracked. He couldn't help emphasizing his own, possibly crucial, link with this. 'I'm glad the private eye who contacted me after the match on Saturday proved useful.'

Lambert smiled. 'Clive Bond. Not a man with a prepossessing appearance, but I'd say a highly competent operator in a difficult trade. Not one I'd ever contemplate myself. I couldn't envisage operating without the police machine supporting me at every turn. And Bond knew when to come to us with information, which not everyone in his trade does. Perhaps he feels a certain loyalty to Preston, who must have paid him a lot of money over the last year or two.'

'I believe Bond had new material for us on Preston's wife.'

'Indeed he did, Chris. With times, places and personnel efficiently detailed. Edwina Preston has a lover, Hugh Whitfield, whom she met on the night of Preston's death. We already knew that. What we didn't know and what Bond was able to tell us was that neither she nor Whitfield took dinner in the hotel, as we'd previously thought. Edwina Preston drove out of the hotel at ten past eight and returned at ten twenty-seven. She turned towards home but Bond lost her quite quickly. She says she parked for a long time near Sudeley Castle and considered her future – principally how she was going to divest herself of her husband so that she could marry Whitfield when his mortally ill wife dies in the near future.'

Rushton made a note of the times to add to his computer file on the widow. 'That leaves her ample time to have driven to her home, dispatched Preston, and returned to the hotel.'

'Yes. She looked duly shaken when we pointed that out. She agreed that his death was very convenient for her.'

'Would she have had access to a pistol such as the one that killed Preston?'

'That is a problem with most of the candidates for this crime. It's possible of course that Peter Preston kept a weapon like that in his study. It would accord with his taste for secrecy and intrigue. In which case, Edwina Preston would almost certainly have known about it.'

Hook said, 'We can't discount the possibility of a contract killer, can we? Marjorie Dooks or Edwina Preston certainly had the money to employ one.'

Lambert grinned at him. The empathy they had built over the years was such that Bert knew immediately that the chief had divined what was behind this reminder: Hook didn't want Sam Hilton or Ros Barker to be guilty of this. But Lambert didn't reject the suggestion. He said, 'We should bear that in mind, and possibly add Sue Charles to that list as well, though I would query whether any of these ladies had the underworld connections to know how to contact a hitman.'

Bert said stubbornly, 'Marjorie Dooks would soon discover that information, if she put her mind to it. She's a capable and resourceful woman.'

'Fair point. And we've now got more details of her work record in the Civil Service. As a senior bureaucrat, one of her responsibilities in her last working years was to direct the people involved in the collection and disposal of illegal arms after the Irish agreements at the beginning of the century. It's quite possible that she acquired an ex-army pistol at that time without there being any record of it.'

'And Preston was threatening her in a way she'd never had to endure before – threatening the future life of the man she plans to marry in due course. She's a proud woman, used to controlling her own destiny. She wouldn't take kindly to being threatened. And her alibi is suspect. She's admitted that although they were at home together, she and her husband often spend the evenings apart in a big house. She could easily have left the place for an hour or more without his knowledge, as he took some pleasure in revealing to us. Marjorie says that he's a philanderer and their marriage is over. And over the last nine months, she's been conducting an affair with an old flame from her Civil Service days who plans to become an MP. Preston had it documented and was trying to blackmail her. Not for money; he simply wanted to take over the literature festival and direct it along his own lines. I'm sure Marjorie didn't take kindly to his attempts to pressurize her, any more than she welcomed the threatening letter he'd sent to her a few days before he died.'

Rushton said, 'Marjorie Dooks certainly seems to be the one with the capacity to plan this and the nerve to carry it out. What about Sue Charles? I suppose most people would think that as a crime author she's made a study of murder and its methods.'

It was Bert Hook's turn to smile. 'She's sixty-eight and widowed. She makes no secret of the fact that her novels are escapist whodunits rather than sordid crime-face stuff. She hasn't an alibi for the time of the killing, but as she lives alone you wouldn't expect one. Apart from her writing, her main interests are her cat and her garden. As a murder suspect, she's hardly convincing.'

Rushton nodded. 'Sam Hilton?' He could hardly conceal his eagerness. The DI was a great man for statistics, and the statistics proved that a man caught out in one crime was likely to be guilty of others, once he had embarked on the primrose path to the everlasting bonfire. Chris couldn't have said where that phrase came from, but it had surfaced from his subconscious and rather appealed to him. Even DIs who spent most of their days in front of a computer were allowed poetic flashes. Bert Hook might now be an Open University BA, but that didn't allow him a monopoly of these things.

Lambert nodded soberly. 'Hilton lied to try to give himself an alibi for that night. Fortunately, the girl he tried to use is highly intelligent but basically honest. She did her best to lie for him, but it soon became obvious that she was doing just that. He now admits he was on his own in his bedsit on the evening of the murder. His old Fiesta could have been the car an independent witness saw outside Preston's house at the time of his death.'

'The independent witness is a felon who was carrying out a burglary in a neighbouring house, one Wayne Johnson,' Hook reminded them sturdily.

'Nevertheless, a man we consider a reliable witness in this matter,' said Lambert.

'But Johnson was preoccupied with his own crime at the time. He was never close to the car and he can't identify it, beyond the fact that it was small and a dark colour. There are a number of other vehicles owned by suspects which would fit the bill equally well. Sam Hilton is a minor drug dealer and has admitted it. He doesn't have a history of serious violence.'

'He does not. But then, we may have to accept the fact that this crime was committed by someone without a previous record of violence. The only suspect who has previous as far as we are aware is our painter, Ros Barker. Not with a firearm, but with a knife. Without a good lawyer, she might well have had a conviction for assault with a dangerous weapon.'

Rushton remembered all the details of the artist which he had fed into his computer file. 'She was also alone on the night of the murder. Her partner was away visiting her family. Whether that was at Ms Barker's instigation or not, we don't know. What we do know is that she had a lot at stake if Preston had chosen to mount a campaign against her and her art. She's just got her first exhibition at Barnard's Gallery in Cheltenham. She might even have lost that if Preston had chosen to be really malicious. Both she with her paintings and Hilton with his poems seem to be flavour of the month at the moment, but we all know how transient a reputation in the arts can be. And apart from the material considerations, people can be very sensitive when their creative work is attacked. Young versifiers and artists aren't as thick-skinned as we simple coppers quickly learn to be.'

John Lambert grinned at Chris Rushton's mention of thick-skinned coppers. Hook and he had enjoyed some fun in the past from taunting an over-serious Rushton, who was never quite sure when the older men were extracting the urine. Chris was more balanced since the entry into his life of Anne Jackson, the lively primary school teacher who was ten years his junior and had been briefly a suspect in a murder investigation. Lambert said patiently, 'Does that complete your list of major suspects, Chris?'

Rushton looked down at his notes for a moment, though he knew what he was going to say. 'I don't think we should rule out Kate Merrick. As far as I can see, she's devoted to her partner. She'd be very sensitive to any attack on Ros Barker's integrity as an artist or a person. She's younger than Ros and very much under her spell. She wouldn't be objective or balanced in her reactions to any attack on Ros.'

Lambert nodded. He had been awake since five and an idea that had at first seemed preposterous had become increasingly credible over the hours since then. There was a second or two of silence before he said gnomically, 'I think we shall find that affection for a partner is a major factor in this case.'

TWENTY-ONE

It was an agreeable moment in the leafy Oldford suburb. Monday afternoon was a quiet time for cats, with the world back at work and most of the birds resting in hedges and trees after a sunny, song-filled morning. Roland sat on the gatepost and surveyed the warm world through half-closed eyes. The tiger in him was merely quiescent; at the first sign of prey or danger he would be instantly alert.

At two o'clock the sun was high, the day was at its hottest, and Roland's eyes had closed completely. At one minute past two, his eyes were wide with apprehension and hostility. Bert Hook drove the police Mondeo carefully past him and into the drive of the modest bungalow with the immaculate gardens. Bert eased himself from the driving seat, waited for his chief to rear himself stiffly to his full height on the other side of the vehicle, and looked round appreciatively at the spring-green lawn with its sharply cut edges, the weedless beds with their newly planted bedding plants, and, in the furthest border, the luxuriant pink of the peonies and the thrusting stems of the roses that would follow them into bloom.

'I wish I could say it was all my own work, but my gardener was here yesterday. He's a good man.' Sue Charles was framed by honeysuckle in her front doorway, enjoying Hook's obvious approval of the work she had done with Brian on Sunday afternoon. She led them into her home, not closing the door until Roland had sprung from his watchtower and followed the trio inside.

'I've made some tea,' she said, as she ushered them into the cosy sitting room and installed them upon the couch opposite her favourite armchair. 'I think Brian has left some of my flapjacks for you!' she called from the kitchen. She bustled back in with a tray containing cups and saucers, a teapot, and a plate with the five remaining flapjacks from her

Saturday baking. 'I'm glad to see people enjoying them. They just sit in the tin when I'm on my own.'

John Lambert, who wished that she had not done this, left Hook to offer the conventional thanks for her bounty.

He did not say anything for a long time, watching Hook bite appreciatively into the flapjack he had himself refused to take. Eventually his gaze settled upon Sue Charles. He studied her for a moment, apparently more in sorrow than in anger, then took a belated sip of his tea. The author was a highly intelligent woman, despite the efforts she sometimes made to disguise the fact; his look had already told her more than many words would have done.

But she might be mistaken. She would keep up the front for as long as it was necessary and worthwhile. 'I'm always glad to have visitors – the writer's is essentially a lonely life, especially after she has lost her partner of many years. But I confess I'm surprised to see you again so soon. You must think I am in a position to help your investigation, which surprises me. Or have you come here to tell me that you have made an arrest?'

Her blue eyes were bright and attentive beneath the neatly parted grey hair as she settled herself back into the old-fashioned winged armchair, which might have been designed to house her still supple and agile body. Her head was a little on one side, which they now recognized as one of her mannerisms when asking a question. She looked, Hook thought, like everyone's favourite aunt, the understanding and encouraging relative, which as a Barnardo's boy he had never had.

Lambert was as composed as his hostess, but firm beneath his reluctance as he answered her query. 'We have come here this afternoon not to tell you about an arrest but to make one, Mrs Charles.'

She would play it out until it became hopeless. All might yet be well, she told herself determinedly. She looked at Roland, who had leapt up to his favourite place upon the sunny windowsill. His tale was lashing behind Lambert's head, almost as if he had understood the words which had come so quietly from that long, grave face. She must make a final effort, if only for his sake. 'You cannot possibly mean that you think I killed Peter Preston!'

'That is exactly what I mean.'

'He didn't like me and I didn't particularly care for him. That is hardly reason for murder. Do I strike you as the type of woman who would commit murder because of a few insults to my writing from a man like Preston?'

She addressed her question to Hook, as if turning to a balanced man for a more balanced view. But it was Lambert who answered her. 'You do not strike either of us as that sort of woman, no. Perhaps that blinded us to things we should have followed up earlier. The fact that you collected the deceased's wife immediately after she had been informed of his death and brought her here, for a start.'

'I gave poor Edwina a little tea and sympathy, that's all. She was sorely in need of both.'

'I expect you did, yes. But you also informed yourself about when the murder had been discovered and what had been revealed to the widow at that point. It was no coincidence that you were waiting to pick her up that morning. You knew what had happened and hoped to find a distressed Mrs Preston in Oldford. You took care to let us know that she was very shaken, as someone might have been who had committed a serious crime.'

'Or as someone might have been who had lost a much-loved husband.'

'Perhaps. Except that you took care to emphasize when we saw you for a second time that Edwina and her husband were living separate lives and that their marriage was probably over.'

'As a case against me, this is pretty thin stuff, Chief Superintendent. You'd have difficulty proving that I tried to make you believe Edwina was guilty of murder.'

'You're probably right about that – it's just interesting to follow the way your mind was working. Your initial tactic was to try to divert us right away from the people like yourself around Preston. It was you who pointed out that Preston must have made enemies in his earlier and more successful life at the BBC and elsewhere. You pointed out without any real evidence that these were "rich and powerful people, with the money and contacts to employ a hitman".'

Sue forced a smile. 'Thin stuff, I say again, Mr Lambert.'

'I agree; not the stuff on which to base serious charges. You did, however, make one very definite mistake, one which I think would be damning even in a criminal court. You knew how Peter Preston had been killed, which only the killer and our detection team knew at the time.'

She showed no immediate sign of dismay. Lambert was filled with a reluctant admiration for her insouciance. In the same instant, he realized that perhaps she did not much care, that perhaps she had always anticipated that it would come to this in the end. You could never approve of people who took the law into their own hands, but there were rare occasions like this when you felt despite yourself a strange sympathy and understanding for those who did.

Sue Charles stared at him for a long moment before she said, 'And how exactly did I make this "mistake" which you see as so crucial?'

Lambert nodded at Hook, who flicked open his notebook. He knew the key phrases well enough, but he found it was easier to read them out than to look directly into the face of this most unlikely murderer. 'You said that you found it difficult to believe that "someone took a pistol to his house and shot him". You should not have known at that moment the manner of Preston's death.'

'I expect Edwina told me when I brought her here after she'd been told of the death.'

'Mrs Preston was told only that her husband was dead when she arrived back at her house that day. She did not know that he had been shot.'

'But what possible reason could I have for killing Peter? He'd made a few scathing references to my writing, but I found them pathetic rather than wounding.'

'I agree with you on that. I think you are too sensible a woman to kill a man because of his opinions of your work, however derogatory they might be. But it was you who pointed out that "few of us are completely objective about our own work". You were trying to convince us at the time that Preston's contemptuous dismissal of Sam Hilton's poetry and Ros Barker's paintings might have driven them to kill him. You even took the care to point out that "young people seem to react more violently to criticism than my generation".'

'I still think that's true, you know. Perhaps it just reflects a tendency in our present society to resort more quickly to violence.' She seemed to be weighing his point as if she were engaged only in some complex intellectual argument that interested her.

'But Preston was a malevolent and unscrupulous man, not just a petty critic. He knew how to hurt you: by revealing the stuff he had grubbed up on your husband.'

'You told me about that. I didn't know anything of it until then.' With the mention of her husband, her face had turned to stone.

'Oh, I think you did, Mrs Charles. Preston used his material to threaten the other people on the literature festival committee. He was hardly likely to deny you his unwelcome revelations, particularly since he thought of you as the most vulnerable, as he recorded in his notes.'

She said dully, 'I couldn't let him attack George like that. I couldn't let him go around saying and writing these things, as he threatened to do.'

It was her first admission of guilt. Hook made a note of it, though he knew in his heart that it would not be necessary to quote this in court. He referred again to his notes and said gently, 'You said to us on Saturday, "It doesn't happen often, but I can be very direct when I'm upset". You were very upset when he made these accusations about your George, weren't you?'

It was less an accusation than a helping hand towards the confession they all knew was coming, and she took it as such. 'It was George's pistol I used on Peter Preston. That seemed like poetic justice to me.'

'It was a weapon your husband had retained from his army days, I suppose.'

'Yes. I always wanted George to get rid of it, but he said he wasn't going to live in fear of the young ruffians who practised burglary as a hobby. He was rather an old-fashioned man, my husband, but I loved him.'

For a moment, it looked as if she would weep at the memories that besieged her. Hook said softly, 'Loved him enough to kill the man who was besmirching his memory.'

She glanced at him for an instant, as if she was surprised to see him sitting there, as if she resented his intrusion into her memories. 'I don't know what I intended to do when I went to see Peter that night. I think I thought that if I threatened him with the pistol I'd frighten him off. But he laughed in my face – he obviously thought an elderly middle-class lady wouldn't use a firearm on him.'

'As we did also, for rather too long,' Lambert said quietly, with a strange combination of grimness and tenderness.

'I waved the pistol at him and asked for a guarantee that he wouldn't speak and would destroy whatever vile notes he'd made on George and his business career. He refused and laughed at the idea. When I levelled the weapon at him he grabbed it and we struggled for a few seconds. It was quite ridiculous, two people of our ages struggling like that. But then the gun went off – twice in quick succession – and it wasn't ridiculous any more. I couldn't believe what had happened for a moment, but I could see that he was dead without even checking. I got out as quickly as I could.'

'And took the pistol with you. Where is it now, Mrs Charles?'

At the bottom of the River Wye. I can take you to the spot, but I doubt you'll recover it.'

Lambert doubted it too. But it wouldn't be necessary now. There was material for a plea of involuntary manslaughter in her account, once it had been shaped by a clever defence lawyer. But the prosecution would argue that she had gone to see Preston with murderous intent, with a loaded pistol in her handbag. That was fortunately not police business. Hook stepped forward and pronounced the words of arrest in a muted, almost apologetic tone.

She nodded her recognition of the formal phrases familiar to any crime writer, then stood and signified that she was ready to accompany them. She said, 'I wouldn't have allowed it to go to trial, you know, if you'd arrested someone else. I'd have come forward immediately. It's important to me that you know that. I suppose I just hoped that it might go down as an unsolved case.'

Hook had the completely unprofessional thought as he stood beside her that he might not have minded that. This killer was worth much more than her despicable victim.

She strode steadily before them to the door of her sitting room, then stopped and turned. There was no need for words. Lambert said quietly, 'We'll make sure that Roland is looked after, Mrs Charles. He'll have a happy home.'